Merlin's face was as pale as the waning moon. "Did Arthur learn?" he asked. "Did he send you to kill me?"

"What?" Mael said in surprise. "Kill you? He sent us to tell you to let the dragon loose against the Saxons."

Merlin burst into cackling laughter. "Let it loose? It's about to let itself loose, don't you see?"

Another jet of flame slashed through the hillside. For an instant the wyvern's head thrust through the opening.

Now the head was almost a yard long from crest to muzzle. . . .

"A cunning conceit, a masterful passion, an artful storytelling style: three furies David Drake brings to bear on the traditonal Arthurian legend. The first sword-and-sorcery novel I've read in years that made me want to cheer, rather than toss the book in the dustbin. T.H. White would have loved this new view of that ancient, wondrous fable."

—Harlan Ellison

The DRAGON LORD

By
David Drake

TOR

A TOM DOHERTY ASSOCIATES BOOK

Copyright © 1979 by David Drake

A TOR Book

Published by Tom Doherty Associates, Inc. 8-10 West 36th Street, New York, New York 10018

First TOR printing, December 1982

ISBN: 48-552-2

Cover art by Howard Chaykin

Printed in the United States of America

Distributed by:
Pinnacle Books
1430 Broadway
New York, New York 10018

To Karl Edward Wagner—
Excellent friend, excellent writer,
and an excellent inspiration for a would-be novelist.
"Yet, be warned; call not to you that
which you may neither hold nor forbid."

Acknowledgments

This book owes a great deal to a great number of people. Among them are:

Joanne Drake, my wife, and Glenn Knight, who read portions of the work in progress and pointed out several forests which I couldn't see for the trees;

Sharon Pigott, who proofed the typescript and found four pages of errors I had missed;

Dave McFerran, an Irishman and a godsend to my research;

Karl Wagner, MD, a source—among other things—of crucial medical data;

Andrew J. Offutt, whose request for a plot outline was the proximate cause of my sitting down to write a novel;

Dave Hartwell, who pointed out a problem and then stepped back to let me fix it my way;

and Prof. Jonathan A. Goldstein, who taught and I trust still teaches his classes to enter the minds of ancient peoples through their own writings.

PROLOGUE

"I want a dragon," said the king. His voice was normal, almost too soft to be heard by the man across the table. "I want a thing that will fall out of the night onto a Saxon village, rip the houses apart . . . leave everything that was alive torn for the neighbors to find in a day or a week." The king's voice began to rise. Centuries under Roman rule had smoothed the accents of most British tribes, but the burr was still to be heard among the Votadini. "I want a thing that can breathe on a field at harvest time, can turn its grain and beasts and the men among them to ash!

"Can you do that for me, wizard?"

The other man waited with a half smile for the echoes to die. He was small and should have shaved off his beard. It was dirty, sparse, and ridiculous. He could have been merely a frail old man, except for eyes that bit what they stared at. "You have your army," he replied, using the willow switch he carried to dabble in the ale spilled on the intarsia tabletop. "Your Companions kill and burn well enough."

"Oh, I can *beat* the Saxons," said the king offhandedly, "but that won't make my name live a thousand years." He was lying Roman fashion on the bench, his long cloak pinned at the shoulder and draped so that it completely covered his feet. He always hid his feet if possible, though all men knew that the right one was twisted inward from birth. The Saxons had named him Unfoot in derision when they first saw him leading a troop of cavalry against them. The name had stuck, but by now it had the ring of Hel or Loki in Saxon ears. "I can beat them a dozen times . . . but I'd have to, wizard, because they won't surrender to me and there's too many of them to kill them all. I can bring fifteen hundred men to the field at a time. If the Saxons stood in rows for a week, my Companions' arms would be numb with throat-cutting. And there still would be Saxons in Britain."

The wizard looked down at the parquet table and muttered something under his breath. The spilled beer shimmered. For an instant the liquid showed two armies facing each other. The ripples were sword edges and silvered helms, teeth in shouting faces and the jewel-bright highlights of spurting blood.

The king pretended to see nothing. "I'll give them a symbol, since they won't surrender to a handful of horsemen. But I want it to be a symbol that kills and burns for a thousand years, kills unless I tell it to stop—or nothing remains. I want a dragon."

The willow whip nodded, throwing nervous shadows against walls where years had cracked away most of the frescoes. The paint had been replaced by patterned fabrics, tapestries and brocades. The wizard said, "There have never been many who could raise dragons, Leader. The knowledge it takes, and even with the knowledge, the very considerable danger, yes . . ."

The king's beard and hair were cut short—hacked short, rather, for he could not bear a blade in another's hand to lie so close to his throat. Perhaps he would have let the hair grow and run across his torso in rich, syrupy waves had he not once seen a man try to dodge back from a dagger point—and find that his enemy gripped a handful of his beard. The king's moustache alone was full. "Can you do it or can you not, wizard?" he demanded. "Can you raise me a dragon?"

The older man had heard that tone too often in the past to dally with his answer. "Yes," he said, "I can raise a dragon—and control it—if you can get me the ingredients I need and cannot supply myself." The wizard toyed with the beer and murmured again. A thing trembled on the inlay. Its neck was as long as its body, and its tail was as long as both together to balance it on its two legs. There were no forelegs. From the shoulders sprouted a pair of scaly black wings. The beast could have seemed childish, but it did not, even before one realized that the irregularities beneath the feet of the illusion were Saxon longhouses.

Nodding, reaching through the simulacrum for the ale pitcher to refill his jeweled bronze cup, the king said, "Of course, of course. What will you need?" His forehead glistened with sweat, but he still said nothing about the illusion.

"The major thing . . ." began the wizard. He paused to rephrase his thought and continued, "My magic works from lesser to greater; for a matter of this magnitude, however, 'lesser' by no means implies 'little.' There are monsters in the Pictish lochs. I need the skull of one of them."

The bronze cup gouged the tabletop as it slammed and splashed. His cloak swirling as he leaped erect, his eyes bright with sudden fury, the king shouted, "Am I God Almighty that you ask this thing of me? Or—" and his hand dropped to the hilt of the long dagger thrust through his brocaded belt—"do you think this is an easier thing than saying no to me? Wizard, if I believed that . . ."

Except for tiny lines around his eyes, the wizard's face was unwrinkled. He kept it bland as a waxen death mask as he said, "Leader, I will not lie to you." He paused, holding the willow branch so still that not even the leaf eyes at the tip, bared when the wizard had stripped away the bark in long threads, trembled. "I need a skull."

The king let out his breath and with it much of his anger. "I can't fight the Picts," he admitted. He stepped over to a side table set with napkins and a wide clay bowl for washing. The king's limp and the thick-soled buskin that gave his right leg back its height were evident when he moved. "The Saxons fight like a big slow bear. My troopers can prick an army of Saxons and run off, prick it again and again until all the blood runs out and the army dies without striking a blow. But the Picts, now . . . the Picts swarm like bees. My horsemen don't have enough hands to swat them."

He tossed a linen napkin to the dining table. The wizard mopped at the ale shining in pools on the parquetry, never taking his eyes off his king. The club-footed man continued, saying, "They dismounted me. A naked Pict rolled out of a clump of heather that couldn't have hidden a toad, and he put a spear up into the belly of my horse. Then I was on the ground and I tried to stand . . . and they swarmed at me. . . ." The king slipped his foot out of its buskin and rubbed its calloused knob on his left calf as he remembered. "Cei got to me before they did, swung me over his saddle. That time. Oh, the Picts can be beaten—" his voice changed as he spoke and he was again the strategist and not the frightened cripple—"and one day I'll do it, send an army of Saxons against them to trample their heather flat and spear them in their burrows. But not yet, wizard. I still have the Saxons to conquer. And there isn't any way I can bring you a monster skull from the middle of the Picts."

The wizard pursed his lips. A thin line of bark still traced down the side of his switch. He began to worry it loose as he thought. "Can you get a man into Ireland?" he asked.

"Perhaps."

"They say the creatures once swam in Irish

lakes. I don't think they still do now, but all *I* need
is the skull of one."

The king sat back down on the bench. His dark
face lost a little of its hardness. "Yes," he said. "I
couldn't send one of my captains . . . any of my
Britons, I think. Matters between us and Ireland
are well enough—given what they were ten years
ago, or a hundred. But there are men on that
island still with long memories and long swords.
Men who haven't forgotten that raids on Britain
stopped when I drowned them in Irish blood. Still,
I've got a few Irishmen in my squadrons. If they
sold themselves to me to fight Saxons, they ought
to be glad of a job this easy. One of them will be
able to bring you what you need." The king got up,
calmly this time. He walked to the door of the entrance hall and threw it open. His six guards
looked at him, scarred men whose eyes were as
hard as the iron links of their mail. In its case in an
alcove behind them, meant by its builder for his
household gods, waited the war standard of the
army. It was a tube of red silk, ten feet long from
mouth to tapered end. When the wind filled it, the
scales of gold writhed and whispered on the
fabric. Uther, the king's father, had borne it. It
was the Pendragon, the King of War Standards,
for which both Uther and his son were named. But
its history was longer than that, longer than any
man now living could recite. Four centuries before, the standard had come to Britain with a
squadron of Roman cavalry. It had remained on
the island, victorious and venerated, ever since.

From behind the king, the wizard asked curiously, "A mercenary? Do you think you'll be able to trust a hireling with something as important to you as this is?"

The king's eyes were fixed on the dragon banner. He was not seeing it as it was, but rather waving over greater triumphs than any it had yet known. The guards looked away uneasily, aware that their Leader's expression was skewed a little to the side of madness. "Well, wizard," he said, "we'll have to make him trustworthy, won't we? Find one with a wife, say, or a son . . . or perhaps a comrade he loves more than life itself. I'll have my dragon, Merlin. Depend on it."

Behind him the wizard nodded slowly. "Yes, my lord Arthur," he said. There was no doubt at all in his voice.

CHAPTER ONE

The amphitheatre had been built as a rich man's toy in the palmy days after Constantius Chlorus had replaced a British usurper with a Roman emperor, when for the first time in decades the armies of civilization were able to fight pirates instead of each other. The structure had never been richly adorned; it was only an oval arena fifty feet by a hundred, surrounded by a five-foot curtain wall of native sandstone. On either side sloped turf mounds which once had been laid with wooden bleachers. In the early days all the countryside, slave and free, had turned out to watch the shows. Sometimes there would be imported gladiators, the acts alternating with local boys battling with quarterstaffs. There were beast hunts, too, though they only used bulls. The bulls were dangerous enough, to be sure, and available

—but even more important, they could not leap the low wall the way a hungry wolf had done on one long-remembered afternoon. Gymnasts had performed in the arena, horse-trainers and fire-eaters as well. Once a magnate of intellectual pretensions had even imported a troupe of Greek mimes to put on a comedy of Terence. The actors' Latin had been so pure that the West British crowd had howled them offstage as foreigners mouthing gibberish, as indeed they had been to the listeners.

Those were the good days. Time passed. Bit by bit, the Empire had passed as well. Trade slowed as markets burned. The amphitheatre became used mostly as a sheepfold, and the bleachers rotted away. The villa of which it was part was too far west for the Saxons to raid it, too far south for the Picts to be a problem. Its owners and their friends met in the evenings and murmured about the state of the Empire, vowing to plant more wheat the next year since the wool market was so uncertain. Then, in the night, Niall and his reavers had landed.

The metal and fabrics, the tools and the weapons, the women they wanted—all those things the Irishmen sent back to their curraghs. The humans they did not take were marched to the amphitheatre where their throats were slit, thirty-seven of them. The Irish joked that a man as fat as the owner of the villa should have had so little blood in him.

Arthur was the first man in a hundred years to find a use for the enclosure after Niall had left it.

There had once been a gate at the western end of
the curtain wall, but it had long since rotted away.
The men who now entered the dark arena did so
through the gap. There were thirty of them of two
distinct groups. Six of the men were of Arthur's
Companions, afoot now but obviously horsemen
from their rolling stride. Despite their evident
discipline, they marched no better than did the
shambling recruits they accompanied. Their dress
was uniform: leather breeches and jerkins,
polished black by the links of iron mail that
covered the leather in battle or on campaign. The
rounded leather caps were padding for helmets.
Though the Companions did not wear their full
armor, a sword hung from the belt of each.

Except for their captain, the Companions themselves were as uniform as their garb. They were all
stocky men of middle height with faces darker
than exposure alone could account for. Arthur had
men of all races among his Companions, but for a
variety of reasons most of his training cadre was
British. They carried flaring torches, the only light
in the amphitheatre since the moon was new. The
breeze was channeled by the viewing mounds. It
whipped the yellow flames. Occasionally it lifted a
droplet of pitch to bring a curse from the man it
touched.

The chief of the Companions was set apart by
more than his arrogance. He stood six feet six,
almost a foot taller than the tallest of his subordinates. He was slim at the hips, thick in the wrists
and the shoulders. While the other Companions
cut their hair short to fit safely under their helmets, the chief's curled out in long auburn ringlets

which had as much of art as of nature about them.
The tall man had no torch, nor was there a real
sword on his belt. In his left hand he carried a
buckler with an iron boss, and in his right was a
pair of training swords. Each of the swords was a
yard long, fashioned of thick wood and strengthened by a rod down the center. The captain swung
them one-handed with a nonchalance that belied
their weight. In the middle of the arena he paused,
looking over the recruits. He let his lip curl under
his moustache, forming the quick sneer that came
so naturally to it.

The recruits were varied but by no means des-
picable. Man by man, they looked to be as for-
midable a pack of killers as could be hired.
Most of them were Germanic—half a dozen
Franks besides Goths, Vandals, and Herulians—
but there were other folk represented as well. A
Moor in a robe of stinking black goat's wool, his
fingers nervous because they no longer held his
pair of knobbed javelins; a Greek with a black
beard to hide a neck scar, still wearing the ac-
coutrements of the Eastern Empire; and the Irishman who called himself Mael mac Ronan and
whose six-foot frame was utterly dwarfed by the
huge Dane who stood beside him.

Starkad Thurid's son was as tall as the captain
of the Companions in the center of the arena; he
looked twice as broad. For a game, the Dane sometimes straightened horseshoes with his hands and
flipped the resulting bars to gaping onlookers. The
torsion-heated metal would sear the men who
caught it as surely as if Starkad had plucked the

horseshoes from a fire. A buckler swung from Starkad's neck on a leather strap, ready to be raised if he wished it. Generally he waded into battle swinging his axe with both hands. Even now the Dane stood with the weapon's head on the ground before him, its oaken helve upright beneath his cupped palms. All the other recruits had obeyed the command to turn out with shield and padding only, leaving their mail and weapons at their tents. Starkad's hands and the carnage his axe left behind had earned him the nickname Cruncher; alone of the men in the amphitheatre, he would have said his Irish friend was the more deadly of the two of them.

For ten years Mael—who admitted to being of the Ui Niall and would change the subject if pressed further—had closed the Dane's back in battle, drunk him cup for cup in peace, followed Starkad's whimsies or led the Dane where a black Irish fancy called. The two of them had spent the decade as soldiers and merchants, pirates, and even for one season farmers. That had ended in strayed cows and seven men dead in the garth to which the cows had strayed. Mael and Starkad were outlawed in Tollund for that, but they had made it to the coast before the posse was raised. It was neither's first outlawry.

The chief of the Companions cleared his throat, a signal to his men. They stilled their banter at once. The murmuring among the recruits, low-voiced and uncertain at all times, died away as they too realized something was going to happen. "Get in a line," the tall captain ordered in Latin.

He sneered again, watching the recruits form awkwardly against the crumbling wall. Some had not understood the order; if they did not guess its meaning from the others' motion, Companions thrust them into place. The Irishman whispered in Starkad's ear and the two took places at the end of the line. There they waited, giving the nearest of the Companion's stare for stare.

"I am Lancelot," rasped the chief of the Companions. For five years he had greeted in this same way each gathering of the mercenaries who sold their swords to Arthur. He explained to his peers that his "demonstrations" served a double purpose: the recruits learned to respect the unfamiliar techniques in which they were to be trained; and they learned to respect Lancelot himself—Arthur's chief adviser and Master of Soldiers. There was a third reason that Lancelot admitted only to himself. He took great pleasure in humiliating barbarian warriors. All the recruits were symbols of the tribes which had brought down the Empire in two continents and eviscerated it even in the East. To Lancelot, Arthur's dream was not an adequate substitute for the past, but it was a suitable tool for revenge.

"I am the chief of Arthur's Companions. It's therefore my duty to start you on your way toward becoming . . . not Companions, I suspect—there's few men anywhere up to that standard and probably none among you—" his lip writhed again—"but fair soldiers, perhaps."

Mael had heard the speech eighteen years before. Then it had been spoken in Irish on the train-

ing grounds of the Ard Ri's Guard. He knew what
Lancelot was leading toward and he listened with
only half an ear. With his right sandal, the Irishman scraped at the soil to test the footing it would
give. It was an amalgam of sand and sheep dung
rammed into the clay substrate, a pocked, irregular surface but hard as concrete and unlikely
to slip out from under a lunging man.

Starkad leaned toward Mael. In Danish and in a
voice not really meant to be private, he rumbled,
"What does he say, brother?"

"You!" Lancelot called, pointing at Starkad
with his right index finger instead of the practice
swords he held in that hand. "Do you speak
Latin?"

Mael cleared his throat. In Latin as good as the
Companion's, he said, "Starkad speaks your
British tongue well enough."

For a moment Lancelot did not reply. When he
spoke there was an edge in his voice. "He'll speak
Latin soon." The captain's eyes swept the line like
a challenge. "You all will—because Latin is the
tongue Arthur's Companions speak. There's no
time in battle for a translation, no place for a
missed command. And you'll learn to shoot a bow,
ride on horseback, thrust with a sword—all these
things, because that's what Companions do. And
you think you can be Companions." Again he
glared at the recruits, one by one. This time he
spat on the ground. "You should live so long," he
said.

"He's both self-important and a fool," observed
Starkad almost soundlessly. His lips were pressed

close to the Irishman's ear. The two men had spent
years together in situations where concerted ac-
tion meant survival. That long experience made
the burr of sound intelligible to Mael where
another man would not even have known the Dane
was speaking. "Let's you and I walk away from
here."

Mael leaned his shoulders back against the
stone. He knew—as perhaps Starkad did also—
that Lancelot, for all his posturing, was no fool. "I
think," Mael replied in the same battle whisper,
"that the lancers on guard out there would ride us
down in a hundred yards. They make a god of
order, here."

Staring at Lancelot as if he were really listening
to the harangue about the necessity of training,
Mael waited for the Dane's reply. At first it was
only a sigh. Then, "You were right when you
warned me, my black-headed friend. But I was so
sure the war pickings would make up for the
trouble . . ."

"Right now I'm going to teach you how to use a
sword," Lancelot was saying. The interest of the
recruits revived. They had been restive though silent during talk of discipline; swords were another
matter. "Most of you carry one, don't you? And I'll
wager there's not a man of you who knows how to
use it—by thrusting, not slashing. 'The edge
wounds, the point kills.' *Always* remember that."

"I've killed my share with the edge," retorted a
Herulian in the middle of the line. His hair was
black but there were gray speckles in his ruff of
beard. Though he was of no more than middle

height, he was broad and had the arms and shoulders of a blacksmith.

The Herulian's jaw was cocked up, expecting a snarled insult and ready to reply in kind. Lancelot instead smiled and said, "Fine. I thought somebody would be stupid enough to say that. Come on out and show me how you use a sword." The Companion tossed one of the training blades so that its polished sides made a yellow ripple in the torchlight.

The Herulian caught the hilt in surprise. His own face lit in a slow grin. Just below the edge of his deerskin cap, a long scar crossed the recruit's forehead. It flamed like a white bar as he flushed with anticipation. His eyes took in the ground, its irregularities and the heavy blocks of sandstone that had fallen from the wall. "Not much of a surface," he grumbled.

Lancelot's smile was as cold as a king's thanks. "Before we next fight the Saxons," he said, "shall we have them rake and roll the field?"

The Herulian slipped his left arm through the loops of his iron-bound target. He began to advance on Lancelot without replying.

The torch-bearing Companions were spread in a forty-foot arc around their captain. Lancelot raised his light buckler in his left hand, gripping it by the double handles on the back of the metal boss. Other than their shields, the antagonists were similarly equipped. Lancelot wore only his gambeson and a cap. The Herulian's cuirass was similarly of leather, boiled and sewn with half a dozen iron rings the size of large bracelets. The

two men eased together with the mutual confi-
dence of persons who had killed frequently and
were both sure they knew the techniques of the
business.

Ten feet from Lancelot, the German shrieked
and charged. The Companion moved with the
lethal grace of a swooping hawk. His right leg slid
forward while his left straightened to give him
thrust. Lancelot's left arm and buckler swung
back slightly, just enough to balance his right arm
and the thick practice sword which stabbed out
unstoppably. Its tip caught the Herulian in the
middle of the right thigh, just below the edge of
the shield. The rounded end of the sword did not
penetrate, but its impact—doubled by the victim's
own momentum—was as bruising as the kick of a
horse. It spun the Herulian to the ground. His own
overhand swing had slashed the air harmlessly.

Lancelot backed a step as if to let his opponent
rise. The Herulian rolled to one knee and winced
as he put weight on the right leg. He touched his
shield rim to the ground to steady himself.
Lancelot lunged again, smashing his point into the
center of the German's chest. Even through the
reinforced leather, a rib cracked. The Herulian
was flung backward. He groaned but tried to
stand again. Though the fight was already over,
the battering had just begun.

"Shift your footing with your weight," Lancelot
said, demonstrating by skidding his right foot forward as he drove at the Herulian's pelvis. Wood
and bone clacked together. The Herulian's skin,
torn between the hardnesses, began to leak blood

onto his linen tunic. "Never, never let yourself lose your balance," the Companion continued. The Herulian had kept his feet after the last blow, but a feint at his thigh brought his guard low. The real thrust broke the left side of the German's collarbone.

Screaming more with frustration than pain, the Herulian dropped his lath sword. He let the target slip from his useless left arm, then seized the heavy round of wood and metal by its rim and hurled it backhand at the face of his tormenter.

Even that was expected. The Herulian's fury and thick shoulders spun the shield with enough force to kill, but it sailed harmlessly over Lancelot's head as he ducked away. When the shield struck the ground thirty feet distant, it clanged.

"You can drive down a battlefield, killing a man at every step," Lancelot said to the other recruits in a conversational tone, "if they're all as inept as this fool." He lunged a last time, his body a perfect line from his left heel through his extended right arm. The sword point buried itself in the pit of the Herulian's stomach. The German doubled over, somehow keeping his feet though his knees wobbled. He was retching uncontrollably.

"There's one other thing that we'll take up later," Lancelot said as he rose gracefully. "Since you've already seen it done wrong tonight, though . . . Shield fighting. Your shield is a useful weapon, but don't *ever* let it out of your hands." The captain stepped to the bent-over Herulian and clubbed him behind the ear with the metal edge of his buckler. All the Herulian's muscles went slack as he dropped. "You see?"

None of the recruits made a sound, not even the two remaining Herulians.

Lancelot's chest was heaving but his voice was under perfect control. Its timbre was normal as he demanded, "Well, do any of you women think you could do better than this one did?"

Starkad turned his head and spat deliberately into the darkness beyond the wall. He faced back around without speaking.

Lancelot pointed the wooden sword at him. "You, Dane!" he said in German. "Can you take me?"

"I can kill you, Roman," Starkad said without raising his voice or lowering his eyes. He matched the Companion's angry stare.

With his foot, Lancelot indicated the lath sword the Herulian had dropped. "Pick it up, Dane," he said.

Starkad's knuckles tightened, but he did not shift his grip on the axe helve. "I won't fight you with toys, Roman," he said. "Get yourself a real sword and we'll holmgang."

No one in the arena doubted that the Dane seriously meant his offer to go to an island for a death duel with the Master of Soldiers. The recruits drew up, weighing the alternatives of mutiny or brutal exercises like the incident they had just watched. The six Companions tensed as they awaited decisions over which they had no control.

Mael stepped forward. "I'll fight you," he said to Lancelot in Latin. He scooped up the wooden sword. Lancelot smiled at him; but then, the captain had never let his smile slip, even when baiting Starkad.

Mael could have been a model for Lancelot in nine-tenths scale. He was six feet tall, large-boned and covered with muscles that looked flat until they tensed and stood out in knotted ridges. In battle the Irishman wore a mail vest to mid-thigh and a rimless steel cap. Tonight he had turned out as ordered, bareheaded and with only a gambeson of laminated linen covering his torso. Without headgear his one affectation became obvious; he still shaved the back of his head to above the ear peaks, in the fashion of the High King's Guard. Whenever someone asked Mael about it, he told them loudly that he was a coward who feared to be seized from behind when he fled, and Mael's eyes dared any listener to believe him. The shield the Irishman carried was a heavy target like the Herulian's, a round of plywood three feet in diameter with an iron boss and a seamless rim of the same metal. The rim had been shrunk on like a tire to a fellie. The shield was plain and serviceable—and of course new. A good sword was an heirloom that father might pass down to son through several generations. A good shield served once in a hot fight, and its owner thanked his gods then if it got him through that one encounter without disintegrating.

Mael and Lancelot edged toward one another, rotating counterclockwise to keep their shield arms advanced. The Irishman refused the first blow. Lancelot thrust from six feet away, his long

sword and longer arm flowing in one supple
motion that brought the sword tip to within an
inch of Mael's chest. The Companion recovered as
smoothly as he had struck, but there was a glint of
surprise in his gaze. Mael had jerked back at the
waist, just enough for the thrust to clear him—
and no more. There had been no counterattack,
though, neither the roundhouse swing to be expected from a barbarian nor the lightning thrust
of which Mael's cool precision suggested he might
be capable.

Lancelot feinted at Mael's face and lunged low
at the left shin which only the high-laced sandal
protected. The point should not have rung off the
Irishman's shield boss, jarring every bone in the
Companion's lower back, but somehow the shield
was there. Still Mael did not strike back. Lancelot's smile was as stiff now as the leather of
his jerkin, but he kept his curses within him as he
and the Irishman circled tensely.

Lancelot's third thrust was smooth and precise
and guided cleanly past Mael's face by the edge of
the Irishman's sword which redirected it harmlessly. The missed stroke almost threw the Companion off balance, but practiced reflexes allowed
him to recover. The Irishman's reaction seemed to
give Lancelot his first real opportunity, however—
Mael screamed something Gaelic and bloodthirsty, raised his sword high over his head, and
let his target swing to the side where it did not
cover his body.

This was the fatal error Lancelot had expected
from the barbarian, the triumph of bloodlust over

discipline. He reacted instantly, lunging again in a
spray of sand even though his weight was not
perfectly centered nor was his left leg set with the
care he would have demanded of a trainee. The
captain had been rattled by the Irishman's skill,
after all, and he needed a quick victory to retain
the prestige that was his life.

Mael's timing was dangerous but perfect. His
left foot lifted as if drawn to the Companion's
blade by magnets. Even if Lancelot had seen the
parry coming, he was already hopelessly com-
mitted to his lunge. Mael's hobnailed sandal
caught the sword. The weapon and the man holding it spun to their left. The point glided past Mael
again. This time Lancelot's shield was no longer
between him and his opponent but rather on the
other side of his body. Lancelot could have left the
buckler in his room for all the good it did in stop-
ping Mael's sword.

The Irishman's practice blade scissored down in
the same motion that had brought up his left foot
to block Lancelot's thrust. The sound Mael's
sword made on the Companion's cap was like the
first slap of lightning before the full weight of
thunder rolls across the sky. The oaken blade
shattered, leaving the hilt and reinforcing rod in
Mael's hand. Lancelot skidded on his face, driven
by his own lunge and the force of the blow. His
head stopped inches short of a block of stone.
There was a collective intake of breath from the
other men in the amphitheatre, recruits and Companions alike. For the first moments after the
blow, there was no sound at all from Lancelot.

Mael backed toward his place in line beside Starkad. There was a wild light in his eyes. He looked at the vibrating remains of his practice sword and giggled. "'The edge wounds . . .'" he quoted. He giggled again. Then he flipped the rod over his back into the darkness.

Lancelot raised himself to one elbow and stared at Mael. The Companion's nose was broken. Blood from that and from his sand-abraded face smeared the ground. It shone black in the torchlight. If the Irishman's eyes were wild, then Lancelot's were hell-lit. Without taking his eyes off Mael, the captain felt for the block of stone and grasped it with both hands.

The block was coarse sandstone, a rectangular piece of the wall larger than a man's torso. Lancelot faced it and locked his right knee under him. He was a big man and hugely strong even for his size, but there should have been no way a single human could have lifted that mass of rock. Grunting, Lancelot gripped it by the ends and cleaned it, bringing the block to chest level and rotating his palms under the edges. The right side and shoulder seams of his gambeson ripped. The leather flopped loose over muscles as stiff as the stone they lifted.

One of the Companions dropped his torch and ran to Lancelot, his hands washing each other in the same terrified indecision that knotted his tongue. Lancelot ignored him, did not even see the man although his eyes were open and staring. Before Lancelot was only the red blur of sandstone and the brighter red of the blood bulging the veins

behind his retinas. The captain straightened his
legs and arms together, jerking the monstrous
weight overhead.

There was silence in the arena save for the peep-
ing of frogs in the low spots beyond the wall.
Lancelot stood, a caryatid whose face was no
redder where blood smeared it than where the
blood suffused the flesh within. Then the towering
figure took a step forward, toward the Irishman
who no longer laughed. The Goth to Mael's left
blundered away from him, stumbling because his
eyes were fixed on Lancelot. It was a scene whose
like had not been played out in the fifteen centuries since Ajax lifted a boulder and advanced on
Hector beneath the walls of Troy.

Lancelot took a second step. Dust puffed from
his boot toe and the hard ground shook. He was
eight feet from Mael and only a chest's width more
from the wall against which the stone would pin
his victim. Mael crouched, his shield raised but
useless.

Starkad stepped forward, his buckler swinging
like a bangle on its neck strap. The Dane had
gripped the four-foot shaft of his axe with both
hands. Using the doubled strength of his arms, he
brought the ten-pound head up in an arc that shimmered because speed blurred its glittering highlights. The peen led, square and blunt and
tempered to take shocks that would shatter the
glass-hard cutting edge on the other side.

The axe struck the center of the sandstone
block. It rebounded, ringing with a shrill sound
that was nearer a scream of anguish than a chime.

The metal could shriek and leap back; the rock had no such resilience. It would hold or would crack, and the weight of Starkad's blow left no choice but the latter.

Lancelot's breath *whuffed* again with tension released as the stone split in the middle. It fell backwards out of his hands. The twinned blocks thudded to the sand together and rolled once, dice that gods might have thrown. Lancelot, his balance gone and with it the hysterical strength that had worn his flesh like a cloak, toppled and fell back between the stones. He lay there, his eyes beginning to focus for the first time in minutes.

Starkad's right hand had been leading on the axe helve. That whole arm was numb to the shoulder. With his left hand alone, the Dane raised the axe over his head. Its bearded edge still quivered like a live thing with the shock. "They call me the Cruncher, Roman," Starkad boomed in British. "Shall I show you why?"

The tension broke in the shadow of that axe. Like a force of nature, a storm or an avalanche sweeping all before it, the weapon was for the instant a thing that no man present could imagine withstanding. Surrender brings an absence of conflict; recruits and Companions relaxed accordingly. When the six mounted cataphracts rode through the entrance to the arena, the men gathered within were too drained of emotion to do more than glance at the newcomers. Minutes earlier, their arrival would have jangled nerves and led to bloody mutiny because the recruits would have thought they were about to be attacked.

The six riders were Companions in full armor. Their gear jingled as they cantered into the amphitheatre. They were of normal height for West Britons, averaging around five and a half feet tall, but in armor and mounted they bulked larger than life. Two of them wore scale mail, tiny leaves of iron sewn individually to a leather backing where they lay in overlapping rows. The result was not as effective as a fabric of rings, each interlocked with four others, but it was within the capacity of any smith and seamstress to manufacture. Scale armor was both cheaper than ring mail and far more readily available.

The four other horsemen wore rings, however; their chief's had been washed with silver so that his torso danced in the torchlight. Among Arthur's Companions, as in most professional armies, it was customary to flaunt wealth in fine equipment. The only proviso was that one's arms must not appear more valuable than one's ability. Besides their mail shirts, the cataphracts wore leggings faced with scales or rings on the outer sides. The insides of their thighs were covered only with leather, not simply because armor was unnecessary there but because iron would have robbed the riders of the firm grip they needed to stay on their horses. Their saddles had four low horns, two front and two behind—and no stirrups at all. Keeping mounted in a fight was a major part of the training each Companion received.

"Lancelot, what in the name of the crucified God are you doing?" demanded the silver-armored horseman.

Lancelot used the broken stone beside him as an

anchor and pulled himself into a sitting position. He tried to speak but blood or a dry throat choked him. He spat out a tooth on the ground. One of his own men knelt beside the Master of Soldiers and ripped a strip of linen from the hem of his tunic. Another Companion splashed the rag with beer from the goatskin bottle hanging at his waist. Together, as carefully as artificers preparing a pharaoh for eternal burial, the two soldiers sponged away at the damage to Lancelot's face.

"Lord Gawain," one of the training cadre blurted, his eyes flicking back and forth from Starkad to the mounted man, "it was—"

"I'll wait for your captain to tell me, thanks," interrupted Gawain with a mildness that bit. The trooper bobbed apologetically. No one else spoke aloud while the two Companions worked on Lancelot.

Nearer the wall, two Herulians and a Frank were tending to Lancelot's object lesson. The remaining recruits had drifted toward them. The nursing gave the men something to focus on instead of the cataphracts and their battered officer. Hot looks came out of the motley throng, directed against the isolated Mael and Starkad. The torches had burned down to embers and a trickle of fire, but they had dimmed gradually enough that those present could still see each other.

"I think they've just written us out of the human race," Mael said to the Dane. He tossed his head toward the recruits in lieu of a more respectful gesture. "They think they'll all be punished for what I did to that prancing dandy . . . and they've seen enough of Arthur's discipline to worry about it."

"What *we* did to that one," Starkad corrected softly, staring at his right hand as he clenched and unclenched it. Feeling seemed to be returning. "Men and dogs, Irishman, men and dogs . . . Give me a wolf pack any day. Wolves tear out no throats but their enemy's—or their dinner's, of course. But wound a dog and the ones he's been running with'll be the first on him. Since they're the nearest." The Dane flexed his hand again, turned it over to show curls of hair as heavy and dark as copper wire crawling down the back of it. Even Starkad's fingers were hairy, except for the skin over his knuckles. Those patches gleamed pale in the torchlight for not being shadowed by hairs. "We could run," he said in the same tones of bored unconcern.

Mael had been watching the riders with a frank, friendly smile on his face. The Irishman looked as if he could not imagine what their dismounted fellows of the training cadre were telling them in low murmurs. "No, I don't think so," Mael said. "I don't feel quite like I'm about to die yet, and I surely would die if we ran." He grinned sidelong at Starkad. "Of course, *you* may be about to die, my friend. That stone was probably a valuable Roman relic—and you've heard how this Arthur is about Roman things."

The Dane chuckled, reaching across to knead Mael's skull brutally. They were in this as in most things—together. Call it friendship or a wish to

die. "Next time I'll have sense enough to use the
edge on his skull," Starkad said. "At least I'll be
able to use both hands if I have to, later."

Mael continued to study the Companions. Men
in armor were no rarity now in any army apart
from the Irish. Long past were the days in which
Rome's legions faced hordes of shrieking Germans
protected by no more than a loin clout and a
wicker shield. Rome had educated her barbarian
neighbors. Part of the process had been by ex-
ample, survivors around camp fires telling how
their points skidded from bronze corselets. Even
more destructive of Rome's superiority had been
her practice of hiring enemies as auxiliaries, training them in armored tactics for twenty-five years
—and all too frequently having the men return to
their tribes across the Rhine or the Danube to pass
their training along. When the naked mobs became effective heavy infantry, Rome's own period
of lordship was soon to end.

But while the Companions' armor was common
enough for warriors who could afford it, their
army of weapons was not. From the right side of
each saddle, just ahead of the rider's knee, hung a
quiver of arrows. A bow was cased to the left,
balancing the quiver. Horse archers had been a
staple of Oriental warfare for centuries, but they
had never been popular among the armies of Western Europe. Even in nations to whom mounted
bowmen were standard, the nobles who could
afford full armor carried swords and sneered at
the drudgery of daily archery practice. These
Companions were equipped with both armor and

bows. Either Arthur had issued expensive mail to
all his forces, or his discipline was so rigid that
even the wellborn were forced into finger-burning,
muscle-knotting archery exercises. Perhaps both
were true. Brief experience suggested to Mael that
they both were. The Irishman wondered where
Arthur got the money and the authority to put
such a program into effect.

Like the dismounted cadre, the riders all carried
swords sheathed along their left thighs. The varied
richness of the weapons suggested the rank and
wealth of the bearers. The hilts ranged from plain
wood, in the case of the two troopers wearing
scale armor, to Gawain's, which was of iron forged
in a single unit with the blade and quillons. The
metal was carven and heavily inlaid with gold and
ivory. Its owner's calloused hand had smoothed
the hilt to a perfect fit for him, proving the weapon
was no useless toy for ceremony.

One further weapon completed each cata-
phract's arsenal, a weapon which Mael knew
for the most deadly and difficult to master of all.
In tubular sockets hanging from the right rear of
the saddles stood twelve-foot lances. The heads
were four-sided pyramids, narrow and a foot long.
A tang joined each point to an ash shaft two inches
in diameter and as smooth and straight as an
artisan could fashion.

Lances have only rarely in history been popular.
A lancer gets the first stroke at an enemy, but if he
misses, the speed of his charge thrusts him into
the hands of his foe with no way to strike again. A
light javelin can be flung from a distance or its

shaft raised to block a hostile blow. A lance is like
a glacier, massive and unidirectional. It is too
heavy to throw, too clumsy for protection. Worse,
when saddles lacked stirrups as these did, a
clumsy lance thrust was as likely to dismount the
lancer as to slay his opponent.

And yet trained lancers were the terror of every
field on which they fought. Lances killed with the
unanswerable certainty of catapults, but even
greater than their material effect was the moral. A
line of glittering lance-heads plunging nearer,
backed by dust and thunder and tons of armored
horsemen, was soul-shattering.

Mael frowned inwardly, though his face remained bland. He could appreciate the Companions, for he had been raised a fighting man and
spent his life in the service of war. But these men
were simply too good, too perfect. To conceive of
and train them had been works of genius—but a
damned bloody genius it must be. It was natural
for men to kill and, aye, to make a business of
killing. But to turn slaughter into an intellectual
exercise was as warped as for a woman to lust
after a bull, and the progeny was apt to be as evil.
Lancelot sucked beer into his mouth, wincing at
its astringence. He spat after swizzling it around.
The second mouthful he swallowed. Only then did
he look up at Gawain who was waiting with a
hunter's patience while his men fidgeted. "Well?"
Lancelot said, shaping the word very carefully.

"The Leader needs to talk to two of the new recruits," Gawain said. Both men spoke Latin but
with markedly different accents. The variation

was less regional than a matter of education. Although Britain had scholars and orators the equal of any on the Continent, Gawain had never been trained by such. The Votadini, his tribe and his Leader's, valued other skills than those of civilization. "He sent us to bring them now—the Irishman, Mael mac Ronan, and the Dane who joined with him."

Mael looked at his friend. He popped the big man's shoulder with the heel of his hand and said, "See? That's why I hate to do anything final. You just can't tell what's going to turn up."

Starkad snorted, oblivious to the staring faces around them. "They could still be taking us out to chop us."

"They didn't have any reason to chop us until now," Mael responded cheerfully, "and nobody got a message out of the arena to those guys." Tugging Starkad by the left shoulder, the Irishman stepped toward Gawain and his half squad. "Here we are, friend. Much as we hate to leave this happy gathering."

Gawain's chuckle was full and appreciative without being in the least friendly. "I'd intended to put you both on pillions to get you to headquarters," the slim captain said, "but now that I've seen your friend I'll be damned if I have a horse try to carry him and one of my boys besides. You can walk, and we'll all be happiest if you don't waste time at it." Gawain glanced back at Lancelot. "Good night, Master," he said with an ironic salute. Then, to his men and their charges, "Let's go."

CHAPTER TWO

The horsemen wheeled and rode out of the
arena. Gawain set a pace that brought Mael and
Starkad immediately to a jog. Beyond the gateway
the Companions formed two lines abreast. With
the recruits sandwiched between them—as much
escorted as under guard, but under guard beyond
doubt—they rode back through the darkened
countryside toward the villa that was Arthur's
main base and headquarters. The nearest town,
Moridunum, the market place for the region, was
five miles southward. There were no civilians
closer than that except for dependents.

The route to the villa took the company past the
recruit lines near the arena. They were of wattle
and daub with thatched roofs, recently built and
broken up internally into tiny one- and two-man
cubicles. There were a hundred units in blocks of

ten with common walls. Each had a door in front facing the latrine, a window in the back, and barely enough floor space for beds and the personal effects of the occupants. Only transients and trainees were quartered there; veterans had billets attached to the main building. The semi-private rooms were not intended as benefits to the recruits. There was no enclosure in the area in which more than a dozen men could gather and conspire because of the separation. When the trainees assembled, it was either under the eyes of the cadre or during meals in the huge mess hall in the main building. Then the new men were mixed with no less than equal numbers of hard-bitten veterans.

Arthur was under no illusions as to how his discipline would be received by mercenary recruits, and had the recruits not been bloody-handed killers already, they would have been of no use to the king. His control measures were as carefully considered as every other part of the training.

Mael jogged along with the horses easily, holding his shield close to keep it from battering him at the end of its neck strap. His legs were long, his chest large, and if the Irishman had not deliberately trained for running in the decade since he left the Ard Ri's Guard, then still he was not a man to be concerned about a half-mile jog. He looked over at Starkad. The Dane had dropped back two steps and caught the nearest horseman's quiver in his left hand. Using the horse to smooth his own pace, a psychic rather than physical crutch but no

less real for that, Starkad was pounding along
without evident concern. He and the horseman
had exchanged brief glances when he attached
himself. Sensibly, the Companion had made no
protest. The Dane was ignoring the light shield,
letting it flop against his breast. In his right hand
he carried his axe at its balance near the head. Its
shaft worked up and down behind him like a pump
handle as he ran. Mael grinned and stopped worrying about his friend.

The villa they approached was a two-story building of stone and stucco. A taller block of apart-
ments had been recently constructed of lath and
plaster along the back. The kernel of the villa had
been raised in the time of Trajan and expanded
piece by piece over the centuries following. At the
villa's zenith and that of Roman Britain in the
early fourth century, the building had been filled
by slaves who lived in its rambling halls and
turned raw wool into fine woven cloth under awn-
ings in the central courtyard. With the change
from sheep to wheat, the surrounding country had
been broken into tenant holdings and the slave
gangs had disappeared. Rooms were closed. In
earlier ages the owners had been occasional visitors from London or the Continent; now they
became permanent residents.

Then the Irish came. Though they did not burn
the building, for the next century it was occupied
only by travelers and the bandits and deserters
who were an increasing feature of the times. When
Arthur grasped power, he found in the villa his
safe base in the center of what remained British in
the face of the Saxon onrush.

Gawain drew up at the front entrance. Once a portico had led to it, but the columns had been wood and long since burned in cooking fires. The high oak doors had been replaced. They stood open, displaying the lamplit hall and the remainder of the squad on guard duty that night.

"Pass on through," Gawain said to Mael with a sardonic smile. Turning a little further he added to Starkad, "You'll have to leave your axe."

"I'd as soon die holding it," the Dane replied. His chest was heaving and his face was flushed from the run.

"Well, that's the choice," Gawain agreed without emotion.

"Give me the axe, lunk," Mael said. He reached out, touching the shaft with his fingertips but not trying to grasp the weapon. "Indeed, they may kill us. Assuredly they will if you insist on posturing." Mael spoke in Danish, softly enough and more quickly then he thought the Companions could follow. "This one doesn't posture, my friend. He'd as soon kill us as not. And that'd be a damned foolish way to die." The Irishman closed his hand over the axe. "If they attack us, I'll let you use my rocky head for a club." He lifted the weapon from Starkad and handed it to Gawain.

The British captain weighed the axe and tried its balance. "Sometimes I wish I had the size for one of these," he said to Mael with a grin as lethal as a wolf's. Mael grinned back, knowing that if he had toyed with this man as he had with Lancelot, one or both of them would already be dead. Gawain would simply not have accepted any conclusion short of death in such a challenge.

Mael and Starkad passed through the doorway
and its gauntlet of lounging guards. The roof of
the hall was opened by an impluvium which fun-
neled rainwater down into the decorative cistern
in the center of the hall. The architectural design
was normal in Italy, miserably uncomfortable
during British winters. The concession that Mediterranean style had made to northern weather was
to close the three doorways off the hall with solid
panels instead of leaving them open.

One of the Companions tapped deferentially on
the left-hand door, then opened it to an order
grunted from within. Mael started through.
Starkad touched his shoulder and said, only half
in jest, "No, I lead and you cover my back. Just
like any battle." He entered the room ahead of the
Irishman.

There was no obvious danger inside, only two
men reclining at the head and side of an intarsia
table. Neither man was prepossessing, Mael
thought. There was certainly nothing in the
younger of them to make fighting men refer to him
so naturally as Leader. And then the two looked
up, and Mael felt their eyes on him. The Irishman
grinned, because he had to do something with his
face before these men, each in his own way as
deadly as Gawain.

"Starkad Thurid's son," Arthur said, not a question but a vocalization of notes jotted somewhere
inside his skull. "Starkad Grettir."

The Dane nodded, stiff-backed and hostile. He
had already measured the distance to the king. He
knew he could leap it in time for a single skull-

cracking blow, even if a spear from behind had gone through him.

"And Mael mac Ronan." Arthur was not the hulking bear of a man rumor on the Continent had him. The Saxons who returned from Britain needed an excuse for their fears, a snarling monster to lead their enemies, a beast with swords the length of flails and muscles that could lift an ox. This man, forty and slim except in the shoulders; more gray-haired than gray-bearded, but with much of gray in his beard as well; three or four inches less than Mael's height, though the unclasped cloak over his lower legs hid the exact length they stretched—this was no creature for whom a Saxon warrior could articulate a terror that his fellows could understand.

Mael didn't care who understood. He had seen the Companions and had now seen Arthur himself. Both the man and what he stood for were frightening.

"I need an Irishman to take a trip home for me," the king said. "Merlin here—" he nodded toward the older man on the side bench. The wizard's lips had been working silently ever since Mael and Starkad had entered the room—"needs the skull of a water monster as lived once in your lakes. Have you heard of such?"

Very formally and carefully, Mael said, "I left Ireland for reasons that seemed good to me—and better yet to some who stayed home. I have no wish to die and less to return to Ireland—which may well be different ways to say the same thing."

The king took a swallow of ale and brushed

foam from his moustache with the back of his hand. Merlin beside him continued to mutter, using the butt of his willow whip to divide a puddle of ale. The two dollops of thin fluid stayed separate after the wand passed instead of flowing back together. Arthur was saying, "You're Irish, after all. You can blend in, not attract attention as Lancelot would or Gawain. Call yourself something—oh!" And the king broke off with a gleeful chuckle at his insight. "Of course, of course—you already do. It's a matter of only a few days and back, you see, nothing to tax a disguise."

Merlin said *something* aloud and the puddles of ale rejoined with a pop of blue fire.

"Well?" Arthur demanded.

"Perfect," said the wizard. "Exactly what you wanted." The old man looked up at his king. "None of my spells kept the two pools apart after I'd given the names of these two. Not women nor wealth—nor fear. They won't abandon each other."

"And duty?" the king asked as if the two mercenaries were not in the room.

"Duty means standing by your friends," Starkad rumbled in German before Merlin answered.

Arthur laughed. "And trust means being sure of what a man will do," he said, "not thinking that he's a friend and so he'll back you. Sit down, Irishman—and you, too, Cruncher, though there's no work for you in this except for waiting here until your friend returns. I'll explain what it is we have in mind. . . ."

* * *

The fishing village—six houses, each owner kin to the other five—had been built at the higher end of the rocky beach. Above, the long, rank grass stretched eastward over the Cambrian hills, furring the spine of the promontory so that there was no one place on which a man could stand and see why it had been named Octapitarum—Eight-headed.

To the inhabitants, the baylet was a separate thing and not merely one facet of the seven of the headland. Indeed, the village was part of the greater world only as they chose—in normal times. About once a month the villagers emptied their drying sheds of the fish stacked there, layered with salt baked from tidal pools by the sun. They loaded the fish on ox carts which then creaked along rocky paths in an all-day journey to the nearest of the great farms. There the fisherfolk would barter their catch for cloth and metalwork and sometimes ale better than their own sour, salty brew.

Had the villagers wished, the magnates inland would as willingly have come for the fish themselves. The price would have been effectively greater, since then the fishermen need not have kept oxen. But little as they cared to leave their notch in the island's wall, their home, the fishermen cared less to show visitors to it. Thus the arrival of King Muirchertach's embassy had been almost as unpleasant a shock to the villagers as if the fifty strangers *were* hostile, as they thought at first.

Mael listened to Arthur's account of the landing,

grinning broadly. "What did they do?" he asked
the king. Like Arthur, the Irishman had remained
on his horse when the column halted. Starkad had
dismounted as soon as the glittering sea announced they had reached their destination.

"Oh, they sent a boy running to the nearest
villa," the king said also smiling. "They don't run
very well either, you know. The owner of the villa
whipped off a messenger to me and ran along behind with all his household as quick as he could.
He thought it was a raid, too, and he knew these
hovels—" Arthur nodded to the drystone huts—
"weren't going to occupy the murdering Irish
long.

"So . . . I took the half squadron I had on hand,
rode thirty of the horses to death or to bonebreak,
got lost twice pushing on at night. We got here at
dawn, just in time to see these damned fishermen
lugging their nets to their boats, pretending there
wasn't a curragh pulled up on the shore and fifty
men trying to sleep around greenwood fires while
the locals ignored them. If we'd been half an hour
later I wouldn't have seen the fishing boats. I'd
probably have killed everybody on the shore."
Arthur looked sidelong at Mael. "And then how
would we have gotten you to Ireland, my dragon-
snatcher?"

"Oh, you'd have found something," Mael said,
his humor chilled at the thought of his mission.
They were a huge company for this quiet opening
to the sea. The Irish embassy had been loaned
mounts for its return to the shore. Arthur accompanied Muirchertach's men with two hundred of

his cataphracts, fully equipped as he himself was. The king's mail was silvered and the general sheen picked out by links washed in gold instead. A helmet with a long nose-guard covered his head. The helm had a faceted appearance because it was made of welded steel plates, carefully resilvered after each time dents had to be beaten out of it. To either side flared a gilded wing. Behind Arthur, a bearer raised the ancient war standard to snap and snarl in the wind.

"If this is such a peaceful embassy," Mael remarked, "why does it look like they're being escorted back to the coast by a warband?"

Arthur chuckled. "Oh, just honor due a fellow monarch, perhaps. Muirchertach's more than friendly, yes—to me. It seems there's trouble in Ireland—" and again Arthur's eyes darted unexpectedly at Mael—"and though he's not king of the Laigin yet, Muirchertach has notions for the future. He needs help. For the time, I've sent him one sword as a gift by way of his war chief Dubtach there." Arthur nodded at the burly leader of the embassy. The chieftain's red hair was bound back with a linen fillet and his chest was deliberately bare to display the battle scars on it. "Muirchertach hopes that one day I'll send more swords—and men of my own to carry them."

"You want Ireland, too?" Mael asked bluntly.

"It's part of the world, isn't it?" the king replied, and his words were too offhand to be a joke. Arthur looked out over his accompanying troops. They had formed in a double row as soon as the terrain had opened enough to position a hundred

men abreast. To the right, the ground hung in
terraced pastures sufficient for the goats and
oxen; goats ran loose beyond as well, supple-
menting the grass with mast from stunted hardwoods. The Irish, with Gawain alone of Arthur's
men riding along with them, were filing down the
gentler slope toward the houses and the shoreline
beyond on foot.

"In the meantime, I thought this would be a
good time for a little . . . friendly demonstration,"
Arthur continued, obviously pleased at a chance to
flaunt his abilities in front of a new listener. By
now the king had to have heard about Mael's
destruction of Lancelot the night before, but he
had made no reference to it on the ride to the coast
—unless requesting that Mael and Starkad be
placed beside him was in itself a comment.
"Thanks to you Irish becoming Christians—"

"*Some* Irish becoming Christians," Mael cut in
sharply.

"*Most* of you Irish becoming Christians," the
king went on smoothly, "and Vitalis' daughter
marrying your High King . . . and most of all, I
suppose, the Plague and the squabbles on your
island that seem to have left fewer cutthroats to
amuse and more at home to amuse them—"
Arthur paused but Mael said nothing, only grinned
across at the slender king. Arthur was baiting
death as he dreamed of empire—"perhaps there
wouldn't have been many raids here even without
my Companions to deal with them. But it can't
hurt to get word back that the Companions *are*
here—and *can* deal with raiders—can it?"

Arthur nodded to his cornicine. That tallish
Briton raised a coiled bronze horn to his lips and
blew a single note. Downslope, close to the nearest
outbuilding of the village, Gawain bent to speak
briefly to Dubtach. Then the Companion cantered
over to a smokehouse built of heavy timber. The
building stood a score of yards to the right of the
main path. Using the neck strap, Gawain hung
from the ridgepole the plain shield he was carrying in place of his usual ornately studded one. He
waved up the hill to Arthur, then rejoined the
Irish. Dubtach challenged him, though the words
of their argument were not intelligible at the distance. The Irish waited, bunched together, while
Gawain and their leader spoke. Some of them
watched the shield, their hands a little tighter
than usual on their own weapons. The low, slate-
roofed houses of the village had their shutters
latched as if the visitors were a storm, but the
boards trembled sideways and eyes within caught
the light in stray reflections as the women looked
on.

Arthur himself was in conversation with Cei, the
two men leaning together so that their shoulders
and helmets touched. Their hands twitched in ges-
tures that meant nothing except to each other.
Starkad tapped Mael lightly on the right knee and
used a tiny gesture of his head to indicate on the
other side of Arthur the six riders who had moved
up when the horn blew. Now they waited, talking
among themselves in mild, high-pitched voices.
They sounded from a short distance like the sing-
song giggling of a girls' school. Their horses had

no reins or saddles. The riders held bows with nocked arrows in their hands.

"Oh, yes. . . ." Mael said quietly. He had not noticed these men on the march. Perhaps they had been used as outriders, scouting the line. It was the sort of work they gloried in.

"You know them?" Starkad asked.

"I know of them. Huns." Mael stared openly. They were little men with black, coiled hair and flat faces. One was bare-chested. His skin was hairless and almost of a color with his breeches of supple leather tanned from rabbits or other small mammals. Only in size and the ease in which they sat on their mounts, knees high and calves flexed sharply backward, were the Huns uniform. Two more wore leather corselets, black from being hardened in boiling vinegar. The ancient bronze medallions of a dead legionary, traded eastward over the centuries and so polished with age that the reliefs had been worn almost away, glittered against one corselet.

Two of the other Huns wore mail, but while one set was of the highest quality—each ring a double coil that left almost no interstices for a point to enter—the other shirt was of scales of a type almost unknown in the West. They were large, up to three inches across the base, and made of aurochs' horn instead of metal. The scales were translucent gray and they shimmered as if still alive.

The sixth Hun wore no more armor than the first, only a linen tunic over his breeches, but despite the warm sun, he had a cape of marmot furs pinned at his shoulder. Its cowl was thrown back and the lustrous brown fur rippled down behind him.

"I fought them once with Hjalti's army," Starkad said. He ran an index finger along the peen of his axe as he counted silently. "Fourteen, fifteen years ago, that would be. Maybe if I live another hundred years or so, I'll want to fight Huns again."

Gawain shouted to the king from the midst of the Irishmen. The Companion waved his helmet as an all-clear signal.

"Now," said Arthur. His cornicine sucked a chestful of air, then blew a long note. The six Huns fanned forward at a gallop without noticeably directing their horses. The riders were shrieking like files on stone, each a different note and as bloodcurdling as the cries of the wounded when crows alight on their faces. The Huns shot as they rode, reloading in a single, natural motion with the draw and release. Their bows were short but heavy, recurved and stiffened with plates of horn and bone. The staves averaged between a hundred and a hundred and twenty pounds of pull, so that only the flicker of points and white fletching was visible as the arrows slapped out at the target.

At the first shout and volley, half a dozen of the Irish dropped flat. But the Huns' target was the shield and the men standing twenty yards from it were as safe as if they were in Ireland. Despite the range and the gallop, none of the Hunnish arrows was more than a hand's breadth off the mark.

The shield wobbled. Arrows hitting it squarely

made a double *thunk* as the shafts penetrated and struck the shed behind. Arrows that missed the shield sank to half their length in the heavy timbers. The target area was suddenly a deadly garden, the feathered ends of the arrows trembling like horizontal flowers in the sunlight.

As the riders yipped and thundered downslope, they opened gaps of about six feet between each man and his neighbor. For those on the ends of the line, the final volley was almost an edge-on shot at the shield as the charge swept around the smokehouse, three men to a side. The last arrows smacked into the target as surely as the first had.

In the gravel yard between two buildings, the Huns drew up and reformed. They cantered back around the shed, laughing and gibing among themselves. They utterly ignored the Irishmen who now clustered around the shield. There were over twenty arrows in or near the target. Dubtach tried to pull one out of the timber and found that the shaft splintered before the barbed head would release. There was awe in the faces of those who looked at the swarthy little men. Two of the Christian Irish surreptitiously crossed themselves.

"What do you think of my demonstration?" Arthur asked.

Mael jumped to realize that the king was again speaking to him. The Irishman smiled. His right hand rested on Starkad's shoulder in an unconscious gesture of affection, and from his saddle he looked across the big Dane's head toward Arthur. "Very nice," he said. "There's not a man down there—" his thumb generally indicated the Irish—

"but believes every one of your Companions can ride and shoot like that. At home they'll spread the story and piece fable onto it—though by the Dagda's club, the truth is enough! You'll have an island defended by devils, here, and no place at all for a pirate to think of landing."

"But you aren't fooled," said the king, his lips still curved in what was either good humor or the start of a snarl.

"I've heard of Huns—and I've seen your . . . desire for discipline," Mael replied. "If you could find anybody else to do the job they do, you'd never in hell let these Huns parade like a troupe of buffoons, would you?"

It was a smile. "Yes," Arthur said, "and when they're drunk—which is generally—it *is* a devil's job to keep them from cutting every throat in reach before raping the warm bodies. But they have their uses, as you say."

The king looked back at the beach where the Irish were gathering about the curragh, preparing to launch it. "Time for you to join your kinsmen," Arthur said. He drummed his fingers, thin and paler than the backs of his hands, on his pommels. "Bring me back what I need, Irishman. Bring me back the skull. . . ."

Mael swung off his borrowed horse. "I'll walk, I think," he said.

Starkad echoed, "We'll walk. To the boat."

Arthur made no response. His eyes were as unfocused as a drugged man's, though his seat on his horse was firm.

Flints in the soil clacked beneath the hobnails in

Mael's sandals as the friends trudged toward the sea. Starkad's huge feet were encased in boots sewn from single pieces of cowhide, supple and silent as he walked. They were laced around the outside. In colder weather the boots could be stuffed with rags for insulation and tied with one or two fewer wraps of the thongs.

Gawain rode past on his way back to Arthur, giving Mael a nod and a grin that could have meant anything. When they were beyond him but still long out of earshot of the Irish, Starkad said, "If we both got in the boat, friend, we could be well out to sea before any horsemen reached us. I've always wanted to see Ireland again."

"Umm," Mael said. "You watched that little archery practice just now?"

"They'd kill half the embassy if they started shooting at us in the middle of the boat," Starkad protested, starting to raise his voice.

"That's going to bother Huns?" Mael asked. "Or Arthur?"

The Dane chuckled. He said, "Umm. Yeah, he is mad, isn't he?" Then, "I wish I were leaving with you, friend. I really do wish that."

They were among the houses now, square, one-story buildings. Their east walls, away from the sea and the salt droplets the wind lashed from it during storms, were high and moss-furry. The doors and windows were there, now shuttered but able to be opened to the sun when it rose over the harsh ridge line. The roofs of the houses were slate, black stone frosted with the gray-green lichen despite the salt scouring. They sloped seaward more steeply than the hillside, so that the exposed western walls were only two or three feet high.

Mael glanced back at the seaward lines as they passed. The walls were blank, courses of limestone laid without mortar or even mud to fill the chinks. They were not relieved by windows or openings of any kind. Did the women of these fisher-folk not look up from their evening cooking, the eternal fish stew and bread baked in the coals from bartered flour, to see if their men were returning? To watch for the bobbing coracle that held father or brother or husband—or all three, perhaps, in the same man?

But the walls were as blind as the cliffs from which they were quarried, as expressionless as the sea they faced. And perhaps that was the explanation: the sea would have her way. To search her face for disaster was to multiply that certain disaster by as many days as she, laughing, withheld it. A stoic who ignored fate could be hurt only once—at a time.

"I wonder," Starkad said, wagging the axe on his shoulder just enough to call his friend's attention to it, "why Arthur let me and this so close to him today? Last night it was our lives or our weapons before he'd let us come near. Does he think I love him now for making me a hostage?"

"I doubt he thinks anyone loves him," Mael said after brief reflection. "Mad, yes, but not stupid. . . . But you've noticed his foot?"

"He was whelped when the clay of his flesh was too wet," the Dane said. "Back home, a brat like that—well, the nights get cold on the kitchen middens, even in the summer. And there's always something hungry prowling there for what might be thrown out of the back doors.''

Mael touched his lips in what could have been distaste, but man differed from man, and customs differed among peoples. One individual and another could cross lines of race and tribe to find friendship—but that did not make the differences less real. "On his horse," Mael explained, "Arthur's as steady as any other man with four legs under him. On his own feet, he—fears."

"He was born with more than his foot twisted," muttered Starkad.

The Irish had carried their curragh ashore rather than simply drawing it up on the beach at high tide. The crew had leaped into the surf when the boat grounded and put their shoulders to the hull while their hands found such purchase as they could on the slimy oxhides. When the men heaved upward the whole vessel came, dripping and lurching as the bearers lost their footing on the stones or a wave swept the legs from under several like a soft flail. Shouting and laughing, their steps quicker and more certain as they advanced beyond the slick buffeting of the sea, the Irish had carried their boat up to where the house walls announced safety from the waves of even the fiercest storm. As Mael and Starkad approached, the crew was launching the curragh again as easily by reversing the process.

The curragh was lightly built but not light. Its transport was a function of the fifty strong men beneath it, rather than an absolute lack of burden. There was no true keel or skeleton of ribs, only a wicker lattice anchored in the center to a thirty-foot sapling. The flexible ends of the tree had been bent up to mold the identical stern and prow. Over the framework were stretched oxhides, sewn to the lattice and to each other with linen cord. The seams and thread holes had been carefully tarred, leaving a shiny black pattern superimposed on the brown and black and white blotches of the hides. The seams still leaked, of course, but most of the water that would slap in the vessel's interior would come over the low sides.

If the outside of the hull was simple, its interior was almost nonexistent. There was no oar benches or true strakes, only withies crossing from gunwale to gunwale every yard or so. With luck, that flimsy bracing would keep the wicker frame from opening out at sea like a bud in spring-time. There were no oarlocks or even oars; the curragh was paddled like a huge canoe, twisting and snaking across the waves. It was as limber as a sea serpent and as large. In its crew, the vessel carried a venom more lethal than anything with scales could match.

"Well, do as you please," Starkad said as he eyed the Irish who were beginning to load the cur-ragh. It quivered in the surf. "You will, anyway. But I'd rather that if you have to throw yourself in with those fine ambassadors that you'd at least go armed."

"Oh, I'm armed," Mael laughed, tapping the dagger in his belt sheath. It was a serviceable weapon with a twelve-inch blade, unmarked but of good steel. Its thick tang ran the length of the sharkskin grip to the butt cap. The knife was not a toy, but neither was Starkad's concern misplaced. Besides the dagger and the leather scrip balancing it on the other side of his belt, Mael wore only a tunic and breeches of dark wool, his sandals, and a cloak he carried rolled and slung under his arm. His sword and coat of ring mail, his shield and steel cap, all were back in the room he shared with Starkad in the recruits' barracks. "After all," Mael said, "If I'm to be safe where I'm going, I've got to look harmless and Irish. In all my gear, I wouldn't look either."

Dubtach, soaked to the waist, stepped out of the sea and noticed them. "You're going with us?" he demanded. "They told us one. Gets damned crowded on one a' these bitches, though I don't suppose a land-lobster like your king up there'd know."

"I'd know, wouldn't I?" said Mael speaking the liquid Irish of his youth. It was a tongue that already had more of a lilt and a bubble to it than the remainder of the Celtic language stream. "Haven't I raided the coast south of here in a boat no bigger than this and with twice the crew?" And Mael had, of course, twelve years before in a force led by Cearbhall, the High King's brother. Cearbhall, a few years older than this Dubtach but with the same bright hair, the same muscular chest and arms . . . "The Dane is here only to see me off; I'll be going back with you alone, and you'll have no need to worry for my stomach."

"Irish, are you? I'd taken you for a Briton," said
Dubtach. In his eyes was a glint that further in-
creased his resemblance to the Ard Ri's dead
brother. Nor had the reference escaped the war
chief—there had been few raids in recent years.
"And you say you sailed with Cearbhall? He was
the last real man Ireland raised so near the throne,
Manannan knows. The day of his murder was an
ill one for the country."

"He's dead, then?" Mael asked in lying ignorance. The speech and the warriors around him
were pulling his mind back to another beach,
another curragh, and it was all the same except
that now there was no blood. . . .

"Dead?" repeated Dubtach. "Of course he's
dead, throat cut in his own tent ten years—say, if
you sailed with him, how is it you wouldn't know
that?"

Starkad stood a step to Mael's right and a little
to the rear, as inconspicuous as a 250-pound axe-
man could be. The Dane's eyes were measuring the
distance to Dubtach. Mael spread his hand, palm
backward, as if just stretching the fingers, and
told the war chief the first outright lie, the
planned lie: "Oh, I didn't come back from the raid,
I took a block of stone on the head the night the
Britons ambushed us. . . . You've heard about
that?"

Dubtach's nod was agreement, and the smile
spreading across his horsy teeth was proof that he
had heard the rest, too; the payment Cearbhall had
drawn from the villagers who had dared defend
their goods.

"For seven years I was a slave," Mael continued, "and for five more a freedman. Now the king is letting me go home." And the strangest thing about the lie, Mael realized, was that in a psychic way it was no lie at all. He had not been wounded on the raid, but something of him *had* stayed behind in the West Country. It had been nailed to the hut walls like the villagers themselves—men, women, and children. The lucky ones had been dead. Of the rest, some were screaming and some were silent, but all of them screamed when Cearbhall gave the order and his men began thrusting torches into the roofs of the plundered huts. That screaming was a thing to which Mael could have grown hardened in time; he could have come to accept it as a necessity of life, like the shriek of a pig on the butchering ground or the grunt of a warrior who has just taken your point through his rib cage. Even twelve years ago, Mael had known he was no better a man than most of those around him. The shock, the realization of what he had been helping to accomplish, was just too sudden, that was all.

And as the flames rose, Cearbhall had turned so that Mael could see his eyes. There was nothing behind them but arrogance that would not brook the slightest hint of opposition. Mael had collapsed. His fellows thought it was a delayed reaction to a blow, but in reality Mael had been bludgeoned by an insight more damaging than a stone could have been.

Later he had dreamed about the empty eyes, nightmares that at first had ended in sweaty terror. Then, as months and a year went by, Mael woke in red, killing rages instead. About two years later, the dreams and Cearbhall had ended together.

Red-haired, scar-chested Dubtach clapped Mael on the shoulder. "Ireland needs more of the old breed," he said. "Come and see me after you've looked about your homeplace long enough to satisfy kinship. Muirchertach's an open-handed man, and he'll have a need for men to follow him soon. Real men."

"Gear's stowed," shouted one of the crewmen standing in the curragh while a dozen others held the hull parallel to the shore and steady. The boat bobbed in the shallows, waiting for the burden of men to fill its mottled sleekness.

"Then start boarding," Dubtach called back. "You too," he said to Mael. He turned to supervise the boarding.

Mael looked at Starkad, then up the slope toward the cataphracts. The sheen of their points and armor would, by Arthur's design, be the last image the Irish carried away from Britain. Mael rapped Starkad in the middle of the chest and said, "See you soon."

The Dane caught the outstretched wrist and squeezed it. "Make sure you come back," he said quietly.

"I wouldn't leave you," replied Mael, hurt that Starkad thought he might abandon his friend to Arthur's whimsy.

Starkad snorted, nodding his head contemptuously toward Arthur and his troops. "Think I care what *they'll* do to me if you don't show up? Don't

worry about that. But I've gotten used to having
you around." The big man squeezed Mael's wrist
again, then used its leverage to turn the Irishman
toward the sea and the waiting curragh.

The vessel was riding thirty yards from the line
of wet gravel. Waves staggered Mael twice as he
strode outward. The second time the water rose
mid-thigh and almost threw Mael down with its
purchase on his tunic. Out of practice, he thought,
not that he cared. Reaving in skin boats was, like
plucking hens, a skill with which Mael had some
acquaintance but no desire for proficiency.
Besides, half the men trying to restrain the curragh had gone down in the last wave, too.

Most of the crew was aboard by the time Mael
gripped the flexible gunwales and let the men to
either side of his handhold pull him in. It was not a
hard pull since the loaded vessel showed only a
foot of freeboard. Last within were the two wolf-
hounds who until then had paddled around the
curragh in happy circles. The dogs launched themselves out of the water like hairy porpoises, buffeting men aside as they landed. Somehow they
managed to avoid impaling themselves on spear
points. One hound shook itself and turned around
three times before flopping down with its head
across Mael's feet. Its tongue lolled. The grizzled
paddler beside Mael glanced over and said apologetically, "Blood and old Terror, here, they can't
bear for a boat to put out without they're aboard.
Even though we aren't raiding."

Mael nodded and grinned back at the rangy dog.
He knew why the beasts accompanied raiders. The

long, toothy jaws were not to kill but to hold ransomable fugitives. The dogs' masters would do the killing if whim and economics required.

"Stroke, damn you, *stroke!*" Dubtach was shouting from the stern. There was no rudder or steering oar on the curragh, but stern or bow were the natural places for the captain to seat himself anyway. Loaded with fifty men and their gear, the vessel drew considerably more water than it had empty. Furious paddling thrust the curragh forward, but the next wave cost all of the gains. The bottom scraped. Every man aboard knew what the shore would do to the oxhide hull if it caught them fully.

Up the slope, Arthur's warhorn sang. Mael looked back, saw the six dark-skinned riders detach themselves from the group around the standard and ride for the beach. Mael saw Starkad, too, his axe-helve slung through the double loops on his back and the ocean hammering his chest with foam from about the curragh's stern. The curved stern-post slipped backward despite all that fifty straining paddlers could do. Then the Dane's great hands blocked it. The supple wood gave a little but Starkad did not, despite the weight surging against him. The sea turned and the curragh shot outward beyond the shelf of the shore. The next swell only lifted it. Starkad turned and the Huns drew up, even before the horn ordered them to recase their bows.

Mael let his breath out very slowly. Dubtach looked forward again, still shaking his head in amazement. "A strong man, your friend," he said.

"He's that, all right," Mael agreed. "One day he's going to decide he's strong enough to live with a dozen arrows through his chest, though. I'll be sorry for that day." And for the men who kill that foolish blond bear, Mael added bleakly, but that was to himself and unspoken.

CHAPTER THREE

It was a normal voyage by curragh: wet, cramped, and queasy. Without a sail—the vessel was too flimsy for a mast to be stepped, much less to take the strain of a filled sail—the crew had to paddle constantly in shifts to make way. In theory, the men not paddling could have slept. In practice, the chill sea sloshed across the open belly of the craft and made sleep both unlikely and dangerous. Part of the crew bailed at all times. If the water within rose too high, the curragh would sink like a stone. It was lightly built but not of positive buoyancy.

"I had a piece there in Arthur's camp, one of his captains' wives," Dubtach began when they were out of the surf. "So blonde she looked white as an old lady. But when she threw her cloak back she hadn't a stitch on under it and there wasn't a

wrinkle in her skin. I swear by the MacLir . . ."
The rest of the story was a paradigm of the conversation for the whole of the voyage. It was indeed, the conversation of every group of soldiers since war began. Only the languages change.

Muirchertach's men were a relic of older times, still normal in Ireland. Their shields were light, generally of oxhide strapped with bronze or iron. Almost none of them wore body armor. In the ancient past, battle nudity had been of magical significance, an ultimate sign of faith that the gods would save the man who trusted in them. Now even in Ireland it was more conservatism and braggadocio, acceptable enough on an island whose only contact with other peoples was at the islanders' choice. Niall's reavers, for all their savagery and their king's reputation, would have fared no better arrayed against a legion than had Boudicca's naked warriors three centuries before. But the reavers had proven quite adequate for murdering civilians while Rome's sparse troops marched from the site of one raid to another.

When Mael fled Ireland, he had considered armor and made his own decision about it. If he were to earn his living by war, he would arm himself so that he could fight at the front of any battle on earth. That meant weapons which would cut without breaking or bending, a shield that could last an afternoon of strong men and hard blows—and a good coat of mail, for in the midst of war no man could avoid all blows from his blind side. But now, looking at the naked warriors around him, a fierce surge of freedom shook the exile. He grinned in its throes, and the grin was unpleasant.

The voyage took half a day, lasting from daylight to dusk and then three miserable hours of pitch darkness besides. Dubtach tried to make sense out of the stars. Finally the shore loomed up, richly odorous and—for all its dangers—still home to Mael.

Dubtach and his chiefs held a lengthy, querulous conversation as they tried to decide where the curragh was about to fetch up. Most of the other crewmen joined in. Even the hounds, smelling land and a chance to run, began to whine loudly until a frustrated warrior booted them to whimpers.

"We'll land," Dubtach said finally. "If it's not Muirtaig's reach, it's Eoghan's, and we've no foes so great in the Laigin we need fear to camp on their beach for a night."

They drew in, the men in the stern paddling while those in the bow poised to leap into the grumbling surf at the least tremor from the bottom. To the right was a headland jutting high enough that a clump of three stunted junipers could grow in despite of the salt spray. One of the crewmen called out, pointing to the landmark. Dubtach cawed in triumph, "Who says I can't navigate, hey? Not fifty feet from where we put her in the sea, are we?"

No one contradicted the war chief, least of all Mael. Having listened to Dubtach wrangling about their bearings with men equally ignorant, Mael knew the curragh might as easily have made landfall in the Hebrides.

Mael joined in the quick dash for the beach with
the hull of the curragh flexing over his shoulder
like a silent drum. Laughing in relief at their safe
return, the crew carried the vessel high up on the
beach to where the grass displaced the pebbles.
The night was warm and friendly, lighted by the
silver moon just edging up over the sea. A trio of
wattle huts in a palisade were within a hundred
yards of the beached curragh. No one came to a
door despite the halloos of some of the men. Well,
thought Mael, he wouldn't have come out himself
to meet such a mob. At least not until dawn or an
attack required it. The exile smiled, thinking of
the householders tremblingly alert, each with a
fish spear or a gutting knife clenched in his hand.
This time the residents would be lucky.

"These are Muirchertach's lands?" Mael asked,
stretching his arms high to ease the cramped
muscles of his back.

"King Muirtaig's," Dubtach corrected him. "He
sends his tribute to the Laigin as we do not. But we
have no coast, so we borrowed this curragh from
Muirtaig against a dozen horses pledged for its return."

"Can you show me the road for Lough Conn?"
Mael asked, naming a lake in the shadow of the Ox
Mountains, far beyond where he intended to go.
He wanted to be clear of Dubtach and his troupe
as quickly as possible. With them Mael was an
outsider—always dangerous when among armed
men. Besides, he was sure to attract comment as
"the man from Britain" so long as he accompanied
those who had brought him over.

"We'll be heading west tomorrow," Dubtach
said. "Travel with us."

"Umm, I'll be back when I've done the business I
need to do," Mael replied mildly. "For now—
well, I've been gone twelve years, and I'd not add
another hour to them for choice."

The war chief shrugged. "I'll point you to the
road, then," he said. "It's past the orchard, is all."

They walked together between the rows of apple
trees on the high ground west of the shore. The
trees were well kept but as gnarled and ingrown
as only old fruit trees become. In the flat moonlight they looked more mineral than alive. The air
among them was a little warmer, a little sweeter,
than that of the shore. The trilling of katydids in
the branches washed away the raucous jollity of
the warriors below.

"Right there's the track," said Dubtach, pointing to a dirt path bounded on the far side by hedgerows. "Go left here and just follow whichever
branch seems western at a fork if you can't get
better directions. Now, I think there's a spring
here if—umm, hel-*lo!*"

Figures moved, two horses and a woman standing in the shadow of the hedge to the right.
Dubtach shrugged as if to loosen clothing from
about his bare torso. Mael touched his tongue to
his lips, darting his eyes about the darkness and
silently cursing the katydids. Their sound, so
welcome a moment before, would cloak the rustle
of bandits creeping to attack. The woman's presence made sense only if she were a decoy.

The woman walked closer while the horses

stood where they were on their dropped reins. She
was not tall, perhaps a little over five feet, nor was
she heavy. Her slim fingers were loosely inter-
twined in front of her. She wore a gray cloak
pinned at the right shoulder. The shift beneath it
was of linen, but it was bleached and silver-gilt by
the moon so that it showed as a gleaming wedge.
Then the woman shrugged her cowl back and Mael
could see the shift was no brighter than her hair.
Her face was perfect and unlined. Glancing at the
contrast, Mael was reminded of Dubtach's tale of
his ash-blonde conquest in Britain. Mael was surprised at the sudden hatred for the war chief that
boiled through him at the thought.

Dubtach stood, arms akimbo, and said to the
woman, "And what would you be doing here,
lady?" Mael was behind him, but even there he
could feel the tooth-baring smile in Dubtach's
voice.

"Waiting for a man," she said, looking at Dubtach and looking away to Mael. Her voice was full
without being either deep or loud. "I've found him
now."

"That you have!" brayed Dubtach. He reached
out his long, thick-muscled arm and drew the
woman closer by the shoulder. "Two of us,
indeed."

"No." The woman nodded at Mael. "I'm waiting
for him." She squirmed, which should have made
no difference to Dubtach's heavy grip, but the
cloak rippled under his fingers, leaving the
woman free and a yard away, staring coolly at the
war chief's fury.

Dubtach's left hand toyed with his sword hilt, raising it an inch or two to free the blade in the scabbard before dropping it back. The gesture was unconscious and a suggestive one. Dubtach reached out again with his right hand. Mael touched his elbow. "Wait a minute," the exile said quietly.

The red-haired warrior snapped around like a released spring. "You're going to tell me she's kin to you?" he shouted at Mael. "That she knew you were coming here when I didn't myself?"

"I'll tell you damn-all but the truth," Mael said, his own voice controlled and as tight as the muscles of his rectum. They were drawing up and chilling his whole body with the fear of death. "She's no kin, she's no acquaintance—by the Dagda's dick, she's not even Irish, you can hear that in her voice." Which was true; the syllables were perfect but too flat for a native speaker's. "But this I will say, I'll not be a part to a rape in a stranger king's territory, not with me not an hour landed in Ireland again."

"You just hold her bloody arms and leave me to worry about Muirtaig," Dubtach snarled. He turned back to the woman.

Mael caught him again by the arm. Dubtach cursed as he jerked his hand down to his sword hilt. Mael kicked him in the groin, his hand locking Dubtach's down so that the war chief could not draw. Dubtach's gasp as he doubled over choked the call for assistance that was already halfway up his throat. Mael hit him on the back of the head and cursed as Dubtach ignored the blow and tried to rise. Mael kneed him in the face, then drew his own dagger and chopped the red-haired man with the butt of it twice behind the ear. This time Dubtach sagged all the way to the ground.

Mael spun, crouching, his dagger out to take the charge and the life of anyone who might have followed him and Dubtach through the orchard. Breeze and the terrain blocked all sound of the men at the beach. Mael prayed that all sound of Dubtach's struggles had been masked as well.

He turned again, both fearful and threatening. The woman with white hair had not moved, nor had the hedges spilled her suspected companions. Mael was breathing heavily. "I need one of your horses," he said, pointing his dagger downward. He did not sheath it, not yet. "I'll pay you for it, a fair price."

"I brought it for you," said the woman. "I've been watching for you to come."

"That was a fine story the first time," Mael snapped sarcastically. "It nearly got me killed and you raped by a boatload instead of the chief only. But it's no good with me, you see. You don't know me and you can't have been expecting me."

"I've been waiting for Loeghaire o'—"

"Don't say that name!" Mael shouted. For the instant he forgot the men on the shore and the others a cry might bring to find him over the bludgeoned Dubtach. He forgot everything but the far past and the icy fear of discovery. Mael had convinced himself that it would not happen on a brief return. After all, there had been a decade for men and memories to age.

"Come," said the woman, "we have to ride."

That was good advice. Besides, Mael was beyond planning for himself, not then. He sheathed his dagger as he followed her, two quick steps and a vault that took him astride the larger of the two horses. The woman mounted the bay mare as easily. Mael's stallion walked, then trotted to quick heel pressure. They were following the path westward as Dubtach had directed.

"Where are we going?" the woman asked, keeping station to Mael's right and half a pace behind.

"Don't you know that, too?" Mael retorted. The measured gait of the horse was a comfort to the exile's mind, especially after the greasy smoothness of the curragh in the waves.

"I was told to meet a man," the woman said, her tone quiet and certain. She sounded like a mother drawing an answer out of an unruly boy. "And if you don't want me to call you by the name you were born with, you have to tell me what you go by now. I'm Veleda."

"Mael mac Ronan," Mael said unwillingly. Veleda was not an Irish name, but that was no surprise. German, perhaps? But not really that, either. There was no accent at all in her speech; rather, she had a suspicious lack of accent. And— but Mael broke into his own thoughts to add, "I'm riding to Lough Conn," repeating his lie to Dubtach.

They went on in silence for almost a mile, through a landscape of small fields and occasional small turf houses. Most of the dwellings were surrounded by fences that served both as corrals and for protection from attack. Once a horse whinnied as Mael and Veleda passed, but their own mounts made no reply.

They reached the first fork in the road. Veleda pointed to the right without hesitation. They continued on. "What are you?" Mael demanded abruptly without looking at his companion.

"A woman," she replied.

He turned in his saddle and her eyes were on him already, her face shadowed by the silver frame of her hair. "There's ten thousand women in Ireland," Mael said, "and not one of them but you knew where I'd be landing—any more than I myself did. What are you?"

"We're all of us together in the world," Veleda said, "all of us a part of it and of each other. Some are born a little more aware of that togetherness than others. I hear things, I'm told things. I was told that I should meet you, and where I should and when . . . and I did. I don't know who or what it was that told me, or why—not really. If all that makes me wise, then I'm a wise woman, as some have called me. But they've called me a demon, too, and a goddess—and I'm none of those things. I'm a woman."

She smiled and tossed her head. The road jogged south at the same moment, and the thin moon lit Veleda's face like a still pool in the sunlight. Mael grinned back, then laughed aloud as he found himself believing her. A pressure lifted from him. "I won't complain that you hear voices," he said, "if they've saved me a hike I was dreading."

For a while Mael's face sobered, but it did not

fall into the grim lines it had worn at the beginning of the ride. He held his horse for the half step that brought Veleda abreast of him, then asked, "What are you going to do, then?"

"There's something very important and very near," Veleda said. "Very . . ."

"A king rising?" interjected Mael into the pause with his mind on mad, brilliant Arthur and his boasting. "An empire?"

"No," said Veleda with the curtness of one who understands something completely for one who never would. "Not men, not anything of men. That's like saying the sun sends down its light to warm us. We're not that important. But whatever is about to happen, you're a part of it. I want to stay with you, at least until I understand more than I do now." She smiled again. "That's a fault of mine. I like to know things."

"Umm," murmured Mael as he considered. Indeed she was a woman. An attractive one who had done him a favor. Clearly it was not safe for her to wander alone in a country as unsettled as Ireland now. Even the leaders, unless Dubtach was the exception, seemed to think it no disgrace to rape in peacetime as if they were at war. . . . "We'll see, then," Mael said. "Do you have any relatives around here?"

"None at all."

"Well, we'll see then," Mael repeated. "For now, I think we're far enough from Dubtach and his friends for safety, and I, at least, could use a soft place to sleep in. Though I doubt we'll do better than a haystack. It's damned late, and nobody with

good sense is going to open his house to
strangers."

"I've slept in haystacks before," said Veleda.
"There's one a quarter mile ahead on the right—
near the path and far enough from the house that
we won't trouble the owners. Or they us."

"Oh, you've been this way—" Mael began. He
stopped himself when he realized that if the
answer were "No" he would not want to have
heard it.

The haystack was where Veleda said it would
be. It was a six-foot dome notched by use to half
that height on one side. The two of them unsaddled their horses. Mael stripped the reins off
his mount and started to use them as a makeshift
hobble, but the woman said, "No need—they
won't stray." She had already unpinned her cloak
and was wrapping it around her in place of a
blanket.

Mael shook out his own cloak, a thick, gray-
white rectangle of wool. It had not been either
bleached or dyed. The lanolin still in the wool
made the garment almost waterproof. He eyed
Veleda as he worked, fascinated by her grace and
the economy of her movements. Odd—generally
he liked his women tall, with a little more bone
showing than was most men's ideal. Mael's mind
flashed him a memory of a tanned, rangy woman,
her eyes and hair black and welcoming. He
shivered with the force of the thought, shaking his
head as if to free cobwebs from his hair.

This woman, Veleda. Was it her hair that drew
him? It fell in silky perfection to the small of her

back when she shook it from beneath her cloak. Or again, the attraction might be her face; serene and smooth, its youthfulness was a stunning contrast to the white tresses around it. Veleda's lips were thin—*thinner than those other lips*—though not cruel. But a knife blade is not cruel either, only lethal, and there was a quality of lethal determination in the blonde woman's lips and face.

Veleda's hands were small and gentle, as delicate as filigree brooches. They clasped the cloak about her in the moonlight.

Mael grunted and rolled himself down in the yielding hay. He found the woman interesting as a person, and the fact concerned him. Interest in women as people was a practice Mael thought he had given up ten years before, in a bloodstained bedchamber. That was not a scene he ever wanted to repeat.

Sleep was a longer time coming than it should have been.

CHAPTER FOUR

In the morning Mael told Veleda their real destination, the wide slough of the Shannon that was
Lough Ree. The roads were crooked and narrow,
frequently muddy ruts where their course followed a creek. Mael and Veleda moved as fast
as the well-being of the horses allowed, but Mael
knew it would be at least an honest three days'
travel to the wayside shrine that was his goal.

Though travelers were rare, the two of them at-
tracted little attention. Veleda generally rode with
her cowl up to hide her striking hair. They were
both too simply dressed to arouse greed. Mael,
though not heavily armed, had a killer's look
about him that twice turned casual bullies to look
for other prey. All around were signs of an unsettled land. Men tilled their fields with spears
lashed to their plows where they could be seized at

need. Women called their children sharply out of the road when the strangers appeared. But two riders who gave no trouble and looked able to defend themselves were safe enough anywhere.

Veleda traded brass armlets for boiled mutton and porridge along the way, bargaining with the householders while Mael stood back with just enough of a frown to encourage a quick resolution. They dipped water from springs when there was no house nearby to barter them beer.

And each night the two of them slept on the ground, close enough together that Mael could feel the heat from the woman's body—or thought he could Mael's knee had swollen where Dubtach's tooth had cut it, but the pain and swelling had disappeared when Veleda applied a poultice of leaves and spider silk. Mael's only pain was that of his groin which was as tight as an inflated bladder. It ached, especially when his mind wandered back to times past. Mael talked incessantly as they rode.

Late in the afternoon of the third day, Mael and Veleda topped the wooded ridge that overlooked the black waters of Lough Ree a quarter mile away. There had to be some current, but the surface seemed still for as far as the watchers could see. Reeds grew so thickly in the shallows that the shoreline was hard to determine. The western slope of the ridge on which Mael stood was covered with rhododendrons that linked themselves impassibly to either side of the path. From the water's edge at the end of the path, a rickety pier thrust out beyond the reeds.

Halfway down the hill, between the crest and the pier, stood a tiny stone chapel whose peaked roof made it look taller than it was long. "The shrine of the Unknown Hero," said Mael in satisfaction. "They say a traveler jumped into the lough with nothing but a sword and beheaded the monster there. Quite a hero tale about it—as there are about lots of things, of course. More to the point, there was a shrine built at the spot—here— and the monster's skull inside it. I saw it once."

"And you're going to kill a monster yourself?" Veleda asked mildly.

Mael snorted. "I won't go swimming with fish that size," he said, "not when somebody did the work for me already. Besides, there aren't any of the beasts around, not any more."

He felt Veleda's cool eyes on him. He turned to her, frowning. "Look," Mael said, "it happened a long time ago. There's stories that the hero was Niall, but that's not true—the skull was old even when he was the High King. Maybe it really was Lugh or some other god that killed the thing— that's what the oldest songs say. I don't know. But I don't have years to spend out there in a rowboat, proving that the skull in the shrine was the last one there was to be had, either. I don't care to rob a shrine, and if your voices tell you to go—go. I didn't plan to drag anybody here anyway.

"But the gods can take care of their own. I've got a friend depending on me."

"A man does what he must," Veleda said.

"A man does what he can, you mean," Mael said, and he faced back to the shrine. But of course it was not what Veleda meant, and it galled Mael more than any open condemnation could have.

The chapel was of ashlar-cut limestone. The roof was formed by heavy timbers because its slope was too sharp for slates. There was a suggestion of a wooden lean-to built against the far side, but the angle made it hard to see for sure. On the uphill side toward Mael was a wooden door and a slit window. The latter was unshuttered but too narrow to pass a man or even a boy. A yard of sorts had been cleared of rhododendrons. A solid oak bench sat in the clearing against the wall of the building. It was a moment before Mael noticed the stone cross that now stood at the northern peak of the roof.

"Christian?" he blurted incredulously.

"Many of the old places are now," Veleda replied. "It's coming, you know, all over Ireland."

Mael shook his head. "I've been away too long," he said. He grinned and added, "Or maybe not long enough. Well, this may change things, but we won't know till we check." He clucked to his horse, leading the way down the narrow path through the twisted shrubs.

Chance or the thud of hooves on the peaty soil brought motion at the window. Then the door flew back and a short man stepped out of the building to await them. He was a priest—or a monk, perhaps; there was a difference but Mael did not know quite what it was. The man was old and wore a cassock of black wool in startling contrast to his white beard and hair. His face was more shrunken together than lined, its expression bitter and proud and inflexible. He could have been fifty years old or eighty, but he still moved like a bird.

Mael smiled and waved his right hand, empty, in greeting. The priest nodded stiffly in reply. He stepped to the side of the door. A balding giant seven feet tall walked out of the shrine behind the priest, ducking to clear the lintel.

Mael was not small himself, and he had been around even bigger men for most of his life. This fellow would be, he thought, the biggest man he had ever seen. The giant was barefoot and clad in a plain linen tunic with a wide sash. He seemed to taper toward both ends like a skein of wool. Mael's first thought was that the giant was fat, since his smooth limbs seemed stuffed like sausages and his torso a tun of lard. Then the fellow moved in front of the black-garbed priest. His flesh rippled and bulged instead of dimpling as fat does. The giant was muscular, and there was an awesome bulk of those muscles.

"Fergus!" snapped the priest. "Did you finish your prayers?"

The giant stopped. He opened his mouth and drooled slightly on his tunic. Mael could see that the cloth was already damp. "I forgot," Fergus rumbled, looking at the ground instead of the small man questioning him.

"And do you want the Lord Almighty to forget you in the day of your need? Is that what you want, Fergus?" the priest demanded.

The giant began to twist his right index finger into his left palm. He concentrated wholly on the process and did not speak.

The priest sighed. He wiped spittle from the giant's chin with the end of the sash, then said, "Oh, go sit down. But you *must* be more careful." Obediently Fergus walked to the bench and sat. The oak creaked loudly. The giant's round face was as expressionless as his bare pate.

The giant's appearance had startled Mael out of his original plan of tying the priest, stealing the skull, and fleeing before a chance wayfarer stopped by the shrine. Instead, the exile reined up at the edge of the clearing and said, "Ah, sir . . ." but he could not think of a way to continue.

The little priest nodded. "Yes, yes, I'm Father Diarmid. And you're pilgrims to the shrine, I see— since this path doesn't lead anywhere else."

Mael dismounted, still trying to frame a useful opening. His body no longer blocked Diarmid's view of Veleda. The priest's breath hissed in. His wizened face took on the look of a man who has caught his wife making love to the potboy. "Witch!" he cried with loathing.

Mael blinked in surprise and looked back at Veleda. She was calm, not even frowning. There was nothing unusual about her except her hair— and that, if unusual, was no certain witch-mark.

But the priest was right.

Diarmid pointed at the woman and his voice, never pleasant, rasped like a corn mill as he shouted, "You! God seared Ireland over the coals of his wrath for your sort, witches and druids! He brought the Plague on us as upon the heathen Egyptians, that all this land should know His name and follow Him. Your gods are false, dead and stinking with the corruption of their false-hood. How dare you try to enter this holy place wrapped in sin and error?''

"Men will do as they wish, think as they wish, pray as they wish," said Veleda. She leaned a little toward the old man and added, with a distinctness as forceful as his own shouted polemic, "and god is still the same in all his aspects. For myself, I don't worship a god who died on a tree, and my god doesn't drown the earth with the blood of innocents to fill his churches—and his coffers!"

"Get away from here," Diarmid said, almost calmly. The leash on his tongue snapped and he screamed, "Get away from here, whore of Satan! Cease defiling ground blessed by the feet of the holy Padraic!"

"Now wait a minute..." Mael began. He stepped forward with his left hand raised as much for attention as a sign of peaceful intent.

Fergus moved also. He reached under the bench on which he sat and twitched out what Mael had thought was a loose building block. It was a forty-pound wedge of soapstone, a small boat anchor. A three-inch hole had been bored in the center to reeve through a line. Fergus had fitted the stone with an oak shaft as long as Mael's arm. The streaked, gray mace head was utterly steady though Fergus held it one-handed.

The giant stood. Mael smiled and brought his left hand around in a slow arc to the side, no-thing threatening, just an easy motion to draw eyes away from his right hand and the dagger in his belt. He could slip the knife out and throw it point first, knowing that at seven feet he could bury it to the hilt in Fergus' chest. Mael knew also that while the dagger would kill the giant, it would assuredly not stop him. The sweeping counter-blow of the mace would literally tear Mael's head off if it connected. His fingers poised—

"Wait!" Veleda cried. Mael froze, turned his head toward her. She was white with the same fury that was shaking Diarmid, but the command in her voice was certain. "This isn't a fight be-tween men," she said, "and I'll not stay to make it one. But I've one last thing to say before I leave, priest: men get the sort of gods they deserve." She wheeled her horse. "Mael," she added, "I'll wait for you at the top of the hill."

Mael and Diarmid both watched her ride off. Fergus simply grunted and flicked his mace back under the bench as easily as he had taken it out. "Wipe your mouth, Fergus," the priest said. Fergus stared at him blankly. Diarmid muttered, then daubed spittle from the slack chin. Then the giant sat down again.

"You aren't Christian, either," Diarmid said, "but you're not a witch. What brought you here?"

"I came to see the skull of the monster," Mael said. "The one the Unknown Hero slew."

"The monster which God Almighty slew at the behest of the Holy Padraic," the priest corrected him, sharply though without rancor.

Mael blinked. "Padraic killed one of the water monsters, too?" he asked in perplexity.

"There was only one of the creatures," snapped Diarmid, "a child of Satan—as *all* things heathen are. It pursued one of the followers of the Holy Padraic as he swam toward a coracle." The priest gestured vaguely toward the peat-black waters in which his own skiff bobbed at the end of the pier. "The Apostle prayed to God to save his disciple, and the hand of God struck down the monster in answer to the saint's prayer."

"I hadn't heard the story," Mael said mildly. Nor had his father, who had seen the relic before Padraic had returned to Ireland to preach in the year Mael was born. The year Loeghaire was born, that was, but he must not think of that . . . "Father," Mael said aloud to the stern-faced priest, "I've traveled a long way to see this skull."

"You'll find your journey to Hell much shorter unless you repent," the older man gibed, but he motioned his visitor to follow as he stepped into the shrine. Fergus stood also.

Diarmid crossed himself at the threshold. He looked at the giant. "Fergus," he said.

"I forgot, Father," Fergus said. He crossed himself carefully.

With Fergus' huge body blocking the doorway behind him, Mael's eyes took a moment to adjust. There was little enough to see. A wooden crucifix had been added above the altar. It was of rustic workmanship but was carven with surprising vigor. The Christ's eyes bulged as he writhed against the nails. Mael could almost hear the scream from his open mouth. The altar itself was of plain stone, the same slab that had been there when Mael had seen it as a boy. The casket on the altar was the same also. It was a foot and a half

long and about a foot in width and depth, constructed of bronze-bound wood. It was so
obviously ancient that Mael shot a quick glance to
Diarmid to surprise signs of embarrassment at his
lie about it being a relic of Padraic. There were no
such signs. The priest was obviously sincere, even
though his claim for Padraic being the monster-
slayer was untrue on its face. Religion, Mael
thought sourly. He grinned.

The design on the casket was a rendering of the
monster. Its head formed the latch which opened
from pressure on the plate set cunningly between
its open jaws. The head of the beast was oval, with
a blackish-green patina that even looked wet.
Around it was a circular fringe like a stylized
lion's mane or a gorgon's frill of snakes. The neck
writhed around the edge of the casket to the left,
while the pointed tail rejoined the head from the
right side. Presumably the creature's torso and
limbs, if any, were inlaid on the back where they
were out of sight for the moment.

Diarmid murmured a prayer, then reverently
touched the latch. He lifted the lid of the chest.
The interior was padded with heavy scarlet wool
—a trophy itself, cut from the cloak of a high
Roman officer in the days when the conquest of
Britain was still in doubt. The skull within was
flat, about a foot long and nine inches broad. The
brain case was small, no more than the size of a
clenched fist. Mael realized that what he had origi-
nally taken for large eye sockets were only sinuses
in the bone to lighten it. The real eyes had been set
far back and to either side of the head. The sockets

were smaller than a man's.

Most of the skull, in fact, was jaw, or attachment for the jaw muscles. The maxillaries were set with a pincushion of teeth, conical and rear-slanting. The longest—and they varied little from the mean —were only about half an inch long. Fish-eater, Mael thought. He suddenly remembered the big salamander he had once plucked from beneath a rock in a stream so cold it numbed his fingers. That one had been black, slimy, and almost blind, a squirming monster in its way, though only eight inches long. A beast of that sort and this size— well, it would be nothing to meet in the water, whatever its choice of diet.

"Behold the power of the hand of God," the priest was saying.

Mael nodded. There were three vertebrae in the casket along with the skull. Two of them were notched and the third was half-missing where a blade had severed it. That bone had other blade nicks in it. The hand of God should have sharpened its sword, Mael thought to himself, but that was unfair. The drag of the water would prevent a proper stroke, and the thick sheath of muscles and cartilage would dull any edge before it reached the bone.

"Thank you," Mael said aloud. Diarmid's deep eyes burned him as if the priest knew what his visitor was planning ... but no, that was only Diarmid's normal expression. Men get the gods they deserve. . . . "A man beholds the relics of ancient heroes that he may follow in their footsteps," Mael added sententiously.

"Follow in the path of God," Diarmid corrected, but with a hint of approval in his voice. The priest gestured. The room brightened as Fergus moved away from the door. Mael stepped back into the sunlight, hearing the latch click as the priest closed the casket behind him. Blinking with the light, the exile mounted his horse which was nibbling such grass as it could find at the edge of the rhododendrons.

"Thank you," Mael repeated. As he rode back up the slope, he could hear Diarmid scolding Fergus again for missing a prayer. For some reason, the scene chilled him.

Veleda had built a small fire on the far side of the ridge, out of sight of the shrine. Mael unsaddled his horse without saying a great deal. He began to knead ash cakes from the barley flour they had bartered that morning. Veleda used her small knife to prepare a chicken for roasting. She skinned the bird instead of trying to pluck it without a pot in which to scald it first.

"He's crazy, isn't he?" Mael said at last. "Not the big one, he's just lack-witted . . . but that priest, that Diarmid, he—what he's saying is like he said the sun shines here at midnight. But he really *believes* it."

"Why does that bother you?" the woman asked, her hands still for the moment as she looked over at Mael.

He opened his palms. "I've never been much for gods," he said. "They may be, they may rule me and everything else—I don't know and I don't much care. I don't care much about Christians, either, in a way . . . but even when I, ah, left Ireland, they were turning everybody to them. Now this. They don't just convert the men, they convert the holy places that have been there as long as there've been men at all on the island. And they tell lies, and they *believe* their own lies!" Mael clenched his fists in frustration. "Why is everybody going crazy?" he demanded. "Or am I?"

Veleda smiled. She spitted the chicken on a twig. "Men don't want to die," she said quietly. "People don't want to die."

"Nobody wants to die!" Mael blazed. "And everybody dies anyway. What does that have to do with it? Padraic didn't bring all this about by threatening to slit all the throats of those who wouldn't pray to his god."

"No, though that may come later," Veleda agreed. She laid her hands over Mael's, her fingertips touching his wrists. "Do you remember the Plague?"

"Yes," Mael said. The Plague had wracked Ireland only a few years after Mael was born. Limbs blackened and began to decay even before death; abcessed lungs filled with fluid and drowned sufferers; high fevers cooked brains and left behind inhuman things that died later as the rest of their systems disintegrated. Isolation had preserved Ireland for centuries from the diseases which ripped the Mediterranean Basin, but past safety was cold comfort when death began to ricochet back and forth between the narrow shores. "Yes," Mael repeated, "I don't think I'll forget that soon."

"Nobody will," Veleda said. "Most people come to religion for comfort, not truth. There are truths, but they're not for most people to know. Whole villages died then, from the Plague. Half the people on the island died, and the bodies rotted in the fields because there were too few hands left to bury them. The idea that cycles are infinite and that souls are reborn in other bodies —doesn't have any appeal after so much pain. Even though it's true. Especially because it's true."

Veleda began turning the chicken over the coals while her left hand still touched Mael, sending prickles up and down his arm. "The old faith could handle death in people's minds, but not death on that scale. You know that the emperors of Rome were worshipped as gods?" Veleda continued.

Mael nodded.

"That didn't start in Rome for a political reason," she said; "it started in Gaul, men bowing to the power that had slaughtered their kinsmen by tens of millions. And that would have happened here, people praying to death and disease because there was no other power in the land. Except that the Christians had come at the same time."

"Padraic didn't make the Plague stop," Mael argued. "Hell, he died himself just last year. A sailor in Massilia told me that when I asked for news from home."

"But death doesn't matter to Christians," Veleda explained. "They learn that this world is only a doorway to the real existence in their heaven. I don't know where that heaven is or what it is—but people don't need truth. They need a way out of a charnel house, and that Padraic and his teachings promised them."

Mael swore in frustration. He prodded at the coals to scatter fat that had dripped and flared up. The sky above them was growing dim as the sun set, making the orange flames brighter. "You mean their god Christ is false," Mael said flatly.

"No." Frowning again, Mael looked up at Veleda. "No," she repeated, "I don't mean that at all. Padraic's truth wasn't my truth, but he had a power. His vision was beyond that of all but a few of the men who have ever lived. Even the little man here, Diarmid . . . Mad? Of course. But he has a window to truth of a sort. He knew me for what I am, though his twisted mind put twisted labels on what he saw.

"So I won't say their Christ is false. But sometimes I wonder at minds that can take comfort in a truth of death and torture and misery in this world."

Mael chuckled grimly. He shifted his seat a little so that he could lean back against the pine tree beside which they sheltered. "I always wanted to come home," he said. "Oh, I knew I didn't dare, but . . . I was looking for an excuse like this one that Arthur offered me. But now that I've seen Ireland again, I—well, I'll be glad enough to leave it to its Christians."

CHAPTER FIVE

Two hours after sunset, Mael slipped down the pathway afoot and alone. He would have liked to wait longer, but the moon would be rising soon. No light spilled from the priest's quarters. Probably Diarmid and the giant went to bed at sunset, vaunting a poverty that did not allow even an oil lamp. If they were awake praying instead, Mael knew he would have to take his chances. He touched his dagger hilt; they would all have to take their chances.

Mael had left his cloak behind with Veleda and the horses. His tunic and trousers were a dark blue, invisible in starlight. He had considered blackening his face and hands with mud but had decided against it. That was too clear a badge of crime to any chance-met traveler later, and Mael did not want to waste time washing if his theft was

successful. Theft. Well, he'd done worse things in
his life than steal from a holy place.

Before he entered the clearing, Mael crouched
beside the rhododendrons that formed a solid
palisade along the trail. A fitful breeze was blow-
ing from behind him toward the water. He
strained against it to hear any sounds that might
be coming from the shrine. There was nothing,
though a fish slapped the surface of the lough.
Mael took a deep breath and stepped swiftly to the
door of the building.

He had drawn his knife to force the latch, but
that was unnecessary. A simple slide bolt on the
outside held the door against the wind; there was
no lock. Mael pushed the door open gently. At first
he thought he heard a tiny tinkle of sound. He
froze, but the sound was not repeated. He opened
the door the rest of the way.

The casket was still on the altar under the tor-
tured Christ. The room was otherwise empty.
Mael's tautness eased. He had been more afraid
than he would admit to himself that Diarmid
would have removed the relic into his sleeping
quarters overnight. Even worse, the priest or
Fergus might have been waiting in the shrine.
Mael stepped forward to take the casket and run.
The room darkened.

Fergus stood blocking the doorway. The mace
was in his right hand.

Mael cried out, slashing at the giant's eyes.
Fergus bellowed and seized Mael with his left
hand. The doughy fingers wrapped themselves in
the front of Mael's tunic. He jerked upward as if

Mael were weightless. Mael's bare head rang on a roof beam. The giant swung his mace to finish the smaller man, but the weapon caught in the narrow doorway. Flakes of rock spalled off the outside of the shrine.

Mael held his dagger in a death grip that had nothing conscious about it. Fergus flailed him against the walls of the stone room, roaring in his own mindless pain. Blood from his slashed face spattered over Mael and the shrine. The casket had been knocked from the altar. It lay on its side, still fastened.

"Out!" Diarmid cried. "Bring him out!"

Either the words penetrated or Fergus acted without hearing them. He stepped back, wrenching Mael through the doorway in the same motion. Mael's tunic ripped and the battered man flew free. Mael bounced numbingly on the ground. The dagger sprang from his hand. It fell, gleaming softly, a dozen feet downslope where the path continued toward the pier.

Diarmid darted into the fane to examine the precious relic. He came out with the casket a moment later. Snuffling in wild frustration, Fergus turned toward the priest for the first time since Mael had cut him. No major blood vessel had been severed, but a sheet of gore, black in the dimness, had spilled down the giant's face. It was collecting to drip from the rounded chin. Both eyeballs had been destroyed. Clear humor from the eyes emphasized the upper cheeks by washing the blood away from them. "Oh Christ, *Christ!*" Diarmid cried. "My son, *my son!*"

Mael tried to get up. He could not. His whole left side was numb, as much beyond his control as if it belonged to another man. The first shock had been to his skull. That and the repeated pounding of his body against the wall of the shrine had stunned both his muscles and nerves. He could see the sheen of his knife through a haze. He rolled toward it.

"Fergus!" the priest ordered. There was grief and rage in Diarmid's voice, but he was controlling them. The reliquary was under his right arm. His left hand guided his son's arms and weapon upward, then turned him to face Mael. The priest took a step forward, maneuvering the giant from the side. "Now!" the old man said, and he twitched at the mace arm. Fergus struck down with his full strength.

The soil was peat, compacted by the feet of pilgrims for ages. The wedge-shaped stone buried itself to its haft, brushing Mael's chest as it passed. Mael's good hand snatched up his dagger. Fergus effortlessly tore his mace free and started to take another step forward. "Back!" Diarmid cried, and Mael's blade snicked air an inch from the giant's right ankle as that foot halted.

Mael crawled backward, down the trail, putting another few feet between himself and the deadly mace. He used the heel of his right hand to propel him while the locked fingers still pointed the dagger at his enemies.

"A little forward, Fergus," the priest crooned. "No, no, boy. Don't lift your feet, slide them. That's right, now—"

Mael pivoted his body. His feet caught in the impenetrable wall of rhododendrons. The exile shouted, arching backward like a wingless insect. The mace thudded into the ground again. Fergus cleared it with a sideways flick that netted the head among the dense branches. He bawled angrily and tore the weapon free—into the tangled rhododendrons on the other side. Despite Diarmid's cries, Fergus began to slash his weapon from side to side, scattering stems and branches with every sweep. He paused only when an arc in front of him had been cleared and further strokes met no resistance.

The giant was breathing heavily. Still, he held the mace out at arm's length with no perceptible strain or weariness. Mael had scuttled a dozen feet further down the trail, temporarily out of danger. He was unable to take his eyes off the awesome destruction. Diarmid's hand touched Fergus inside the elbow. "A little forward," he said.

Mael's left side was still almost dead to him. A few prickles of sensation were returning, but he had no real feeling. In a way that was just as well. He had long since scraped away a patch of his trousers on the ground, and the skin of his thigh was rapidly going as well. Bluffing, Mael thrust himself up on his right knee and stabbed. "Back!" the priest ordered. Then, seeing the exile was still only half a man, Diarmid shouted, "Strike!" Fergus' blow was harmlessly short. Mael had bought a few more moments toward the time he would have full use of his limbs again. He backed further, to where the trail ended at the pier.

The breeze wrapped Mael in the effluvium of Fergus' body: hot, dry—the odor of an ox which has been plowing in the sun, not so much offensive as overpowering. Mael knew that he himself must stink of blood and fear like a pig in the slaughter pen. The moon had risen. It silhouetted his assailants, the giant and the black-robed priest. They hunched forward together.

Mael made a choice that was no choice. The pier was narrow and uneven, giving him even less room for maneuver than the path had done. But to either side quaked the mire of the slough margin where reeds replaced rhododendrons. To dodge to the side meant to be held in gluey muck while Fergus pounded his body into something of similar consistency. Cursing, Mael backed onto the flimsy boards.

Splinters tore at him. In another minute or two he might be able to stand or even strike back—if he could avoid the sweep of the mace until then. Mael did not even consider throwing his knife. It was the only thing that kept Fergus at a distance. The giant did not need a weapon to kill a man Mael's size. Once the threat of the dagger was gone —even if it were buried in Fergus' heart and inexorably bleeding his life away—Mael was dead. The giant would seize him barehanded and pluck his limbs off one by one, like a boy with a cricket.

The pier swayed as Fergus stepped onto it. He halted. In chillingly normal tones he said, "Father, you never wanted me to walk here."

"This once we'll go together," Diarmid said softly. "Be very careful now, Fergus. I'm right behind you." The older man paused, then added, "When I tell you, I want you to swing your club sideways."

The giant slid his right foot forward, the bare toes gliding over the irregularities of plank edged against plank. There was nothing clumsy about his advance. The pier showed no signs of imminent collapse but it creaked and sagged with the strain. Fergus was too big—and too much of his bulk was muscle—for Mael even to guess at his weight.

The pier had been constructed by driving double lines of posts into the mud of the slough, then pegging stringers to the inner face of each line. The plank flooring was attached to the stringers by leather thongs tied through holes in the wood. Where the leather had rotted away, the planks were loose and ready to spill a man who stepped on the edge. Diarmid's gentle touch kept his son centered safely and lethally.

Mael slashed quickly across the thongs holding three planks to the right-hand stringer. He twisted stiffly, ignoring the fanged splinters as he reached for the ties on the other side. If he could rip a big enough gap in the boards, he would be safe. Blind Fergus could never jump an opening. If the giant tried, his weight would carry him through into the water. He would hit the boards on the far side like a battering ram hitting the wall of a woodshed.

"Step," Diarmid ordered, then, "Now!" and the mace whistled out toward Mael's flattening body. The edge, blunt as it was, stripped away Mael's breeches with both the skin and the underskin fat of his left buttock. At the other side of its arc the mace clipped a post. The post was four-inch oak, a recent replacement for one that had rotted away. Where the anchor stone struck it, the wood sheared off as cleanly as if sawn. Transmitted impact was still great enough to skew the remainder of the piling in the bottom muck and pull it loose from the stringer. The flooring sagged slightly to the side.

Mael was dazed and weeping with pain. He crawled backward more from instinct than from conscious volition.

The priest said, "Hold your mace in your left hand, Fergus. . . . That's right. Now, put your right hand on this post. Keep very close to the side . . . now, step, step . . . let go the post and slide your right hand—*right hand*—that's right, hold the post and wait for me, yes. . . . Now you don't have to hold the post any longer. We're past the bad section. Step, step. . . ."

The weakened portion of the pier had cried under the giant's weight, but it had held. Now Mael had nothing around him on three sides but water. On the fourth, the soapstone mace was rising for a final blow.

Mael was unable to swim in his present condition. He would sink like a stone in the water. If he clung to a piling, if he even tried to flutter toward the coracle floating ten feet away at the end of its tether, Diarmid himself would throw the mace down on top of him.

"Step," said the priest. "Now—*sideways, Fergus!*"

Mael threw himself outward, catching the end

piling in the crook of his good arm. The mace arced straight down to where Mael had lain an instant before. The pine planks exploded upward without slowing the weapon in the least. The mace plunged on into the slough like the anchor it was meant for. Fergus followed it, his bald skull caroming off the post to which Mael clung. The giant's hands still gripped the shaft of the mace as the water sprayed up at his impact. Not even a bubble returned to the surface.

Diarmid stared at the shattered pier and the roiling water. The disturbance was the only marker his son would ever have. Mael was wrapped around the lone piling like a monkey on a stick. His left hand still lacked strength, but he had managed to bend its flesh onto the wood in a semblance of gripping. The priest moaned deep in his throat. He turned.

Veleda leaped down from her horse at the other end of the pier. "Mael!" she cried. She had a knife in her hand.

Without hesitation, Diarmid flung himself and the reliquary into the lough. When he surfaced, he began kicking toward the boat. The casket floated. Diarmid pushed it in front of him, making headway despite the drag of his billowing robe.

Mael cursed. He squirmed to bring his right foot onto the stringer so that he could stand instead of hanging by one arm. Veleda was pattering down the pier toward him, but she would be too late to stop Diarmid from reaching the coracle and casting off. The monster's skull would be gone and the priest would be free to raise a posse to avenge the desecration. Under the circumstances, Mael would be lucky if they burned him alive.

The coracle bumped before Diarmid reached it. The priest's vision was blocked by the reliquary so he did not notice the boat move. Then the black water humped as something opaque and equally black rose through it, spilling the coracle to the side. Diarmid screamed. A head lifted in front of him on a five-foot neck, a column as thick as a man's torso. Only in comparison to the swollen bulk of the body did the monster's neck appear slender. A stiff fringe like a ruff of coral fronds sprouted from behind the creature's skull. They were the gills of a huge, neotonous salamander which never needed to surface in order to breathe. It was not at the flaring gills that Diarmid screamed. It was at the mouthful of needle teeth lowering on him. The priest continued to scream until the jaws closed on his head and pulled him under. This time there were bubbles. They would have been red in better light.

The coracle had overturned and sunk. The reliquary casket rotated alone in little eddies as the water slowly calmed.

Mael looked across the four-foot gap between his piling and the rest of the pier. The stringer, still festooned with the stubs of shattered planks, connected them. "Veleda, I'll fall if I try to get across," Mael said.

"Of course you won't," the woman replied sharply. Her knife disappeared into her scrip. She held out both hands to Mael. "Your left leg will hold you. It's just one step. Now, walk."

Like Diarmid and Fergus, Mael thought, and look what it got them. But the black joke settled the terror that had paralyzed him for a moment after the real danger was past. He stepped onto the 'stringer, then to the planking. Veleda was right. His leg did hold.

Mael clutched her to him like the only buoy in an angry sea. "There, there," she murmured as her fingers brushed over his wounds. She winced more than Mael did at his left hip where the skin still curled in tendrils that had dried to his trousers. "We'll have to do something about that," Veleda said. Her touch brought a quick flash like that of cautery. Mael was not sure whether it seemed hot or cold. Then, though feeling returned, the pains were less than those of the hard ride from the seacoast.

At last Mael broke away. The reliquary floated a body's length from the pier. To Mael's surprise, he was still holding his dagger. He sheathed it, then unlaced his sandals and kicked them off with his trousers. His tunic, ripped all the way down the front, slipped off without needing to be lifted over his head. "Next time, I strip naked first and grease myself," he said ruefully. "At least that'll leave me decent clothes to be buried in." He set his dagger between his teeth, careful not to gash his lips with the edges, and crouched to lower himself into the water.

"No," said Veleda. "Leave the knife."

"Umm?" Mael took the blade out of his mouth and stared at his companion in surprise. "Didn't you see that thing that—got—Diarmid?" he asked.

"I've seen them. That one I called to us. There are very few left."

"Oh." Mael lowered his eyes to consider. "Well, if you called it—" and he did not like that idea in the least, but that could not show in his voice— "then it won't hurt me, I suppose. . . ."

"I can't promise that," Veleda said flatly. "I don't rule those old ones—or any other living creature. I can only talk to them, sometimes. But there aren't so many of us who follow the old truths, Mael, that we should plan to slaughter each other when we meet."

"I don't follow any gods, old or new," Mael said. Veleda met his gaze but made no reply. He grunted, then laid his dagger on a dry plank. He slid into the lough. Nothing touched him but the cold water, and that was further balm to his wounds.

Mael handed the chest up to Veleda and followed it awkwardly. "I should poultice your cuts," she said to the battered man as he began drawing on his clothing.

Mael shook his head. "I want to be at least ten miles away before we stop," he said. "I don't look forward to the ride, but they'll flay the rest of me if anybody catches us here."

Still he took the pad she handed him, linen folded over layers of herbs, and rode with it between his torn hip and the saddle. The casket was tied to Mael's pillion after they had checked it to make sure the skull within was undamaged. Mael found he liked the look of the rows of teeth even less after he had seen similar ones in use.

"We'll ride south to mBeal Liathain," he said. "There's enough trade through the port that I'll be able to buy passage back to Britain. Besides, I don't want to go back the way we came."

Veleda mounted without replying. Mael looked at her in brief doubt, then mounted as well with only a spurt of agony. Except for brief comments where the trail forked, they rode for two hours in silence. At last Mael said, "If this isn't far enough, nothing is. We've put half a dozen farms between us and the shrine."

"There's a grove of pines at the top of the next hill," said Veleda. "The ground there is smooth. The horses can be out of sight, and there's a spring there, too."

The grove was just as she said it would be. There was no altar within it, but in the recent past the ground beneath the big trees had been swept clean of twigs and needles by someone for some reason. Veleda soaked another cloth in the spring. Using it and her little knife, she cleaned Mael's buttock while he bent against a tree, digging his fingers into the coarse scales of the bark.

"I, ah . . ." he began. Carefully formal, he tried again. "When I held you there on the pier, it was because I was, ah, frightened. I didn't mean anything by it. Didn't mean to offend you, that is."

"You didn't." Veleda looked as helpless as a rabbit in a ferret's den, soft and warm and gentle. She laid the cloth down and bound another poultice over the wound. Her touch made Mael's whole body shiver. "There," she said. "It'll be weeks before it really clears up, but you'll be able to ride. Ride further.''

They spread their cloaks on the ground. Mael set his saddle at the head of his cloak for a pillow. He lay down on his back, staring at the starburst pattern of pine branches against the moonlit sky.

"When I use my saddle like that," Veleda said from very close beside him, "I wake up in the morning with an aching neck. It's a little too high."

Mael turned his head. Veleda was facing him, leaning back on her left elbow. Her hair shimmered about her arm and pooled on the cloak beneath her. He stretched his arm out, under her head. After a moment's hesitation, he curved his hand around her neck and pulled her to him.

"I told you I was a woman," she said before she answered his kiss.

And she was, but like no woman he had ever known before. The last thing Mael remembered as he finally fell asleep was the thrill of her slim, white fingers as they urged him to heights he had not dreamed a man could reach.

In the morning, Mael rode bare-chested until they reached a farmhouse. There he traded a copper bracelet for baggy trousers and a tunic of gray homespun. Britons had minted coins before the Romans came, but it would be another four centuries until an Irish king did the same. The remnants of Mael's old tunic were wrapped around the reliquary to hide its unique decoration. Mael whistled a good deal as he and Veleda cantered southward. Occasionally he broke into song.

"Ruadh, but it's been a long time!" he said suddenly, turning toward Veleda with a dazzling smile.

Veleda smiled back. She had thrown off her hood so that the fresh sunlight exploded in her hair. "Since you last had a woman?" she asked, as naturally as another man might have done. The question was incongruous from someone so feminine, but Mael found that it did not bother him.

"I would have said, 'Since I've been in love,'" he explained. "But there's a little of the other, too, since I . . . since a woman last mattered to me more than a few minutes." He was remembering things now which pain had kept him from willingly recalling before. "Ten years," he said. "Ten years."

"She left you?" asked Veleda, not really a question, only an offer to let someone who mattered drain off a part of what had been eating away his soul for a decade.

"She died," said Mael. His voice was normal, but his eyes were now fixed on the road instead of meeting Veleda's. "Or rather, she got killed, but the end was before that, that just resulted . . ." He took a deep breath and, still without turning his head, said, "Her name was Kesair. She had black hair and she was just the same height as me for all our lives. We—grew up together, you see.

"At fourteen I was sent off to train with the Ard Ri's Guard. When I came home on leave—and after the first six months that was frequent enough—it was just the same as it had always been between us. There was never another woman for me until now, until you." Mael looked at

Veleda. She reached out and touched the back of his hand with her cool, perfect fingers.

"You didn't marry," she said.

"No, we didn't do that," Mael agreed grimly. "But neither of us married, not for a long time. Then, ah, her father—her father was an important man"—and Mael's whole body was cold, trembling with the recollection of what he had almost said, but not quite, not quite—"a king in fact, though a client himself of the Ulaid. Every third man's a king in Ireland, doesn't it seem? Her father was a king, as I say. When the High King needed a wife for his brother Cearbhall, to make an alliance an edge more secure, where should he look but to Kesair, my lovely, black-haired Kesair?"

Veleda's fingers squeezed Mael's. He bent in his saddle to kiss her hand before continuing. "There were two years of that. I talked with Cearbhall, ate with Cearbhall—even fought at his side, if you can believe that. And I never once touched Kesair, never." Mael looked straight at Veleda. "And when we saw that it wasn't going to work, we . . . met again. And it was just as good as it ever had been. Only Cearbhall walked in when he was supposed to be a hundred miles away.

"He had his shield and a drawn sword. I suppose some of the servants had guessed and told him. But he didn't bring anybody else with him, either. He didn't want *that* talk in the barracks, and I guess he figured he could handle the matter himself. Which maybe he would have, except that Kesair threw herself onto his sword point before he could get it into me. And then I beat him to death with a bronze candlestick." Mael grinned like a skull. "No, I didn't put it through his helmet; but it was hard to live in a steel drum, and anyway, the helmet slipped off after a time. . . ."

Mael wrapped his fingers around Veleda's, letting them writhe in active contact for the first time since he had begun speaking. "See," he said with a false smile, "that's the kind of person you're running with."

Veleda leaned over and kissed him, startling a shepherd watching the travelers from the shade of a wayside oak. "It won't happen that way again," she said. "I promise. And I'm a witch, you know."

CHAPTER SIX

mBeal Liathain was considerably farther from Lough Ree than Mael's landfall in Leinster had been. Despite that and the battering Mael had taken, he and Veleda rode the distance in the same three days. Both fear of pursuit and a desire to finish a task thus far successful drove them. mBeal Liathain was a fortified village nestled on an inlet, a port and as near to a city as Ireland had at the time save for Cashel and the High King's seat at Tara. There was even a true wharf, though many of the round-bottomed vessels were simply beached to avoid the toll. Men from Gaul and Spain traded on the waterfront. In the market square you might find a blond-bearded Geat bartering with a Phoenician through an interpreter. The pelt of a great, white ice bear for silk brocades woven in war-torn China . . . This was the funnel through which Ireland moved her exports: horses and fine woolens, linen and metalwork the like of nothing cast elsewhere west of the Scythian steppes. But mBeal Liathain was more than that as well. The little village in Munster provided a stable freeport for much of the North Sea and the Atlantic, where migration and the dissolution of the Empire had left very little stability.

Mael and Veleda found a suitable ship at once. The vessel was a beamy, shallow horse transport about fifty feet long. She had been beached parallel to the shore, not only to save the wharfage fee but also because that was the only practical way to load her cargo. Sandbags cocked the shore-ward gunwale down. Planks made a ramp up the side along half the boat's length. The six horses of her cargo would be walked aboard without difficulty. There they could be harnessed between the thwarts before they realized they were no longer on dry land. The crew had already started loading when Mael, after a whispered discussion with his companion, dismounted and walked over to them.

"Who's your captain?" the exile called.

The burliest of the six sailors, a black-bearded man whose forearms and legs looked as curlingly hairy as his face, turned from the horse he was prodding forward with the butt end of his quirt. "Who the hell wants to know?" he demanded.

"Two people who need to buy passage to Britain," Mael said, as calmly as if he had not been challenged.

"Well, go find another bloody ship," the sailor snarled. "This one's headed for bloody Gaul on the next tide."

"I said 'buy,'" Mael remarked, knuckling his purse so that the heavy coins within gnashed together.

The sailor looked around with a somewhat different expression. He tossed his quirt to a companion. "I'm Vatidius," he said. "I'm the captain. Let's go get a drink and we'll see." Back over his shoulder he roared to his men, "Get 'em loaded right or I'll have your bloody hides when I get back!"

While Veleda sold the horses to a drover with a string of twenty, Mael and Vatidius bargained over bad beer and worse wine respectively. Vatidius was not the owner of the transport, merely a captain hired by a Breton consortium. He had no authority to do anything but sail straight for home with his cargo. Mael found the shipmaster brutal and stupid, but also venal. They struck a bargain after two cups of the wine. The bribe was sizable, but Vatidius swore he would have to pay his five seamen out of it for their silence as well. It was Arthur's money, anyway, and with as little direct trade as there was between the islands, Mael was willing to call the price fair.

Veleda and the cloth-covered reliquary, their only baggage, were waiting with the loaded freighter when Mael and Vatidius returned. Mael wondered briefly at Veleda's income—not until she sold the horses had it occurred to him that she must somehow have bought them as well. But that was no great matter; perhaps she told fortunes for the rich. Mael took her hand and nodded. Vatidius was already shouting, "Get your bloody asses on, then, and don't get in the way!"

The ramp had been dismantled so the three of them splashed aboard through the foul harbor water. Mael and Veleda watched in silence as the vessel was poled off shore. When the water was deep enough, four men began to work the sweeps. The remaining seaman watched the harbor over the tall cutwater, while Vatidius himself knelt astern at the steering oar.

The ship—if she had a name, Mael never heard it spoken—was a dozen feet wide amidships. Passage forward or aft was too tight for safety from the teeth or hooves of a nervous horse. All the beasts stood crosswise, their heads to port, lashed to reinforced thwarts intended to hold even horses frightened by tacking or bad weather. The sail was a single square of linen, hoisted to catch the fitful west wind as soon as the vessel cleared the harbor. The two men on the forward sweeps went astern as soon as they had shipped their long oars. The lookout followed. Mael and Veleda were left with only three of the snorting horses to keep them company forward of the mast.

"I don't like either the ship or the crew," Veleda said, her back cushioned from the gunwale by Mael's right arm. There was no chop, so even in the extreme bow they were dry.

"Who could?" Mael agreed with a shrug. "But we'll be shut of them soon enough if the wind holds. Are you tired?"

"Go ahead and nap," she answered. "You're still healing."

Mael smiled and squeezed her. He managed to
nod off almost at once. Veleda did not let a frown
of concern show on her face until after she was
sure the Irishman was asleep. From time to time
her eyes locked with those of one or more of the
polyglot seamen as they worked the ship. None of
the sailors came any nearer than was necessary to
feed and water the horses. Horse dung lay where it
fell. The breeze blew the green odor toward the
bow.

Clouds rolled up from the west to catch the sun
before it reached the horizon.

The sky was pitch-dark when Mael awakened to
the crash of the falling spar. He snatched at his
dagger left-handed. Embarrassed, he immediately
resheathed the weapon when he realized the crew
was simply taking in the sail by the light of a horn
lantern. Vatidius gave his passengers a wave and a
gap-toothed grin. After a moment he came forward, still holding the lantern. His men appeared
to be furling the sail. It was difficult to see the
crewmen because of the darkness and the inter-
vening horses.

"Don't want to go driving up on the bloody
shore, do we?" the shipmaster said cheerfully.
"That's not the kind of arrival you paid for, is it?"

Mael gave a noncommital grunt. Veleda said
nothing, but her body tensed. Vatidius squatted
down in front of his passengers anyway, talking
enthusiastically. "Going to be glad to get back to
Britain, I suppose."

Mael nodded. He had told the shipmaster only

that he was returning to Arthur. It didn't matter
that the Gaul mistook him for a Briton. He said,
"Glad to be back on dry land, anyway."

Vatidius' hand on the lantern kept the light from
his own eyes, shrouding his whole face. Not far
away the water slapped, making one of the horses
whicker in response. "Yes," the captain went on,
"I know you landsmen. I never had any luck on
shore, myself, and little enough at sea. . . ." His
voice trailed off. Then he added, "Tell you one
thing that does surprise me, though—that box you
carry." Veleda was murmuring under her breath,
the words only a bone-felt vibration to Mael. He
stiffened. The reliquary lay between his legs and
Veleda's. As unobtrusively as possible, he cleared
his right arm.

"I mean," Vatidius was saying, "most people'd
have baggage for as long a trip as you're making.
Folk of quality like you, you know. But the box, it's
not real baggage, now, is it? Just wondering, of
course."

"It's just got some bones in it," Mael said. "Just
some saint's relics, that's all." Did one of the
sailors around the mast hold a javelin?

"Now isn't that something?" said Vatidius.
"Now me—you know how sailors are. If you
hadn't told me, I'd have imagined there were, oh—
jewels, say, in the box from the way you carry—"

"Mael!" Veleda shouted. There was a huge
splash behind them. Mael's feet lashed out, skidding the casket hard against Vatidius' knees and
spilling the lantern. Even as Mael kicked, he was
turning. A Syrian seaman was lunging over the

rail with a knife in his right hand. The sailor must have slipped into the calm water and pulled himself along the boat's side while Vatidius occupied the passengers. Mael's right elbow caught the sailor in the throat with all his strength behind the blow. Gurgling, the Syrian pitched back into the sea.

Vatidius struck in the darkness. He rang an oak belaying pin off the side of the Irishman's skull. Mael bounced against the gunwale and fell back. He was conscious, but none of his limbs seemed to work. The captain's black bulk raised against the sky, readying a finishing blow.

At first Mael thought that Veleda had cried out and thrown something. She stretched her right hand toward Vatidius. A worm of purple fire uncurled from one slim finger and struck the Gaul. The flame-thing did not seem to move swiftly, but even before Vatidius could scream, its flattened ribbon had wrapped about his throat. One end of it buried itself deep in the captain's chest. Then the scream came and purple fire burst with it out of the burly man's mouth and nostrils. The flash lit the whole forepart of the ship.

The purple glare caught the remaining seamen running toward the prow. Each had an upraised weapon. The sailors froze as their captain, his torso shrinking in on itself and the fire licking all about him, threw himself overboard. Steam hissed when he struck the water. Veleda spoke again. Two more serpents of fire rippled from her hand. One of the sailors hurled his javelin. The metal popped and sizzled as the purple flame coursed

through it. The air stank with the harshness of a
lightning strike.

All six horses went mad together. The harness
and attachments that might have been adequate in
a storm disintegrated as supernatural terror
drove the animals. Showering wood fragments,
the beasts plunged into the sea in near unison.
They carried two of the sailors with them in their
rush. A third seaman overbalanced when the
three-ton cargo leaped to port and sent the vessel
pitching. That man flipped over the starboard rail.
The last crewman deliberately jumped, an inch
ahead of the flame that had darted for his eyes.
The purple light winked out as the intended victim
cleared the rail.

The moon came out from behind the clouds.
There was no longer any sign of the living flames.
One of the seamen was still afloat, swimming
blindly away from the vessel. He was dwarfed by
the frothing horses. They neighed in panic as they
kicked white pools of foam in the calm water
around them. The beasts could swim well—for a
time—but the immensity of the sea terrified them.
They tried to lunge higher in the water to sight the
shore. Two of them reached the sailor at almost
the same moment. They battled viciously with
their teeth and front hooves, each seeing the man
as a place to rest. Long before the horses had
parted, their feet had pulped the sailor and driven
his remains deep into the sea.

The boat rocked and pitched at the fury of the
big animals around it. One of them approached
the vessel. The horse's fear of the witch flames had

been dwarfed, as everything else was, by the huge expanse of salt water.

Mael pulled himself upright. A javelin stuck up from the planks halfway between him and the mast. He stepped to it and tugged it out. The blade was warped and dulled by the fire that had touched it, but its point was sharp enough to serve. The nearing horse, a chestnut stallion, kicked upward. Its hoof rang on the hollow side of the ship. Its head sank, then rose again from the water in a froth of effort. This time the horse swung its left foreleg over the rail. The vessel lurched toward its weight.

Mael lunged, driving the javelin into the horse's chest at the junction of neck and shoulder. The beast's jaws started and it screamed like a human. Both forelegs kicked straight up, the left fetlock shattering the railing as they glanced together. Mael jerked his weapon free. The chestnut dived backwards into the water. It did not come up again. Two more of the horses paddling frantically around the vessel came nearer.

A bow and a spilled quiver of arrows lay amidships. Mael saw them and judged the distance of the approaching horses. He tossed the javelin sideways to Veleda, shouting, "Hold them off a minute!"

"But they're *horses!* They'll *drown!*"

"Hell drink your soul, woman!" the Irishman cried. "They'll drown *us* by trying to get aboard!"

Mael snatched up the bow. Veleda, weeping, slapped the nearest horse across the muzzle with the spear shaft. The horse shied back and sank to nostril height. Its companion, a black mare, kicked and knocked the spear away. Mael shot the horse behind the ear. The animal went limp and sank without a sound.

The arrows were crooked and the boat provided a shaky weapons platform. Mael locked his hip against the rail and leaned outward so that the point of his arrow was almost touching the other horse before he released. The arrow penetrated half its length but missed the brain. The beast turned away, whinnying and leaving a swirling trail of blood.

There were twelve more arrows in the quiver. Mael fired them all. When he was finished, the sea was clear of all life but himself and his companion. Mael set the bow against his knee and snapped the staff into halves. Then he leaned the halves against the gunwale and broke them again with his foot. When he was finished, he hurled the fragments as far as he could into the sea. They floated over the bodies of their victims.

Mael leaned against the rail. Veleda's cool hands touched his neck and right biceps. Memories of her fingers skittered through Mael's mind: comforting him with their pressure—stroking his groin to unbearable lust—*burning Vatidius' lungs away with a ribbon of fire—*

Mael screamed and jerked away from the woman.

Veleda stared at him as if he had slapped her. "I had to!" she cried.

"I'm sorry," Mael said, pressing his hands together to have something to do with them. He would not meet her eyes. So delicate, so . . . "I know you had to, I really do, it was your life and mine and maybe Starkad's, too. . . . And I'm really glad you could, could do something about those sailors, because I sure as hell couldn't. But just for now I, well, my mind is . . ." He looked up at Veleda and bit his lower lip. Then he burst out, "Manannan MacLir, woman, I just don't want to b-be touched right now! That's all."

Veleda stepped back from Mael's pitiful anger. "No," she said, "that's not all. But it's not your fault either." She looked back at the western sky. "I think we're going to get some wind soon," she said. "If we can get the sail up, we can get out of this . . . stretch of ocean. I think we'd both be happier for that."

The breeze was sudden and strong. The vessel was squirrelly with neither cargo nor ballast, but the wind was dead astern. There was no real danger even in their undercrewed state. Mael wondered briefly whether that was a result of Veleda's art, too, but he put the thought aside hurriedly.

Veleda had saved both their lives.

Mael steered by the stars and an inner compass that failed him about as often as it brought him where he wanted to go. At the moment he felt he would be just as happy if the boat gutted itself on a rock in mid-ocean, so of course his luck carried him straight to his destination with an accuracy no practiced navigator could have guaranteed. Seas rustling on the shoreline to the north brought Mael to steer that way. Half an hour later, Veleda

pointed to the river mouth that gaped blackly be-
tween the fringes of surf to either side. "That's the
Tuvius," she said. "We're within ten miles of
Moridunum and the villa."

Mael did not bother to ask her how she knew.

A mud bank brought the ship to a halt that
seemed fairly gentle, until the mast snapped and
went crashing over the side. Mael was jarred off
his feet. He stood, picked up the reliquary, and
walked to the bow. It rested a dozen feet from
shore. Veleda followed, her face calm. Mael
looked over the rail, then back at Veleda. "I'm
sorry," he said. "I really can't tell you how sorry I
am about—the way I acted." Very deliberately, he
extended his right hand to her. "I'll lower you
down, then I'll jump."

Veleda smiled with tears bright in the corners of
her eyes. Grasping Mael's big hand with both of
hers, she lowered herself into the shallow water
and waited for him. Mael tried not to shudder at
the touch of her fingers. The two of them waded to
shore together, into a small crowd that the noise
had brought out of bed with torches and half their
clothing.

One bulky spectator was mounted on a good
horse. He trotted forward and demanded, "What
happened? You aren't just going to leave your ship
like that, are you?"

Mael eyed him flatly. "No," he said, "I'm going
to trade it to you for two horses."

The rider blinked and pulled his maroon cloak
closer about him. He was fully dressed but his
tunic was inside out. "Trade?" he repeated. "Why,

that's—I mean, how do I even know you own the thing?"

"Look," Mael snapped, "either I own it and you're getting one hell of a bargain, or I cut the throats of the people who *did* own it and you aren't wearing a sword. Now, do you have another horse handy or—"

In ten minutes Mael and Veleda—on a pony that was adequate for her weight and the short distance—were riding north along the east bank of the River Towy. The casket was again lashed to the back of Mael's saddle.

CHAPTER SEVEN

The night was warm. The six guards on duty at the villa's front entrance were outside, under a torch. At that distance the sounds of their dice game would not disturb the chieftains quartered within the building. When the guards heard the approaching horses, they swept up the dice and checked their weapons. A messenger was more likely than a sudden attack, but—it was cheap enough to be ready, that was all.

Mael reined up in the circle of torchlight and dismounted. He began to unstrap the reliquary. "We've got to see Arthur," he said. "At once."

Two of the guards laughed. None of them answered.

Mael pulled the last tie loose and turned in fury with the casket in his hands. "Look, ye cunt-brains," he snarled, a little of his Erse lilt quivering through the anger in his voice, "it's five hundred miles your Arthur has sent me to fetch this back—with my friend's life the forfeit if I failed. I'll have Arthur awake now to see it, do you hear?"

Hands hovered near weapon hilts. The guard officer said, "No, I recognize him. He's the one we escorted off to Ireland. Godas, knock on the Leader's door and see if he wants to talk to this one now."

Doubtful but obedient, the named guardsman slipped into the villa. A moment later the door reopened. First through it was the guard. To Mael's amazement, the second man was Arthur himself. The king must have been asleep, but even so he had slid into his boots and pulled his coat of mail on over his bare shoulders before coming to the door. The links would be uncomfortable without padding beneath them, but they were less uncomfortable than a spear thrust through naked skin. Kings had died before through neglecting to arm themselves as they rushed out into the night. Behind Arthur was his seneschal Cei, a short, stocky man who was also in armor. He carried a drawn sword in one hand, in the other a lantern. Cei blinked in its radiance, looking as logy as a denned bear and as ill-tempered.

There was soft motion from the darkness to Mael's right as well. Mael turned and squinted. Unsummoned but not unexpected, Merlin stepped into the converging spheres of torch and lantern light. The wizard was barefoot and wearing the same simple tunic as before. His fingers toyed with another willow switch. Merlin's eyes searched Mael and the casket eagerly. Then his peripheral glance at Veleda penetrated and he froze. He glared at the woman. She stared back at him, overtly as calm as a stone.

"What's *she* doing with you?" Merlin demanded of Mael.

The Irishman's eyebrows rose with his temper. "Bringing a bloody lizard skull back." Mael turned to Arthur. "Where's Starkad?"

Arthur shrugged the question away. "He's here, he's fine. Did you bring the skull?"

"Where the hell is 'here'?" Mael shouted. "If anything happened to Starkad, I'll—" He remembered where he was and let the rest of the threat go unvoiced.

The king smiled and said very precisely, "Recruit, every one of the instructors placed over your friend has requested the Dane be discharged as unfit—too undisciplines to teach and too dangerous to have around. He hasn't gone anywhere, however. You'll find them, perfectly healthy, in his billet. As soon as you can give me the skull."

Mael pressed the latch of the casket and opened it. Merlin and the king crowded around. Cei and the other Companions hung back, curious but more afraid. The wizard traced around the small eyesockets with his left index finger, then ran down the line of the snout. "Yes. . . ." he said. "Tonight we can begin the work."

"Tonight?" Cei blurted.

"Can we start sooner?" Merlin sneered. He

looked at Arthur. "I'll need a man to read the responses," he said. "One who won't run if something goes—"

"All right, I'll come myself," said the king with a nod. Arthur's attention was on the reliquary.

Impatience and the nearness of triumph drove Merlin to retort unthinkingly, "Come and read responses? Read? *Read?*"

Arthur went white. Mael, hearing the grating sound of drawn steel, looked up swiftly to see which guard would strike the blow. But the king took a deep breath and said, "Of course. I'll send for Lancelot, then. He can read."

"Mael will read your responses," said Veleda unexpectedly from behind the Irishman. Even Merlin had forgotten her after the casket was opened.

Mael twisted around to look at her, trying to discern in Veleda's placid expression what she meant to accomplish. There was nothing to be seen. Mael chuckled, acting on instinct. "I'll bet your Lancelot still has trouble talking through the teeth I broke for him before I left," he said. "I'll take care of your responses."

Merlin's gaze flickered from Veleda to Mael and back again. The wizard frowned. "You think I'd be afraid, don't you?" he asked the woman. "You don't think I'd dare display my powers in front of a—" his wand stroked—"a pawn of yours? We'll see." Merlin's eyes shifted back to Mael. "And you think you'd be able to read Latin letters, Irishman?"

To a British warrior, the question would have

been no insult. The wizard might not even have meant it for one. Mael's head snapped back as if his face had been slapped. The Ard Ri's Guard had been an assemblage of scholars as surely as of athletes, ever since it was founded two centuries before by the great Cormac mac Airt. Mael reacted in much the same way as he would have to a suggestion that he could not out-wrestle an old woman. "My ancestors were kings in Miletos, Briton, when wolves chased your scampering forebears into the trees," he said. "I can read Ogam or Greek letters or Latin. If you British were civilized enough to have a script of your own, I would have learned to read that as well in the High King's school."

Cei grunted and started to raise his sword. Merlin laid his omnipresent willow switch across the seneschal's wrist without taking his eyes off Mael. The angry Briton froze with a surprised look on his face. Merlin gave Mael an ugly grin. "You think you're a bold man, do you, Irishman?" he said. "You'll have had need to be before this night is out." He turned to Arthur. "We can finish this within the hour if you'll get us horses. I already have everything prepared at the cave in the bluff west of here."

"The old corral?" Arthur queried.

"That's right. And I intend to use it as a corral again—though for a very different sort of cattle.' "

The king shrugged and called to his guard officer. "Three horses. At once."

Merlin led, riding faster than the overcast night made safe, in Mael's opinion. The road was well defined but showed few signs of use in the recent past. Cei was stumbling directly behind the wizard, trying to light his king's path with the inadequate lantern. Mael checked to be sure Veleda rode comfortably. She grinned back at him, amused that he even thought she might be having trouble. Mael pressed his horse forward a little to put him alongside Arthur.

"Where is it we're going?" he asked.

Arthur's mouth quirked at the suggestion of equality in the question. "There's a row of limestone hills half a mile from the main building," he answered mildly enough. "One of them has a cave in it, a small entrance but a belly the size of a church. It used to be a stable."

"Umm. Then why don't you use it?"

The king's smile grew a little broader. "I said," he repeated, "there's one small entrance. I don't want my people to get in the habit of stabling their mounts in places they can't get out of fast. They only have to do that one night on patrol and I've lost a whole sector of border." He glanced back over his shoulder. "Did you really think you had to bring your whore along?" he asked.

Mael laughed. "Didn't ask her to come," he said, "but I'm glad of her company." He dropped back and rode the rest of the short distance beside Veleda. Neither of them spoke, but Mael knew that he had not lied to Arthur about the companionship.

The cave was in a long bulk of stone, an outcrop thirty feet high rather than a water-carven bluff. It was not sheer, but its one-to-one slope was too sharp for a man to climb it easily without using his hands. The cave mouth was at ground level, an egg-shaped hole squared off by the addition of door posts and a great iron-strapped gate of hardwood. Merlin dismounted at some distance from the opening. He tied his horse to one of a small copse of poplars. "We'll leave our horses here," he said, explaining, "they don't like to feel—power being used."

Mael's chest tightened. He did not speak or look at Veleda.

They all trudged toward the gate in file. Merlin paused and took the reliquary from Mael before he entered the cave. The wizard's eyes met those of the witch woman. "You don't come inside," he snapped. "I know the kind of trouble you'd cause."

Veleda's hair twitched like the mane of a beast. "Be assured," she said. "that god watches you whether I do or not."

"God!" Merlin sneered. "God! You don't know—you can't imagine—what I'm about to do!"

"I suspect that you can't imagine the evil you're about to do," the woman said. "A little knowledge . . . but what will be, will be. Go raise your ravening monster, little man."

The wizard's eyes clouded. He passed his willow wand between himself and Veleda three times. Without a word he touched the center of her tunic with the leafy end of the branch. Veleda laughed and reached up with her right hand. She broke the tip between her fingers, gripped for the center of the wand and snapped it, too, and reached for

Merlin's hand. He snatched himself away with a
curse and flung the wand out into the darkness.

Still scowling, he took the lantern from Cei.
"You," he said. "You stand out here and see that
we aren't disturbed."

The seneschal stiffened at the tone. He looked
doubtfully at Mael, even more doubtfully at the
wizard himself. "Leader," he said, "I don't think
you ought to go in there alone with—"

"Do as the man says, Cei," Arthur snapped.
"Merlin's doing what I told him to do, and I can
handle the Irishman—needs must." The king and
Mael eyed each other appraisingly. Then, ducking
their heads under the low lintel, they followed
Merlin into the cave.

The single lantern could not illuminate the
cavity within. From the opening it expanded so
suddenly that Mael suspected parts of the hill face
must be eaten almost through. It had been
hollowed by water, not the hand of man; wherever
the light shone, from the ceiling down the walls to
shoulder height, the surface gleamed with the soft
pearl of flow rock. Lower down, the dissolved and
redeposited calcium carbonate had been worn
away or fouled by the beasts stabled in the cave in
past times. The air had a still, musty odor. Ancient
dung covered the floor, trampled and compacted
until it had become almost as dense as the limestone beneath. The cave was over twenty feet wide
and its walls stretched back further than the light
could follow, but there was no breeze to hint at a
second opening to this bubble in the rock.

As Merlin had said, his paraphernalia was already ordered within. The wizard stepped first to a seven-branched lampstand and began to light the separate wicks with a spill of papyrus. Mael had first assumed the stand was Jewish. As it better illuminated itself, it became obvious that the object was not Jewish at all—not even as Judaism was misunderstood and libeled by gentile sources. Mael had seen worse things than that stand, but it did not mean that he cared for the lovingly crafted abomination.

The seven lamps displayed the rest of Merlin's gear clearly. Most striking was a brazier resting on a tripod and already laid with sticks of charcoal. A grill was mounted above the fire pan on narrow arms; it was raised more than a foot above the surface of the coals. The metal was black and without decoration, apparently wrought iron.

Two cases of sturdy wood stood nearby. One was a cylinder whose lid was askew to display a number of scrolls resting endwise within. The winding rods were tagged, but Mael could not read the titles without making an obvious effort to do so. He kept a rein on his curiosity. Scrolls of both papyrus and vellum were represented. One of the latter had a gilt fore-edge and a pattern of tiny agates set into the knobs of the winding rods.

The other case was of less common pattern. It was full of chemicals, each in a separate jar in one of the scores of pigeonholes into which the narrow chest was divided. The containers were generally pottery, but a few were stone and one was of glass so clear that a king would have been proud to sip his wine from it. A sliding lid could close the chest, but that had already been untied and leaned against the wall. Across the top of the chest was a silver scriber, an arthame, some two feet long. Mael at first mistook the instrument for the weapon it resembled. Then he noticed that the edges of the blade were blunt and that its rippled pattern was only a depiction of a flattened serpent's body. The tail tip, polished with wear, was the point. The head and neck straightened to form a guardless hilt.

Merlin set the lantern on the floor. His hands twitched absentmindedly. When he realized that they were playing with his missing wand, he cursed under his breath. The wizard plucked a shred of willow bark from under a thumbnail. Shooting a vicious glance at the Irishman, Merlin turned his face to the far end of the cave and muttered an incantation. The lamps cast on the wall the capering shadow of what Mael was blocked from seeing by the wizard's body. When Merlin faced around again, he was holding another willow switch. This one was thin and only a yard long. "The wood has eternal life," the wizard muttered to his audience in fuzzy explanation. He became more alert and looked again at Mael. Then he ran the tip of the wand across the sticks of charcoal in the brazier. Where the willow touched, the black turned white with ash. The brazier itself began to glow and stink of hot iron.

Mael grinned. His stomach was turning over with the memory of other magic he had watched. "You must be a delight on a winter bivouac," he said.

Merlin reached into the case of scrolls and took out one of the parchments. "Read this over," he directed Mael. "Not aloud! I have to ready the— rest of this." The wizard set his wand on the box of chemicals and picked up the arthame. Ignoring both men—he had not paid the king any attention since they entered the cave—Merlin began drawing lines and symbols in the lumpy floor. The design was centered on the lighted brazier.

Mael unrolled the first column-width of the scroll. He began to read. At first he thought there was something wrong with the letters. But no, they were plain enough. It was just that the words they formed made no sense at all. . . . "This isn't in Latin," the Irishman said aloud, thinking Merlin had given him the wrong scroll.

The wizard looked up from the pentacle he was scribing. He smirked. "I didn't say it was. The *letters* are Latin; the language itself is a good deal older than Rome, Irishman. Or Miletos."

Mael frowned but concentrated on the manuscript again. Its format puzzled him until he realized that what he held was a list of long antistrophes, each of them ten or more lines in length. Instead of copying out the strophes as well, the scribe had merely indicated the first speaker with the Greek letter "delta" wherever Mael's portion ended. None of the words made any sense, but Mael felt a compulsion to begin speaking them aloud. His frown deepened.

Merlin finished scratching on the floor. He set the arthame down and picked up the willow again. "Well," he demanded, "do you think you're ready,

Irishman?"

Mael nodded, refusing to acknowledge either
the challenge or the hostility in the wizard's tone.
"Yes," he said.

"Believe me," Merlin went on, "this is no joke. If
you start, you have to finish. If you panic, you'll be
in worse danger than you can imagine."

Mael thought of violet serpents lighting the
shadowed deck. "I can imagine a lot," he said.
"And I don't panic."

"Then stand over there," Merlin directed, pointing to one of the reentrant angles of the pentacle,
"but don't scuff the line. Don't even lean over it
after we start."

Mael obeyed. Heat thrown off by the brazier
brushed his legs below the trousers.

The wizard carefully took the lough monster's
skull out of the reliquary. Barehanded he set the
yellowed bones on top of the grill. Then he bent
over again and took a pinch of something from one
of the opened jars of chemicals. When Merlin
tossed the powder on the charcoal, orange smoke
bloomed up and briefly hid the whole apparatus.
The wizard coughed and swore under his breath.
He took a pinch of white chemical from another
jar. Nothing happened when he cast that as well
into the fire. Nodding approval, the wizard
plucked another scroll from the case. Finally he
took up his position at the peak of the pentagram
across the brazier from where Mael stood. He gave
the Irishman a grin that was almost a rictus beneath his glazed eyes. Then he began to intone the
spell.

Waiting made Mael nervous despite himself.
The wizard's voice was higher than normal when
he chanted. The timbre was not so much feminine
as bestial, that of a small dog yapping something
close to words. Mael shot a glance behind him at
the king. Arthur was hunched against the wall of
the cave. He had drawn his sword and was resting
it point down in the gritty flooring. The king's
hands lay on the cross guard and his long fingers
were twined around the hilt. Arthur's face was as
hard as the steel blade.

Merlin broke off at the end of the strophe. He
dipped his wand at Mael like a choirmaster's
baton. Mael gulped his throat clear and began to
sound the unfamiliar syllables. At first the Irishman spoke slowly, afraid to misaccent or stumble
over the gibberish. When he had begun, though,
Mael found his mouth was shaping naturally to
the words. They rolled out with a rightness not af-
fected by the fact that they were still unintelli-
gible. Even that was changing subtly. Though the
words had no meaning, they left behind them an
aura of purpose. When the passage ended, Mael
stopped. He was breathing hard and listening with
new ears to Merlin taking up the chant. It was only
then that Mael realized that the last of the words
he had "read" were on the next column of his
scroll. He had not unrolled it. His fingers fumbled
as he did so.

Merlin threw something more on the fire as the
Irishman began his second passage. A thin, green
tendril wound upward toward the ceiling. The
smoke trembled like a lutestring at the impact of

the readers' voices. The cave was getting colder.
Mael thought for a time that the chill was in his
imagination, but he noticed puffs of vapor from
Merlin's mouth as he read.

The litany caromed back and forth between the
speakers, proceeding toward the end of each
scroll. Merlin dusted the fire with further
chemicals without any significant effect on the
flames or on the chill that utterly permeated the
cave. Finally the wizard completed his last invo-
cation and, beating the strokes with his wand,
shouted the response aloud with Mael: "Sodaque!
Sodaque! SODAQUE!"

The skull above the coals wavered and collapsed
inward. The air was full of the stink of fresh blood.
On the grill in place of the dead bones pranced a
pigeon-sized creature with strong hams and a pair
of wings instead of forelegs. The beast was
covered all over with scales, black and with the
suggestion of translucent depth that a block of
smoky quartz gives. Its head and neck were serpentine. A long tail, thrust out stiffly to balance
the weight of the forequarters, was the length of
neck and torso together.

The creature's eyes were small and cruel and a
red so intense that it seemed luminous. "My
wyvern!" Merlin cried out joyfully. He dropped
the scroll and began to dance with his hands
clasped above his head. The wyvern launched itself from the grill and sailed around it in a tight
circle. One of the scale-jeweled wings spread into
the air above a sideline of the pentacle. The beast
glanced away as though it had struck a solid wall.

Shrieking with high-pitched anger, the wyvern opened its mouth and spurted a needle of azure flame as long as its whole body.

Mael looked at the capering wizard, then back at the dragon. He stepped away from the pentacle and began to laugh full-throatedly, clutching his sides. It was as much the anticlimax to his fear as the actual ludicrousness of the tiny monster that was working on the Irishman.

The chirping wyvern had had yet a third effect on the king. Arthur's face lost its death-mask placidity. He gaped. Then his expression began to contort with fury. "That?" he shouted. "*That* will lay the Saxons at my feet?" The king stepped around the pentagram with his sword raised. His eyes were fixed on Merlin.

The wizard was too caught up in his triumph even to hear the king's words, but the oil lamps threw multiple images of the sword past him to the cave wall. Merlin turned, suddenly sober. "Wait!" he cried. "Leader—it will grow!"

Mael had backed against the wall. He held his left arm across his body where the tunic sleeve hid his other hand's grip on his dagger hilt. Arthur had paused an instant before striking. Merlin half crouched. His wand was raised, but the fear in his eyes was certain. Whatever the power was he had used to block Cei's hand, the wizard did not care to chance it against his king in a murderous rage. "Leader, this is what I *meant* to do," he said. He stretched out his left hand in supplication. "Other people have tried to raise dragons full grown. That's dangerous, suicide—nobody but a god, perhaps, can control something that big from the first."

Arthur did not relax his stance or gaze, but he began to lower his long sword to an on-guard position. The wizard straightened, letting his wand tip fall in turn. "This one—" he used his elbow to indicate the wyvern so as not to break the lock his eyes had gained on Arthur's—"is small and I can control it. It's going to get bigger—very much bigger, you needn't fear. But I'll still have power over it, because the power will increase, too. You'll have your weapon in a few weeks, and you'll have a weapon you can really direct instead of being something all-devouring and masterless. A less able student might have raised a real monster in his ignorance."

The tension was gone. The wyvern squawked again and perched on the grill. It was apparently oblivious to the heat. Mael said, "You know, I've heard a notion like that before. One of the lordlings in—where I grew up. He decided he'd start lifting a newborn bull calf once a day, so in a year he'd be strong enough to lift a grown bull." Mael grinned at Arthur. "It wasn't near that long before he'd broken his back trying, of course. But it was an interesting notion."

"You can read, Irishman," Merlin snarled, "but don't think you can teach me sorcery because of that! You know nothing. Nothing!" To Arthur the wizard added quickly, "Leader, in a few weeks you'll march beneath a power that no prince has ever equaled."

Arthur sheathed his sword. For a moment he

watched first Mael, then the wyvern, askance.
Then he said, "Explain the dragon to me, wizard.
If I have to feed it to full size, I'll need to make
plans."

"Oh, it won't need to eat at all," Merlin said,
with a return of his giggly good humor. He began
bustling about his paraphernalia, readying it to
leave. "Not in this world at least. You see, what
you think is a dragon, what looks like a dragon, is
really thousands and thousands and uncounted
thousands of dragons. Each of them for—well, not
even an eyeblink. It's nowhere near that long a
time. When the dragon seems to move—" he
pointed with his wand. The wyvern reacted by
screeching and throwing itself forward, to
rebound again from the invisible wall—"it is
really a series of dragons. A whole row of them
moving each for an instant into this universe from
one in which wyverns can exist."

"One exists right there," Arthur said irritably,
pointing at the tiny creature. It was again swooping about its prison.

"But only because of my magic," Merlin replied,
"and only for the briefest moment. Then it's back
in the cosmos I drew it from and another—from a
wholly separate existence—is there in its place for
another hairsbreadth of time. Now, that's what
others have done as well, yes, the ones who knew
the path, the essence of power. But I—instead of
having the same wyvern repeat itself from
myriads of identical universes—I added a time
gradient as well. This way each of the creatures is
a little older, a little larger than the one before.

And so on, forever, as long as I wish."

"As *I* wish, wizard," the king reminded him in no pleasant voice.

"As you wish, Leader," Merlin agreed obsequiously.

"If that's true," Mael interjected, "and I won't say that it can't be, I'm no sorceror as you say . . . but why does the beast snap at you here in this world? You say it's only the moment's wraith from a world in which you aren't there to snap at."

"Yes, that's right," Merlin said, bobbing his head with enthusiasm at having an intelligent audience to display himself before. "But something's there, don't you see? There isn't any end of worlds, worlds with wyverns leaping and squalling and spitting flame. It's my control that chooses which world is plucked of which wyvern . . . that and a sort of . . ." The wizard frowned and sobered for the first time since Arthur had lowered his sword. "Well, a sort of inertia that the process itself gives it. I can't be ordering the creature to breathe or telling it which muscles to tense so that it can take a step. That sort of thing just—" he shrugged—"goes on. And with nothing else appearing, the . . . simulacrum . . . made from thousands of wyverns . . . will act by itself as though it were one real wyvern, here and now."

"And wyverns have nasty tempers," Mael concluded aloud. As if in response, the little creature sent another jet of flame toward the men. Mael's skin prickled even at a distance. He noticed that the fire crossed the wall of the pentagram easily, though the wyvern itself could not.

Arthur walked closer and stared at the details of
the beast that leaped and scrabbled vainly to get at
him. The king prodded at it with his sheathed
sword, chuckling at the fury with which the wyvern's fangs and tiny claws attacked. Merlin
tensed. The king tugged back his sword, stripping
the dragon from it at the inscribed line. Still
chuckling, Arthur twisted the scabbard on the
baldric from which it hung. He saw the leather
shredded where the beast had clawed it.

Then the king stopped laughing. With a muffled
curse, he dropped the sheath and slid the blade
free to examine it. The yellow light gleamed on
deep scorings in the steel itself. Arthur grunted
and shot the sword home again. "Stronger than I
had thought," he said to Merlin in a neutral voice.

"They're not at all like things of this world," the
wizard agreed. "They couldn't even breathe if they
were here, if they had to stay. Things weigh much
more in their worlds and the air is much thicker,
besides being different. That's how they can fly,
even though they're huge when they grow. They're
like whales in the waves of our seas. And they're
very strong, yes. . . ."

Merlin closed and thonged shut the case of
scrolls. He fastened the chest of chemicals as well.
Taking the books and his wand under his left arm,
the wizard walked toward the cave mouth.
Pausing to transfer the arthame to his free hand,
he scribed a single line between the gateposts. He
added symbols on the outer side of the line while
he muttered the same half-sensed sounds he had
used when drawing the pentacle. Finished, Merlin

swung the door open. Cei, standing close beyond it, turned around with hope and concern limned on his face by the lamps still burning inside.

"Leader," Merlin directed, "if you'll pick up the lantern—the stand can stay here, I think."

Arthur nodded and obeyed. Mael picked up the chest of chemicals without being asked and started to follow the king toward the gate.

"Don't touch the line or the words," Merlin warned. "Just step over them." To Mael he added, as if an afterthought, "Oh, Irishman—would you just smudge a side of the pentacle before we leave? There's no problem with the barrier drawn here."

Mael frowned. From the darkness behind the waiting seneschal came Veleda's shout of warning: "Mael! Use the silver!"

Mael reacted before rage had time to flush across the wizard's face; darting his hand out to pluck the arthame from the older man. Warrior and sorceror stared at each other without speaking or needing to. Beyond stood Arthur, amused the way a certain type of dog owner can be as he watches a pair of his animals about to mix lethally. Cei's sword was drawn. The seneschal stood ready to slaughter both men if his Leader allowed him to. Cei did not understand the silent quarrel, but he abominated both participants.

Mael flipped the arthame so that he held it by the grip. He spat deliberately on the ground between him and Merlin; then he walked back to the pentacle. Under his left arm the Irishman still carried the box of chemicals. The angry wyvern watched his approach and redoubled its efforts to claw through the barrier. Mael slashed the air in front of it with the arthame. Screeching, the beast threw itself backwards. It rolled over as it tangled its tail and legs in its haste.

Mael knelt, eyeing the little monster. He drew the tip of the arthame through the inscribed pentagram. The wyvern spat fire in his direction but remained at a distance, curling and hunching itself. Mael straightened and backed away with quick, fluid steps. When the Irishman was halfway between the gate and the marred pentacle, the wyvern launched itself at his face like a bolt from a ballista.

The box of chemicals Mael held saved his left arm, for it was pure reflex that threw it up to block the sudden attack. The dragon's speed was beyond anything its swoops and caracoles within the pentagram had led Mael to expect. As it clung to the sturdy box, the wyvern lanced blue fire which danced over the edges of the wood. It seared Mael's forearm. The Irishman cut blindly with the arthame, the instantaneous sweeping reaction of a man who has felt a spider leap to the back of his neck.

The silver arthame caught the wyvern squarely and slapped the beast away. The creature bounced on the cave floor, knocking the lampstand over. The oil burst up in a flood of yellow light and a rush of heat. The dragon sat in the middle of the conflagration and yowled angrily. A long, red streak swelled where silver had touched the ebon scales. The wyvern bent and licked at the wound,

oblivious to the pool of blazing oil surrounding it.
Mael took two sliding steps and leaped the barrier
drawn at the gate. The other three men gave back
swiftly at his movement. The dragon, catching a
peripheral glimpse of the motion, threw itself suddenly after Mael. The beast was an instant too
slow, rebounding from the line just after the Irishman had crossed it. The creature sent a spiteful
stylus of flame out into the night behind its intended victim.

Arthur still held the lantern. Mael turned the
chest of chemicals to the light. The wood was
blackened in a circle the size of a dinner plate. In
the center, the panel was pierced by a hole large
enough to pass a man's thumb. The ceramic jar of
copper salts within had shattered. The fumes
stank of hellfire. The flame had sprayed Mael's
forearm with half-burned splinters blasted from
the box and raised several blisters. Mael dropped
the chemicals without a word. The chest jounced,
breaking several of the containers from the sound
it made when it hit. The Irishman flung the arthame to the ground at Merlin's feet. Its point
sank several inches into the soil, making the metal
ring with the shock. "Your beast has bad man-
ners," Mael said. "It could be that I should've
fed him the poker sideways, I am thinking. Or fed
it to you, wizard."

If Merlin intended a retort, he swallowed it.
From his other side, Veleda spoke. Her hair
slithered as if in harmony with her words. "You're
a man who rolls a rock down a mountainside and
expects to run with it, Merlin. You can't control a

landslide just because you had the power to begin it. There are no fools in the world so great as the ones who think themselves knowing.''

Merlin snarled with the same frustrated rage that wracked the thing he had summoned. He turned and stalked to his horse, still holding the container of books. Arthur laughed. "You know, Irishman," he said, "I'm beginning to think you could be a credit to my Companions—if you lived long enough.''

Mael still shook with anger and the shock of his near death at the wyvern's claws. "Maybe I don't shit well enough on command," he spat.

"Neither do my Huns," Arthur replied mildly. "Sometimes . . . but I think we've seen and done all we care to, here tonight. Yes . . . You'd better get to your billet. Tomorrow's a day of training, you know.''

Mael laughed. He bowed to the king, then followed Veleda to the horses. Behind him he could faintly hear the dragon hiss and squall.

Mael and Veleda slid from their mounts and unsaddled in front of the recruit lines. They lashed the beasts to the rail placed there, even though the recruits had not yet been issued horses. At the door to his and Starkad's dwelling, Mael paused and said to the woman, "Just a second. My friend sleeps light, and he tends to—react when he's suddenly—" Mael broke off because the door flew open. Starkad's huge right hand caught the Irishman by the throat.

"Wait a minute!" Mael gurgled, choked as much

by his laughter as by the Dane's fingers. Starkad broke his grip and the two men began to hug and pummel each other's backs.

"Figured a dumb turd like you'd get back when any decent man'd be asleep!" the Dane thundered, while Mael was shouting, "You know, I met somebody even bigger than you in Ireland? And may the Dagda club me dead if he wasn't stupider, too!"

"Hey, quiet the hell down!" grumbled a voice in Gothic German from the billet beside them.

Starkad's face smoothed, his mouth dropping into a half grin. He loosed Mael and walked to the door of the other room. He was barefoot and wore only a tunic that fell midway on his hairy thighs. The Dane kicked flatfooted, his right heel catching the hinge side of the door and flinging the whole panel into the room. "Come on out," he invited pleasantly. No one stirred inside. Starkad walked back to Mael and Veleda. "And they say that Goths are tough," he muttered.

"Look," said Mael, "much as I'd like to help you mop up this whole army, I'm just about dead on my feet. I was, even before you started pounding on me. Suppose you can let me rack out and keep the damned cadre away when they come around in the morning?"

"Later in the morning," the Dane corrected him. "Yes, I think I can do that thing."

"Oh," Mael said. "Ah . . . this is Veleda." Starkad's expression changed, not exactly in the fashion Mael had expected. The Irishman misinterpreted the look of appraisal, none the less. He licked his lips and said, "Ah, Starkad, I know . . .

Look, tomorrow they can issue me another room—"

"No problem," the Dane said, bursting into a smile again. "We've shared by threes and fours before. And you needn't worry, I like my women with a little more meat on their bones, you know." He clapped Mael on the shoulder. "Come on, get some sleep so you can wake up and tell me what's been going on."

CHAPTER EIGHT

From the angle of the sun, it was afternoon when Mael awakened. With his eyes still slitted, the Irishman groaned and said, "Starkad, if I'd known how I was going to ache when I got up, I'd have just asked you to slit my throat in the dark."

"Up?" Starkad laughed, twitching the sheet down and slapping Mael's rump.

Mael swore and swung his legs over the side of the bed. "How'd I get in your bunk?" he asked.

"I picked you up and put you there when I saw you really weren't going to share the other one with your lady friend, that's how. You needed a mattress worse than I did."

"Oh," Mael said. Veleda's bed was empty. "Ah, where did she—"

"Out to the jakes," the Dane answered before the question was complete. Even as he spoke, the door opened to readmit Veleda. She was beautiful and perfect in the sunlight.

"There're a lot of women in the camp," she said as she entered. She grinned brightly. "Families, I mean—I'd expected women around an army, but not wives."

"Yes, when we showed up, Cei—he took our names—told us it was fine to bring our families," Starkad said. "Of course, Mael and me were each other's family."

"It's useful to Arthur," Mael explained cynically, "for control. People think again about changing sides in a tight spot if they know it means their son gets used for a lance target."

"I need to find a place to, well . . . listen again," Veleda said in an abrupt change of subject. "I don't really understand what's happening—oh, not in the levels I *see*, that's obvious, but in the ones I feel. And things are moving, weaving, there at a rate that—that I don't like at all. There's a grove on the hill just north of here that should do for my purpose. I'll come back from there as soon as I can."

Starkad raised an eyebrow at the sober-faced woman, but it was to Mael that he spoke. "She going to be all right, wandering around alone?"

Mael hid his wince in a brief stiffness around his eyes. "She'll be all right," he said, turning to Veleda, "but I'd like to come anyway."

"No," she said with a smile. "This I really have to be alone to do. I'll be back soon."

She swung the door closed behind her. After a moment, Starkad threw it open to pass more of the sunlight into the room. "Well," he prodded, "what happened?"

"We got the skull at the shrine where I'd remembered it," Mael said simply. "Had to kill a couple people, but we got out all right. And we came back on a ship from mBeal Liathain."

"Right," Starkad agreed. "We."

Mael looked up into the blue eyes of his friend. His own hands clenched, then reopened deliberately. "She met me in Ireland. She knew I'd be coming somehow," he said. "Starkad, she's a witch, and she *scares* me; scares me like nothing ever has. And dear god, I think I love her." Mael stretched out his hands toward his friend like a captive pleading. "What am I going to do?" he begged.

The Dane chuckled without particular humor. "I'd heard her name before," he said. "So she's a witch. So what?"

Haltingly, but with the fullness of detail he had denied before, Mael reported the events of the voyage from Ireland. "I'd thought she was so helpless," he concluded miserably, "but she killed them with her hands when I wouldn't have had a chance alone. And then when she touched me, I . . . What am I going to do, Starkad?"

Starkad remained silent for a moment after the Irishman had finished. The Dane's beard and moustache flowed back across his face to join the hair of his head. It was tangled and rudely cut, but fairly clean despite that. The individual hairs were golden and very fine, surprisingly fine on a man so gross in other respects. Starkad suddenly leaned

forward and took each of Mael's hands, now
lowered, in one of his. The Irishman's skin was in
dark contrast to the Dane's. Mael's fingers were
long and sinewed, but they were utterly dwarfed
within the huge fists that held them.

Starkad squeezed gently. "You've touched my
hands before, haven't you?" he asked.

Mael nodded, frowning. He tried to pull free and
found that he could not.

"And once was at Massilia," the Dane continued
inexorably. "I carried you out of a crib after the
pimp had decked you with an iron bar. Do you
remember what I did to the pimp first?"

"Starkad, that wasn't the—"

"Your bloody *ass* it wasn't the same!" Starkad
roared. His face was inches away from the Irishman's. "I took his neck in one hand and an elbow
in the other, and I pulled on the bastard until his
arm came out of his shoulder. *That's* what I did to
him. And if you're going to get all hateful about
people saving your life, you can damned well start
with me!" He let go of Mael and sat back, arms
crossed against his chest.

"Yes, well . . ." Mael said. He tried a wan smile.
"Guess I never thought I had to protect you
and . . . all."

The Dane's black scowl softened. "Look," he
said, "did she ever tell you she needed to be
coddled like a nice glass trinket?"

"No."

"Then don't hold it against her that you're a
lousy judge of people. Treat her like a woman and
not a—a—I don't know what." Starkad paused.

With a fleeting return of his previous seriousness he added, "It doesn't sound like she—does what she did for fun. Remember, we've all of us done things we had to do but we'd rather not remember now. All of us."

"Except for you, Starkad," Mael said with more bitterness than he intended.

The Dane laughed. "You think I'm so wide open about everything I do that I couldn't be hiding anything? Sure I could. One thing."

Mael caught the tension underlying his friend's light words. "Hey," he said falsely, "if something's eating at you, I don't want to hear it. I've got problems enough of my own." He was taut with fear that Starkad would blurt a secret and regret it immediately, shattering a decade's friendship.

"Balls," the Dane said, almost as if he were reading his companion's mind. "You've spilled your guts to me, don't know why I shouldn't do the same. It doesn't matter, anyway. . . . Ever wonder why I go by my mother's name, Thurid?"

Mael shrugged. "I've known other northerners who did. There was Odd Kari's son we met that night in Hippo. . . . I figured your mother raised you after your father died before you were born."

"Oh, he lived till I was ten," Starkad said. "Only thing is, he never married my mother. Ran off with her, took three months of her temper and her tongue—which wasn't a bad record; I had ten years of them but I made it a point never to see the bitch after I left home myself. But my father dumped her in Grobin among the Letts. He was a trader, you see."

"It's a better man who makes his own name than takes one left for him," Mael said, glad that Starkad's secret was nothing worse than bastardy.

Starkad laughed again. "You mean, I'm a bastard so many other ways it's no surprise to find I'm one in simple truth? Well, that's nothing that's ever bothered me—as many bastards as I've scattered around the world, I'll not fret to've been bred on the wrong side of the blanket myself.

"But you see, what happened is my mother went back to her father's house—I can guess now how she earned her passage. But she wouldn't tell anybody who the man had been, even when they tried to beat it out of her. They wanted a virgin's price out of whoever it was, for honor's sake, you know. They were respectable people. Except for mother. She was a strong-minded bitch, I give her that.

"I grew—fast," Starkad continued, spreading his big arms wide as much to display as to stretch the muscles. "When I was ten, I was as big as any sixteen-year-old. Any sixteen-year-old to come out of Ireland," he corrected himself with a grin. "And that summer I was in Hedeby with my mother, standing looking at the cutlery in a booth an Italian Jew ran. My mother grabbed me by the shoulder—have I said she was a big woman? She turned me to face down the boardwalk. 'D'ye see the man there?' she whispered. 'He's Steinthor Steingrim's son.'

"Well, I'd sooner have looked at knives and axes, but he was a striking fellow. Bigger than most. He looked old at the time, but I know he can't have been but thirty, thirty-five. He had a bright blue mantle with tassels down one side, and a belt of silver plates that he hung a sword from. And my mother said, 'He's your father, child. When you grow to be a man you must kill him for the dishonor he brought to both of us.' I reached out my hand and took a hatchet from in front of the Jew. He shouted but I was already running down the boardwalk. My father, that was Steinthor, saw me coming but he thought I was just a thief. He spread his arms to stop me and I put the axe to its haft in his forehead. I kept on running and at the docks I jumped aboard a freighter that had cast off. The owner signed me on to his crew. I was big, like I said, and—I still had the bloody hatchet in my hand."

Mael touched his tongue to his lips. He started to speak, realized that the sympathy he had been about to show would only have underscored the uncorrectable. Instead the Irishman said only, "I'm sorry."

Starkad lifted half his mouth in a wry smile. He said, "It's not that I killed him, or that there wasn't reason to have killed him—I've never needed much reason anyway, you know that. . . . But I've never killed another man just because some bitch of a woman told me to. And that won't go away, Mael, however long I live."

Mael leaned over and punched Starkad lightly in the chest. "Some day I'll tell you about the day I killed my sister's husband," the Irishman said. "But just for now I'd sooner leave confession to the Christians and talk about something that matters. Just what *is* Arthur trying to accomplish here? I haven't had a day awake in the camp, but you've been around long enough to notice things."

"Yes, I've talked to some of the long-service folks," Starkad agreed. "Come on, it's a pretty day. Let's take a walk outside and feel how nice it is not to be training some damn fool way or other."

The ground immediately around the recruit billets had been trampled bare. The men walked the fifty yards over into the shade of a small stand of poplars. Children played and called around the buildings, ignoring the pair of warriors. Starkad watched them with a mild affection sharply at variance with the way he looked at adults.

"He's building quite an army, Arthur is," the Dane said quietly. "They say he wants to conquer the world. He's bringing the whole world together under his banner to do it, too."

"Yes, there were men from at least half a dozen tribes in the group they stuck us in the other night," Mael remembered aloud. "And they were all fresh recruits like us."

"Anybody willing to make a business of war," Starkad said. "Didn't used to be that way, though. Arthur started with what troops he could raise from his own tribe. Most of the Britons, though— they're soft; their guts rotted away under Rome. Arthur got a few to join up besides his own tribesmen, the Votadini, but only a man here and a man there. Nothing that was going to stop the Saxons. The landowners and the bishops'd pay Arthur to fight for them, but they wouldn't give him men to fight with. He used their money at first to hire other Romans from the Continent, folk that had been beaten once by the Germans moving into the Empire. Some of them were willing to fight again. That was where Lancelot came from, and Lancelot was when the rest all changed."

"Lancelot," Mael repeated thoughtfully. "Sure, I know where I heard of him before. He was Syagrius' right-hand man."

"That's right," Starkad agreed. "The last Roman to think he was Emperor of Gaul. They tell me Lancelot got away from Vesantio with his life and a fast horse when Clovis mousetrapped the Roman army there. He got to Britain, anyway, and to Arthur . . . and Arthur started hiring anybody who'd sign on, leaving it to Lancelot to figure how to whip them into shape. Everybody gets a horse and a coat of mail if they don't have one. Everybody gets the same weapons and has to use them the same way—lance, sword, and bow. They thought they were going to make me leave my axe behind in a fight because they haven't issued one to everybody."

"Think they'll just ignore you?" Mael asked. "There're a couple thousand of them and two of us, you know."

Starkad nodded seriously. "Yeah, I thought about that, figured if they were as stubborn as I was, they were going to kill me sure. But I looked around and there were the Huns—you know. Wear what they please, carry what they please, *do* damn near what they please, so long as they fight like Huns. So the first morning you were gone, the cadre took us out to practice with swords on six-inch posts they'd set up in a field. And I showed them why I carried an axe, not a sword—and I spent the afternoon hammering in new posts. But they stopped fucking with me about my axe.

"You just have to be good, is all," the Dane concluded complacently.

Mael laughed. Starkad had noted the same point that Arthur had mentioned to Mael at the cave—and made use of it. "Sure, if the Saxons'll just plant themselves ankle deep and wait, you'll play hell with them. But the sort of mix we trained with—that's normal for the Companions?"

"For the last five years," the Dane said. "The old sweats, the Britons who've been with Arthur from the beginning—they complain and they don't care who's listening, Briton or German or Greek. They say Lancelot's doing the same thing the Vortigern"—Starkad used the British title for High King—"Vitalis did fifty years ago, hire Saxons to fight Picts, and hire more Saxons, until—bam! The Saxons cut everybody's throats one night and take over half the country."

The Irishman snorted. "Idiots. I'll call Lancelot a lot of things, but not stupid. Anybody can see the difference between this and what Vitalis did."

"Looks pretty much the same to me," Starkad said flatly.

Mael looked at him. "Hey," he said, "you're not supposed to do the thinking, right? Mess with my job and I'll get mad and, oh, piss on your ankles or something." He punched Starkad's chest.

The Dane smiled. "Okay, so tell me, oh learned man."

"Vitalis hired groups," Mael explained. "He'd bring over a shipload of Saxons and settle them at a river mouth or a favorite landing spot of the Picts. They'd have their own government, their own thegn to lead them, and, after a little while, the kings followed the bulk of their tribes over. You don't come first if you've got a soft place at home, but when things seem settled in Britain and the land's so much better, you move in and be king there. And if there're locals there already who think they're in charge but they don't have any soldiers of their own—well, so much the worse for them.

"But Arthur isn't enlisting tribes, right?" Mael continued. "Just men. And they aren't from one tribe together and they aren't under their own leaders, they're under his. They don't even use their own weapons or their own language in his army—unless they're too good to waste, my heroic friend."

Starkad nodded in slow agreement. "Everyone who's been here any time calls him Leader," the Dane said. "And they don't have any ties but to him, you're right. I guess I could take any of the Companions—never met a man I couldn't—" Starkad paused, looked at Mael and rephrased his statement. "Never fought a man I couldn't take, some things I'll likely die without being sure. But even one at a time the Companions I've seen are good. And they don't fight one at a time, they move every man together, and I think maybe they could beat any army they didn't choose to get out of the way of."

The Dane fell silent and frowned. "I'm not much for following anybody," he continued at last. "I guess that's why you and I've knocked around so many places. But I think most of the Companions I've met here—Goths and such-like as sure as the Britons, anybody who's been around him for a while—most of them would follow Arthur to hell if he wanted to lead them there. And they'd expect to ride back, too."

"He does things I wouldn't have expected," admitted Mael. "He got his dragon. Damned if I see what good it'll do him, but he wanted it and he got it. I'd sooner cuddle an asp, myself."

Starkad's eyes had been picking among the trees and fields around them. They focused. "Your— Veleda's coming," the Dane said.

Mael turned. Veleda had emerged from the wooded path a hundred yards away. Her hair was richly white in the sun's eye. Her face, never tanned, looked more gray than pale, and her expression was as tight and wasted as that of a day-old corpse. The Irishman stepped out of the shade toward her, got a better look, and began to run, with Starkad pounding a step behind him. Veleda fell into Mael's arms, trying to smile.

"What happened to you?" Mael demanded in a voice so calm that only Starkad could have heard the lethal threat underlying it. "Who did this?"

"No, no," the woman protested feebly. "Nobody did anything to me. Except myself. And I can walk."

Mael lifted her, his right arm supporting her thighs and his left hand her shoulders. "Sure," he

said, "and I can carry you—which is how we're
going to get back to the room. What did you do?"
Veleda weighed only a hundred pounds or so, and
the ordeal seemed to have drained away much of
even that slight bulk. She lay supple in his arms,
her hair brushing his knees as he walked.

"You've got enough of your own ways to tempt
death," Veleda replied. "Leave me to mine. We all
of us do what has to be done. There are things I'd
never do for myself that I will for mankind and the
earth."

Beside them Starkad grunted, a comment
though wordless. Veleda raised her head from
Mael's breast and said, "Yes, so urgent as that,
Dane. There's a knot being tied in the fate of all the
world, very soon in the future. Merlin's foolish toy
is part of it, I'm certain. . . ." Her head fell back
and she added in a whisper, "But those who speak
to me aren't ones you can order to speak clearly,
tell this and thus and why. They give answers as
they please, and they care very little for men."

Mael turned sideways to fit Veleda through the
doorway to their billet. He laid her down on the
nearer bed. "Do you know a man named Biargram
Grim's son?" the woman asked unexpectedly.

Mael frowned. "I do," said Starkad, seating himself carefully on the edge of the other bunk.
"Biargram Ironhand, yes; a thegn of some note.
He's a big man, big as me. I remember people
guessing at which of us would win a catch-as-
catch-can if we met—though we never did. But
that was a long time ago. He must be fifty now and
a graybeard."

"A Dane?" Mael questioned.

"A Saxon," Veleda corrected him. "He has a shield and a spear, and I need you to get them."

Starkad chuckled. "Biargram'll be as glad to give them up as he would be his left eye and both balls," the Dane said. "Besides which, we have a trip to make to Saxony and back. Want us to bring you the moon besides, along the way?"

"Starkad," the woman said wearily, "I mean it. And the weapons are here in Britain—that much I'm sure of."

"Why do you need them?" Mael asked.

"I don't know." Veleda saw the Irishman's face close and winced herself in frustration. She reached up and caught his hand, saying, "Mael, I don't know, but there's no doubt at all in my mind that I *do* need them, that I *will* need them soon, in a very few days or weeks—and that you and all the rest of the world besides depend on the weapons being in my hands when the need comes. But if you won't believe me, I can't make you believe."

After a moment, Mael's fingers closed on hers. "I believe you," he said.

"Sure, Biargram could've brought his folks across," Starkad agreed. "From what I hear, the country from the Bight to the Elbe's getting to be as empty as a vestal's cunt. Every Saxon and Jute's migrating to Britain. But I don't see how that puts us any forwarder. It's not just what the Saxons would do if we came skulking around—and believe me, Biargram's shield's been in his family more years than anybody can count—but besides the Saxons, neither you nor I can even get out of this damned camp without being used for archery practice."

"Umm," thought the Irishman aloud. He sat beside the woman, his hand still turned with hers. "I think we could arrange that. You know this Biargram—"

"A little. A damned little."

"—and nobody here is going to be able to prove it's only a nodding acquaintance if you say otherwise. Sure . . ."

"Could I have some water?" Veleda asked Starkad as Mael's mind clicked over plans that began to mesh like clockwork.

Mael's mouth dropped in embarrassment at not having offered something without being reminded. His hand snatched the drinking gourd from its peg on the wall. It was empty.

"There's a well at the south end of the buildings," Starkad said.

"Would you go get us a gourdful, then?" Mael asked, holding the container out to his friend.

Starkad did not reach for it as expected. "She's your woman," he said.

Mael blinked. All he said aloud was, "Yes, I guess that's true." He stood, adding to Veleda, "I'll be back in a bit."

When the Irishman was gone, Starkad said fondly—facing the open doorway rather than Veleda—"His mind works all the time. By the time he comes back, he'll have figured how to get the two of us away from Arthur and then back with the gear you want. Very bright fellow, very." The Dane switched his gaze straight at the woman. His blue eyes struck her like twin hammers. "But he's not German. He didn't sit by the fire when he was a little boy, listening to the women telling stories about the things they only said to each other. About the days when the spirits were all women and their priestesses ruled everywhere. And the most powerful of all the priestesses was the Veleda, in those days that are only dreams now.

"How old are you, Veleda?"

"You won't tell him," she said, not a threat or a question, only a statement of fact like the fact that his hair shaded from blond to red and that the vein in his neck pulsed as his heart beat.

"I wouldn't do anything to hurt him," Starkad agreed quietly. "He thinks you're a witch, and he's found he can live with that. The truth isn't so important to me that I'd hurt a friend for its sake." The Dane's voice changed. "But one more thing I'll tell you. You may be priestess or witch or goddess yourself; you may have any power you please and be able to live forever; but you'll live the rest of eternity in two parts if you harm a hair of that man's head. I don't doubt that you can kill me, but no power this side of hell or the other will stop me if I come after you with my axe."

"I won't hurt him," Veleda said. There was neither fear nor doubt in her voice. She smiled. "A man could have a worse friend than you, Starkad. Or a woman."

Mael strode through the doorway with the filled gourd in his hand. He gave it absently to Veleda. "Starkad," he began, his face vibrant, "this will work. There's not a man of Arthur's who could prove you're lying, and besides—they'll all *believe* it's true. You see—"

He bubbled on, too distracted by his coming triumph to notice the glance that Starkad exchanged with Veleda.

CHAPTER NINE

From the top of a low hillock, Arthur and a dozen men of his staff and bodyguard watched two troops performing mounted evolutions in concert. Lances lowered, the hundred Companions advanced at a trot across the broken pasture in a double line abreast. As they approached the wooded margin of a stream, Arthur gave an order to his cornicine who then blew a three-note call on his silver-mounted cow horn. The horsemen raised their lance points and wheeled left in parallel files. One man fell off. In the center, the formation clotted awkwardly where a swale threw the timing askew.

Lancelot cursed. "Ragged, ragged. They do that in front of Saxons instead of willow trees, and there'll be a massacre."

"That's why we train them, isn't it?" the king

retorted. On horseback his clubfoot was scarcely noticeable.

One of the bodyguards looked away from the maneuvering troops, back along the path that led to the villa. The man grunted. "Sir," he said, to Lancelot rather than the king. Arthur was too exalted to be bothered with details of intruders.

Lancelot turned, his eyes following the bodyguard's. "Face around, boys," he said in a flat voice which none the less carried to all the men around the king. To the cornicine Lancelot added, "Bring the troops in." Two notes and then two more sang out. The exercising Companions pivoted left again and rode toward their Leader.

"The Irishman, Mael, and his Dane friend," Arthur observed.

"So it seems," agreed the big Master of Soldiers. Lancelot unsocketed his lance, bringing it forward though still vertical. Its butt spike rested on his toes. The other Companions were also readying themselves unobtrusively, drawing swords and slipping their arms through shield loops. One of them, an Armenian, carried a bone-stiffened composite bow. He swung his horse sideways so that its body concealed his hands stringing the bow and nocking an arrow.

Mael and Starkad were on foot, fully armed but not actively threatening. Both wore their shields slung behind their backs. Mael's sword was sheathed and Starkad rested his axle helve in the palm of his hand. The bearded head was hooked over the Dane's shoulder. The rectangular peen of it facing forward was no reassurance to Lancelot who had seen it crush the stone from his hands, but it was as innocent a fashion as any in which the big weapon could be carried.

When they were twenty feet away, Lancelot dropped his point at the men on foot and called, "That's far enough."

Neither Mael nor Starkad appeared concerned by the implied threat. Starkad even took another half step before halting. Unlike his guards, Arthur, too, appeared to be relaxed. He rested part of his weight on his hands crossed on his right front saddle horn. "Leader," Starkad thundered at the king, "I claim the right to be freed from my oath to you so I may end a blood feud. That feud I swore long ago, so I must follow it now and leave you."

The berserker spoke clumsy Celtic, his inflections Danish and his idiom, such as it was, more Irish than British. Arthur frowned. Beside him the cornicine started to giggle. As if he had been ordered to explain, Starkad continued, "Kari, Tostig's daughter, married in her first youth the bonder Ulf Svertlief's son of Tollund and then, at his death, Asgrim Walleye, second son of—"

"Blood of God, Dane!" Arthur burst out. "If you've got to tell your story, tell it short or get your butt back to where it belongs. You're supposed to be training this afternoon, aren't you?"

Starkad blinked. He pursed his lips in concentration, then said, "Of this marriage—" he raised his voice as the troops of horsemen reined up noisily behind Arthur, awaiting further command —"was born Asa, niece to me through Tostig's line, who married the Saxon thegn Biargram—"

Arthur flushed and swung toward his Master of
Soldiers, a furious command ready in his open
mouth. Mael forestalled him, stepping forward
with a hand laid on the Dane's shoulder to silence
him. "Lord," he called in Latin. "Let me cut his
tale down."

Arthur calmed slightly and turned. "Quickly
then," he said.

Mael licked his lips. "My friend's niece wed a
thegn named Biargram," he said, "a Saxon. He
sent her home after a year but kept the dowry. The
girl's family couldn't get it back since none of
them wanted to take on Biargram. Starkad, here,
had already been outlawed so there wasn't anything he could do, but he swore he'd kill Biargram
if the two of them ever walked a land with no seas
or mountains between them.

"And in mBeal Liathain last week, a Saxon
sailor told me Biargram had brought his tribe
here to Britain."

"That's right," said Arthur. As though his mind
was riffling through a packet of military
communiques, he continued, "He and his household, all told some two hundred, crossed over
several years ago in four keels. They joined Cerdic
—*the traitor!*" The king's face went momentarily
bestial as he hissed the last words. Calmly he continued, "At last report they'd been settled near
Clausentum and were doing quite well. But what
is that to me?"

Mael was an educated man with an educated
man's trick of assuming someone less well educated was also less intelligent. The Irishman kept

his face smooth, but a clear sight of Arthur's mind at work frightened him in a way the flashes of bloodthirsty madness had not. "Lord," he said, "my friend is headstrong and worse, you know that. Once he gets a notion, you can't drag it away from him with a team of oxen. He's convinced now that he has to go track this Biargram down. We're brothers in a real way, he and I; we've mixed more blood on battlefields than ever womb-mates had in common. I have to go with him."

At the word "have," Arthur's eyes narrowed and a venomous smile spread across Lancelot's face. "Oh, aye," Mael snapped, the Celtic phrasing seeping through with emotion, "you can kill us, can you not? A pleasant time you'll have to do it, aye, but you can. And what will it gain you, to kill two men and save your enemies the labor of it?"

Arthur began to laugh. "And so I should send men on leave into the middle of the Saxons, because somebody diddled somebody's niece out of her dower share? No, I don't think I'll begin running my army that way, not just yet. Get back to your duties."

Behind Arthur, the cornicine added, "Sure, they're likely spies for Cerdic, Leader."

Unexpectedly, Lancelot reached over and laid his fingertips on the back of Arthur's hand. "No, Leader," he said. "Let them go."

Arthur looked at him dubiously. Lancelot continued, "They've asked your leave to go; your authority suffers nothing to grant the request, and your camp discipline, I understand—" he cocked a grim eye at Mael; the Gaul's speech was still slurred by thick lips and a swollen nose—"will improve. Let them go."

"And if they are returning spies?" the king asked, but as a genuine question.

"They'll leave the woman," Lancelot pointed out —that had been no intent of Mael's, but he dared not deny it—"and besides, if they are traitors, it's best we be shut of them."

"Leader," Mael put in, "I brought you—" he realized that Arthur might not want the skull and its purpose released to a hundred men, even his own men—"what you know of. I know you realize . . . how risky that job was. It was harder, perhaps, than even you fully understand. But I brought the thing back where scarcely another could have done; and if you give us leave now, I swear by whatever you wish that I'll come back myself and with my friend here, if there's life in either of us."

"Blood feud," Arthur repeated. He laughed again, loudly and without humor. "I have a blood feud, too . . . with the whole world, I sometimes think. It'll bow its neck to me some day, yes. . . . Go on, take this Saxon's head or leave your own, it's all the same to me. But if you enter the hall of Cerdic your master, tell him what you have seen here—and in the cave. And tell him that one day I will be coming to serve him in the fashion that traitors are served. It would be well for him if he had fallen on his sword before that day."

Mael dipped his head in acquiescence. Starkad, following the motion as he could not the words, nodded also. The two men turned and began walking back the way they had come, the Dane's axe-edge winking as it split sunbeams.

"Leader," they heard Lancelot say when he thought it was safe to speak to his king, "I'll ride back with them, arrange an escort to the Zone for them—and a guard for the woman."

Arthur nodded grimly. His mind was fixed on his memory of Cerdic, the British lordling who had weighed the danger of Saxon mercenaries against Arthur's growing tyranny—and had called in Saxons. The king's right hand twisted on the saddle horn as if it were a sword hilt, the knuckles as white as the skin across his cheekbones. Lancelot clucked to his horse and trotted toward the men on foot before they disappeared around a curve in the trail. Behind him, Arthur was giving orders in a normal voice to the exercising troops.

Mael and Starkad waited around the bend for the Master of Soldiers. The overt changes in their stances were slight but significant. Mael had thrust his left arm through his shield straps. Starkad's axe, though still on his shoulder, faced forward and was ready to strike. Both men were tense, certain that Lancelot would not have come alone to slay them, but knowing also how much the Gaul hated them both.

"Gently, heroes," Lancelot said. His grin had split a scab on his damaged face. A tiny runnel of blood streaked his chin. "I'm going back to make everything easy for you, to see that you're issued food and don't have any trouble with our own patrols."

"Why?" the Dane demanded bluntly.

"Oh, not because I like you," the big Gaul

chuckled. "I've spent every day since—this—" he touched his swollen nose—"thinking about how I was going to kill you both. And it wasn't that easy, you know, because frankly, a duel didn't seem very practical. And though I certainly could have found a group of men to do what was needed, that would have been expensive in one way or another. Then there was always the uncertainty of how the Leader would react. . . ." Lancelot's voice dropped unintentionally as he thought about his king. "He's . . . one can't be sure with him, you know. No one can."

Lancelot cleared his throat, regaining his normal insouciance. The three men were walking down the trail, horseman in the center, like closest friends. "And of course I thought of poison," Lancelot continued, "but there was the problem of getting you both at the same time, and from what I hear of this woman you've brought back, Irishman, maybe poison wouldn't be a good bet so long as she's around.

"But you come and say that you want to walk into Cerdic's kingdom and chop off the head of one of his Saxon barons. That's fine, yes; I'll help you get started any way I can. I never quarrel with the will of God, Irishman."

Lancelot's mighty laughter boomed around them as they trudged toward the villa.

The captain of the Cirencester Patrol was a Frank named Theudas, no more of a natural horseman than Starkad himself was. He dismounted with Mael and the Dane at the furthest point of his patrol area, twelve miles southeast of the walled town that was the pivot of Arthur's domain. The score of men in the patrol began nibbling bits of sausage and cheese in the drizzle, talking in low voices and hugging their cloaks tighter to their mail shirts.

"You're welcome to keep the horses, you know," Theudas said. "The warrant you brought from Lancelot says to aid you in any way short of sending men into the Zone."

The two friends continued to unlash their gear from their mounts. "That bastard Lancelot probably hoped this beast's spine'd open me up to the shoulders from beneath," Starkad grumbled. He arched his back, massaging his buttocks with both hands. "Don't know that I'm sure that it hasn't already. No, I thank you, but I'd just as soon walk some."

Both Mael and Starkad wore their body armor, though their steel caps were lashed to their packs. On their heads were droop-brimmed hats of leather, protection against the traveler's twin foes: the sun that might come out to bake them and the rain that now collected in jeweled ropes sliding from the leather. The packs themselves were thin rolls of oiled canvas containing a week's rations and nothing else. Grunting, the men slung their shields and then the packs over them. They carried spears in place of walking staves. Each spear had an oak shaft as tall as a man and as thick as a woman's forearm. Mael's sword and dagger were sheathed while Starkad's axe was slung under his right arm in its carrying loops, the head nodding free against the iron ringlets of his mail coat.

"Hell of a poor day to go off," Theudas said somberly.

"Not exactly a bloody social event," grunted Starkad in reply. To his companion he added, "Ready?"

"Half a sec." Mael shifted his target so that its lower edge no longer rubbed his hipbone. On an eighty-mile hike, the constant friction would raise a blister the size of a drinking cup, even through the iron mail.

"Don't know why the Leader wants to send spies into Venta anyhow," the Frank continued. "God knows, the Saxons aren't like us, running an army together on thirty minutes' notice. When they mount something it takes weeks, and Cerdic isn't planning anything of the sort. *We* know that, here with the Patrol. There's always somebody slipping into Glevum or Corinium to see a relative—or run away from their master, or maybe just to make a little by trading the part of their crop they hid from the thegn who owns the lands they farm. Sure, Saxons, too. *We* don't care, and Cerdic, he doesn't have the men to stop it, the cavalry. If he put his lumbering infantry out in little vedettes, the Leader'd ring the whole Southern Squadron out. We'd eat the Saxon patrols alive before they could do jack shit. Naw, this sector's quiet. It's Aelle who's about to raise hell in the North."

"Okay," said Mael. "Let's go, Starkad."

"There's going to be fighting, then?" the Dane asked. He wasn't looking at Mael, but he held a hand toward the Irishman to indicate he had heard the request.

"Sure is," agreed Theudas. "Aelle—he calls himself king, has most a' the Saxons north of Londinum—he's raised his levies and must be ready to march by now. On Lindum, likely; he's got big eyes. Tried to get Cerdic and the rest to send some housecarls for the work. The good thing about the Saxons is they don't like each other a bit more than they do us." The Frank scowled. "Or than the North British bastards of the Reged like us, come to think."

"Mael," asked Starkad with a worried look on his face, "do you suppose we're going to miss the fighting?"

"We're going to root here in this goddamn place if we stand around talking much longer," the Irishman snapped.

"Umm," said Starkad. He waved to the Frank and said, "Well, we'll be seeing you again soon, you bet." Mael had already stumped off along the road. Grunting a little with effort, the Dane lengthened his own stride to catch up. The patrol of Companions vanished into the mist behind them, though the clink of their equipment sounded long after the horsemen were out of sight.

Mael's sandals clinked also. The drizzle irritated him. He knew he was in a bad mood, knew also that it was worse than foolish to let his friend's relative good humor irritate him still further. Mael kept his mouth shut and let an occasional remark by Starkad and the dull ringing of hobnails stand as the only sounds between him and the Dane for over a mile.

Finally Starkad said, "Hard damn road, isn't it?" The Irishman grunted. This time Starkad pursued the matter. "I mean, I think if I'd had to walk on this before, I'd have taken that Frank up on his offer of horses, huh?"

Mael's anger swelled. Then the ridiculousness of it struck him. He began to laugh. "Hey," he said, "the least Lugh could have done for us is to give us decent weather to get killed in, don't you think?"

"Huh?"

"Look," Mael explained, relaxing and feeling as if chains had dropped away, "you know damn well what our chances of getting out of this in one piece are. Don't you?"

"Well," Starkad temporized, "we've gotten into some pretty tight places before, too. You always find ways out of them." He patted his axe. "You and this, hey?"

The Irishman snorted. "Sure, and that guarantees that any fool thing we get into is going to be fine, sure. And this August it's going to rain pieces of gold for my birthday. Well, right now I think I'm going to know you maybe three days longer, if we're lucky. I don't guess I want to spend that time pissed at you because I don't like the weather. Forgive me?"

Starkad cleared his throat. "Oh," he said, "that's okay. I don't much like the rain, either. And I sure wish we had something to ride on, now."

"Such chance as we've got," Mael explained, "pretty much makes us walk. On horses we'd get a lot of attention. The British were horsemen long before Arthur mounted his whole army, but on the eastern side of the Zone a horse marks you. I want us to blend in with the—human countryside.''

Starkad looked doubtful. "I might pass for Saxon," he said. "Wotan's eye, I've got a cousin who wed one, though they both drowned. He was no kin to Biargram, either. But I don't see you, brother, looking anything but a black-hearted, crop-haired Irishman to anybody with eyes to see."

"Sure, but that's all right—now," Mael said. "You know what happened when Hengst first made his play against the Vortigern?"

Starkad nodded. "They cut and burned everything British around that didn't have walls, until the British got organized."

"Right. And what happened then?"

"They got their balls kicked between their ears," Starkad answered. "Got too confident. They found the locals might not like to do their own fighting, but if they had to . . . Horsa had his skull nailed to the gates of Lindum; Hengst himself got shut up on an island in the Thames, eating harness leather and wondering if he was going to make it through the winter. A damned near thing, from the stories I've heard."

"Very near," Mael agreed. "And there wasn't a bit of help coming from the Continent to get them out of the hole, either. People don't pull up stakes to migrate into the middle of a disaster. They stay home and plow their own bit of dirt, even if it's sandy and the weather'd make this wretchedness—" he shook his head and scattered a coil of droplets from the hat brim—"look like balmy summer. Or, if they've got to move, they go south to Italy or east to try the Greek emperor's pay for a while.

"And the Saxon kings have learned that. Arthur's planning something. Maybe nobody knows just what or just who's going to be first. But they damned well know what'll happen to them if they wait till their backs're to the wall before they go looking for help. Aelle up north seems to be getting his punch in early, but I'm betting that anybody who can handle a sword can find a bunk in one thegn's house or another's. And I don't guess they'd much care what tongue his mother sang him lullabies in. Wandering housecarls don't ride horses, but looking Irish isn't going to call me to mind, particularly."

The rain was with them all day, and it was their only companion. The War Zone separating Saxon from Briton was a wasteland, proof that if neither side won a war, then both sides lost. Between the two races, across the center of the island, lay a no-man's-land that the British had given up but the Saxons could not hold. In the daytime, both sides might use the irregular ribbon for pasture. Their armed guards stayed nervous and watchful. Despite that, all too often they were unable to protect their herds or themselves against skulking bands of Saxons or a sudden brutal thrust by a troop of Companions.

Evening came late and almost indistinguishably from the wan daylight that preceded it. Although they were well within the territory that Cerdic

claimed and taxed, the country to either side of
the road was as barren as that of the War Zone to
the north. Cattle lowed in the near distance, however. Once the smell of wood smoke disclosed a
cook fire whose plume was hidden in the mist.

To the left loomed a settlement, Saxon but
burned out like the occasional Roman building
Mael and Starkad had passed earlier. Mael
pointed his thumb at the ruins. "They thought
they were safe," he said. "There's no place safe
within a half day's hard ride of Arthur's outposts.
Straight down the road, torching everything
that'll burn and slaughtering everything that's
alive. No time for looting or prisoners, but sure,
you can teach Saxons that civilized men are just as
bloody-handed as the barbarians they despise. Any
houses that stand, even this deep in toward Venta,
are going to be far enough off the road that raiders
won't chance ambush to hunt them out of the
woods."

Starkad laughed. "Well, I wasn't raised to be a
farmer, my friend. And if you were, you hid the
fact well enough the time we tried our hands at
it. . . . No doubt this destruction's very awful and I
should feel miserable about it, but right now I'm a
lot more concerned about whether there's a roof
left to keep some of this damned rain off us for the
night."

Mael squinted at the sky. "Yeah, well," he said.
"Not likely we're going to find a better place."

One of the outbuildings had not been burned. Its
door was wrenched off, and rotted grain floored
the lightless interior. Mael settled himself glumly

in a corner, deciding whether to strip off his
armor for comfort or leave it on for safety. The
metal creaked and galled him every time he
moved. Cursing under his breath, the Irishman
pulled the mail over his head and began to unlace
his gambeson as well.

Starkad ducked back into the rain. Mael heard
his axe *thock* loudly. Mael froze, then realized that
the blade had rung on the wood, not metal or bone.
He resumed undressing as the Dane continued to
chop in the gloom. After a few minutes, Starkad
returned. He was clutching an armload of wood
lopped from the roof beam of one of the houses.

"You're not going to build a fire?" Mael
grumbled.

"Sure I am," said Starkad. He dumped the
billets and leaned his axe against the wall. Drawing his big dagger, he began to slice curls from a
log.

"It's too wet to burn. And anyway, it's not safe.
Even if you don't burn us both up, you'll call down
some patrol of Cerdic's. Then it'll all be over."

"This is dry on the inside," the Dane said, pointing to the billet he was shaving. "Go ahead, you
light it. You're better at striking a spark than I am.
And as for a smoke hole—" Starkad stood, his hair
brushing the thatched roof even though he
hunched. He raised his axe. With a single swift
thrust, he straight-armed the head through the
thatch in the corner diagonal to Mael. A quick
twist enlarged the hole so it could pass enough
smoke to keep the fire from smothering those it
warmed. Water dripped in.

Mael scowled. "You think you can cure everything with your damned axe?" he demanded.

Starkad looked at him coolly. "Yes, pretty much. You think you're going to live forever?" The Irishman stayed silent. Starkad pressed, "I want to be warm and a little drier. This wood may smoke, but it's not going to toss any sparks into the thatch. And as for bringing Saxons down on us, we're going to meet Saxons anyway. Tyr's arm, Mael, that's what we're *here* for. We're going to have to talk our way out or fight our way out. We may as well be a little more comfortable tonight and meet 'em now, as meet 'em tomorrow in the rain."

Mael sighed and hitched around his wallet. With a pinch of dried moss from it and the shavings for a bed, he struck his firesteel on a flint until he had a small fire smoldering. "All yours," he said. "If it goes out, you light the next one."

Starkad, smiling, fed the fire with small doses of wood while he accomplished other domestic tasks. The Dane was generally cheerful on shipboard, too, Mael thought sourly to himself. That was because as a rule there would be killing at the other end of the voyage. Starkad covered the doorway with his cloak, pinning it to the withies supporting the thatch with his shoulder brooch and Mael's. The garment was of unbleached wool, so densely woven that it was virtually waterproof. A baulk of wood at the bottom kept the cloak firm against random gusts of wind. The shed began to warm at once. The stolid orange light of the fire did as much for Mael's disposition as the heat itself. He unlaced his sandals and began to strip the wool leggings from beneath them, humming under his breath. Smoke glazed the air. The odor of wool and bodies ripened as the shed heated. That was normal and inevitable; if Mael had a regret, it was that the fire lacked the peculiar pungency of peat-fueled ones like those with which he had been raised.

Starkad slid his own boots off. He cursed, but more in amazement than real anger. The condition of the ball of his foot would have justified a fiercer reaction. A blister three inches across had formed on the sole and burst. The skin hung in shreds. The cloth with which the Dane had packed his boot was glued to his foot by a film of pus and blood. Starkad dribbled a little beer from his canteen to loosen the fabric. "Told you that damned road wasn't fit for a man," he said.

Mael whistled in horror. "Are you going to be able to go on?" he asked. "That looks terrible."

"No problem, unless they get so slippery I keep falling down," Starkad joked. He was peering at his left sole where the callus seemed intact.

"Manannan, but you've got a nice mind," Mael muttered with a grimace.

"Don't see why you aren't having any problem, though," the Dane continued. "It's a damned hard road. I'd think it'd eat anybody's feet as fast as mine."

"No, I've got the gear for it," Mael explained, toeing one of his sandals over to his friend to examine. The sole was thick and multi-layered, studded on the bottom with a dozen hobnails. The iron was bright with recent wear, but a tracery of rust had already begun to hatch-mark the abrasions. The sandal was bound to the foot and high up the leg by straps that could be adjusted precisely. They gave a firm fit whether they were laced over cloth or leather against the cold, or bare skin in a hot climate. The footgear copied the Roman *caligae*, the sandals that had carried legionaries across the whole Mediterranean Basin and beyond. Mael had found it the most practical gear for a man who might have to walk far on a multitude of surfaces, so long as he was willing to accept weight in exchange for sturdiness. "Those buckets you wear," he said to Starkad, "may keep you dry and work well enough on dirt, but they let your foot slide around inside too much on a solid surface. And these roads were built solid."

"Damn well were," the Dane agreed, wriggling his toes toward the fire as he rummaged in his pack for a biscuit. "What'd they do, quarry 'em out of the bedrock? Must've been built a hundred years ago, too."

"Longer ago than that," Mael said. He leaned back against the wall, flexing his muscles so that the rough wattling would rub his shoulders. "I watched a slave gang trench through a road like this, digging a drainage ditch outside of Hispalia. . . ."

"Hispalia?" Starkad repeated. "Three years ago when the city senate was hiring to stiffen their militia against the Goths? We were both there, and I don't remember any road being cut."

"That's because you were in a whorehouse, as usual."

"Oh." Starkad frowned, then nodded. "You find

the damndest things to do with your time when you could be screwing," he said. "What did the road look like?"

"Six feet thick and built like a fortress wall laid on its side," Mael said. He closed his eyes to remember. "Three and a half feet of rubble base. Six inches of rammed tufa to level it. Six inches of flints on top of that. Ten inches of pebble gravel set in loam. And then on top of everything, six-inch flagstones set in concrete. I tell you, they built roads to last, the Romans did. And they'll last a lot longer than the empire did that built them."

Starkad shrugged. He had taken a whetstone out of his pack and begun stroking the fine edge back onto his axe blade. Mael fell asleep with the gentle *skritch, skritch* of stone on steel sounding a warrior's lullaby in his ears.

CHAPTER TEN

The morning was dim but for a time the rain had stopped. Starkad walked without favoring his right foot. It would have amazed Mael had he not once seen the big man methodically hack apart an archer whose last shaft stuck out three inches on either side of the Dane's chest. Pain simply did not affect Starkad once he had decided to ignore it. Many a civilized warrior had discounted tales of berserkers—until one made for him, bloody but as inexorable as an earthquake. That had driven many a brave man to flight.

They passed near several openly sited villages and met a number of other travelers on the road the second day. Everyone left them alone. Even the six armed men heading north passed with hard glances but no direct comment. Mael and Starkad trudged forward purposefully, speaking to no one and in general projecting an aura of being busy but not too busy to cut throats if annoyed. They were not called on what was indeed no bluff.

That night they spent in the woods, wrapped in their cloaks under a fir tree. Its branches looked thick enough to protect them if the rain should resume—as it did near dawn. The tree was some help, but not enough to make it worth continuing to try to sleep. The tenth milepost from Winchester stared crookedly at them from the margin of the road, unnoticed the night before when they had stopped.

"We'd better cut west pretty quick," Mael said, his foot scraping morosely at the old marker. "Otherwise we'll be at Venta. It's got a wall and the guards there won't ignore us. Even if we just get close there's going to be somebody who'll wonder if we turn off. Besides, farther south is likely to be out of our way, anyhow."

Starkad nodded. "I'm not arguing," he said. "You're chief for this raid. Anyway, I don't mind walking on something softer than this rock, rock, rock."

Half a mile farther on, a track joined to the left through a line of poplars. It was narrow, a slick band of mud and trampled dung gleaming in the wider area cleared by the shoulders of driven cows. Mael pointed. Starkad nodded again, and they turned onto the local track.

It had a gloominess not wholly explained by the constant mist. The two men walked single file of necessity, and without speaking because they did not want to alarm villagers whom the rain might otherwise keep inside. The Roman road had not changed in four hundred years, but it had been built by strangers and for strangers. Even in the midst of Cerdic's dominions, Mael had not felt out of place on those stones. This track was newer in one sense but from an earlier age altogether, and there was nothing eclectic about it. An Irishman would be noticed and watched in silent hatred—perhaps even ganged by the village bravos. But the same would happen to a man from a neighboring village—who might steal a pig or a kiss from one of the womenfolk, and was in any case not "one of us." In armor and in company with a man as big as Starkad, Mael felt there was little actual danger, but it was as well to slip by in silence.

The path forked. The friends looked at each other. They took two steps on the right-hand branch before a goat's bleating warned them of a village nearby. They turned left instead. Three miles further on and an hour later, they almost walked into the fenced garth of a house. Behind the fence in the drizzle bulked other buildings. The path led straight through the center of the village. No humans were visible, but Mael and Starkad faded quickly back into the trees beside the trail. There were murmurs from poultry and a whiff of wood smoke now that the dwellings had called it to the men's attention.

"Well, do we just walk through?" Starkad asked.

Mael thought a moment, visualizing the topography as best as he could from the glimpses the rain had vouchsafed him. "No," he said at last, "let's cut around here to the right. We can pick up the path again on the other side . . . and there ought to be a stream pretty near. I'd like to refill the water bottles."

He and Starkad turned into the brush and through it into the second-growth hardwoods. The area had been cleared for agriculture not too long in the past. Beeches and oaks had overgrown the fields, but pines had not yet started to drive the hardwoods out. There was a slight falling-off to the left. Mael thought he heard the purl of a stream and nodded to Starkad. They stepped between a pair of oak saplings and out into the misty drizzle of a swale too low-lying to support normal trees. A grove of silver birches straggled up at the very edge of the stream some thirty feet away.

Starkad's left hand gripped Mael's shoulder and stopped him as still as an altar stone. The whole population of the nearby village, some forty Saxons of mingled sex and age, was clustered among the birches.

Silently, backing the necessary step without breaking a stick or letting their equipment jingle, the friends eased into the added gloom of the trees they had just left. They might have been seen by someone looking for them, but the rain blurred outlines and washed colors away. Kneeling at the forest edge, their armor gleaming no more in the weak sunlight than the wet boles around them, there was nothing to call attention to the men.

In any case, the Saxons were wholly intent on what was going on in their own midst. At the back of the circle were children, naked or nearly so, clutching the skirts and hands of their mothers. The women wore either dresses, simple tubes pinned at the shoulders and tucked at the waist by belts, or skirts and shawls. Hoods or the shawls covered their heads. Their garments were woolen; some, where the weavers had chosen fleece of contrasting shades, were patterned attractively in soft, natural plaids.

Within the circle of women, nearer the snowy trunks which displayed the only primary color on a gray morning, were the men. Despite the chill and the rain, they were lightly clad in linen tunics and half-cloaks of skin or wool. Most of the Saxon males also wore tight-fitting leather caps, sewn with the hair side in, but these were less clothing than armor—and the only armor worn, save by one of the two men in the very center of the group.

The man in armor was clearly the chief. He was larger and at least as tall as the biggest of the men around him, despite the fact that he was slightly downslope of them. He wore ring mail and a horned helmet that must have been an heirloom from an age when warfare was less pragmatic. The other men carried spears or weapons which were obviously agricultural implements—axes and mattocks and, in one case, a flail. The armored thegn was the only one to have a long sword, besides the spear in his right hand. He faced a smaller, older man across what seemed to be a trench, listening to the other intone a prayer with arms uplifted: "Hear us, oh Lady Nairthus. Be near to us in our sowing and in our reaping, now in our Spring and in our Fall. . . ."

Starkad had slipped his pack off without a sound. His big fingers played over the slipknot that attached his helmet to the rest of his gear. The rawhide had swollen and would not give. Without hesitation or effort, the Dane pulled the thong in half.

Mael laid his lips close to Starkad's hair and whispered, "What's going on?"

Holding the iron cap in his hand rather than donning it at once—the neck flare would separate him from Mael by three inches and there was need for them to talk—Starkad said, "Oh, it's a sacrifice to Dame Nairthus . . . the earth goddess, the crop goddess. They're getting ready to butcher a man to her, I'd judge. In my tribe, we prayed to Thor in the Spring and made do with cutting a goat's throat—you can eat the goat afterwards, too. But some of these Saxons, they're so backward they come to war waving stone hammers. Besides, if you've had a bad harvest the past year you start thinking back to old ways—and you've got more useless mouths in the houses than you do in the fold."

The wizened old man facing the thegn continued to pray in a cracked voice. He sounded nervous. If what Starkad said was true, the priest probably wasn't used to human sacrifice either. His head was bare. Rain had plastered his white hair away from the bald spot at the peak of his skull.

The priest stopped speaking and lowered his hands. The thegn stepped forward, then down into the trench. The crowd murmured, shifting a little.

Mael saw heels flash briefly above the lip of earth as the sacrifice kicked. Already the victim lay face down in the boggy ditch. The thegn had one foot planted on its back. Then the Saxon slid his other foot forward to force the victim's mouth and nose down into the ground water in the bottom of the trench. The sacrifice began to scream in a high-pitched, feminine voice. The big Saxon leaned his weight down on the outstretched foot. The screams gurgled to a halt.

Mael cursed quietly. He put his iron cap on and set the slouch traveling hat back atop it. Starkad touched his arm. "Shall we slaughter the whole village, then?" the Dane asked with no hint of emotion. "We'll need to, if we try and break up this ritual, you know. All we *need* to do now is slip back into the woods and get on with our own business."

The Irishman looked at him. Starkad shrugged and donned his helmet.

Mael stood and took two measured strides beyond the masking bulk of the trees. He did not draw his sword and his shield hung by its strap instead of being advanced toward the Saxons. "Hold!" he thundered in a huge voice, trained to bellow commands across the steel-shattered chaos of a battlefield. Starkad walked to the right, a half step behind Mael in the mist. His axe helve was balanced on his collarbone.

The pair of them loomed up above the startled Saxons, Mael a big man and Starkad a blurred giant in full armor. The leather hat brim flopped low over Mael's left eye as he had planned. The

crowd's small noises were cut off by freezing
panic as the Saxons stumbled away from the newcomers. The armored chieftain stepped quickly up
from the pit. He unpinned his half-cloak and
dropped it, then waited with rain dripping from
the down-curved ends of his moustaches. He had
not brought a shield, but he gripped his spear
shaft with both hands.

Besides the thegn, only the Saxon elder stood
his ground. As Mael strode closer, he could see
that the old man's pupils were fully dilated and
that the wizened face had blanched as pale as his
hair. "Wh-what manner of men are you to
interrupt the gift to Lady Nairthus?" the priest
quavered.

"No men at all," Mael boomed back, walking
steadily but slowly enough that the Saxons had
plenty of time to give way.

It almost worked. The villagers were a dim semi-
circle, some of them ankle-deep in the creek waiting for their thegn to act. The elder shuffled backward a step, slipped on the lip of the trench, and
jumped across it away from Mael. When Mael was
only three paces away, the Saxon chief trembled.
Then he cursed and flung himself at the Irishman
with his spear outstretched. Starkad had antici-
pated him. The Dane took a full stride, bringing
his axe around as smoothly as a boy would a fly
whisk.

The axe blade took the Saxon at a flat angle
where the muscles of his left shoulder joined his
neck. His head sprang off and the helmet flew
loose from it. The two objects spun to the ground

in opposite circles, thudding and clanging as they hit. Starkad's axe had continued, shearing the ring mail and separating the Saxon's right arm at the shoulder joint. The torso and the spear which the thegn's left hand still gripped pitched forward, but the impact of the Dane's blow had rotated the victim enough that the point did not even graze Mael's chest. The corpse struck the ground so near to the Irishman that the last spurt of blood from the severed neck covered his right sandal.

The village priest screamed like a pig with a knife through its throat. He ran, caroming off the trunk of one of the birches without slowing, then splashing across the creek. The old Saxon reached the other side without one of his boots. There he sucked in enough air to continue his screaming. He disappeared into the drizzle, again at a run. The rest of the villagers had already melted away, making less noise but with real terror. It was not death that seared their hearts—they had come to view a death. It was not even the loss of their thegn, but rather the way of his killing. Mael's bluff had raised the shadows of superstitious fear which were never far from the minds of barbarian peasants. Starkad had capped the bluff with a blow that appeared inhuman. It would have been spectacular enough to shock even spirits prepared for it.

For years after in that hamlet there would be no sacrifices save to Wotan and Thor, and the slaughter for those gods would keep the region poor.

Starkad levered his axe free of the boggy soil. It had sunk helve-deep with his follow-through. Trying to halt the blow's inertia, even after its work was done, would have been useless and dangerous, likely to pop a cartilage in the Dane's back. Starkad grinned at Mael and began wiping the metal dry with the hem of the thegn's wool cloak. The air crawled with the stench of blood and the yellowish feces the Saxon had voided at the instant of his death.

Mael walked to the edge of the stream and stuck his right foot into the water. The blood washed quickly from the sandal straps but clung to the wool wrappings. From the ditch behind him wriggled the head and shoulders of the intended sacrifice.

"Get your feet soaked and it's going to be hell marching," Starkad said. "A little blood never hurt anybody."

Mael ignored the comment. He stamped his foot twice on the ground to squeeze out some of the water. "What do we do about the girl?" he asked.

"Uh? Leave her. Or do you need to get laid?"

The Saxon girl looked about seventeen, perhaps younger. It was hard to tell from a face so muddy and hunger-pinched. Her hair was a dirty blonde —the dirt might have been an overlay rather than the natural color—double-braided and coiled on top of her head, the braids caught by a bone pin. The men walked toward her from opposite sides. She shrank back down in the muddy ditch. All she wore was a linen singlet and some sort of arm band of woven leather. She had been held by a heavy staff laid across her shoulders and pinned at either side by forked branches. Her struggles had dislodged that, but her knees were still pinioned by deep-driven forks.

Starkad tugged one stake free, then the other. The girl did not move. Her face was turned upward and her eyes stared at the two men.

"Well, we can't leave her," Mael said. "Her people are just as apt as not to drown her when they come back again. Besides, she's seen us clearly; she knows we aren't gods. There're twenty men out there who'd be on us like flies on a turd if they got a notion of the truth. I don't fancy what they could do to us in this fog, even with sticks and manure forks."

"Well . . ." Starkad muttered. He raised his axe for another blow.

"MacLir take you, you butcher!" Mael shouted, reaching across the trench to grasp Starkad's wrist. "I didn't just save her so we could kill her ourselves!"

"Shall we carry her with us, then?" the Dane queried softly.

Mael grimaced and spat. "Yes, I guess we have to," he said.

Starkad laughed. He reached down into the trench. The girl squirmed to avoid his fingers. They closed on her wrist anyway and the Dane hauled her upright. "Up we go, girlie," Starkad said. Beside his armored chest, she appeared a mud-stained wraith. She was thin except for her stomach which had been distended by long-term malnutrition. "What's your name, hey?" the Dane asked.

In panic or the belief that Starkad's grip had

loosened, the girl tried to bolt. Mael thrust out an arm. Starkad had already jerked his prisoner back, throwing her feet out from under her on the lip of earth. The Dane straightened her up by the wrist until her toes scrabbled on the ground and her arm pointed straight up. She looked as though she were manacled to a high wall.

"Listen, girlie," the Dane said, without raising his voice or needing to add that emphasis. "We've saved your life, and if you're good it can stay saved. If you aren't—well, you won't get away and you won't be the first Saxon I've killed, will you?" He laughed. "Or the fifty-first. Now, what's your name?"

Mael touched his friend's hand and guided it down so that the girl could stand comfortably. "We aren't going to hurt you," he said, half stooping to bring his face nearer a level with hers. "But we've got to get out of here. We're going to take you with us, as much for your sake as ours."

The girl looked at Mael, then down at the ditch in which she had almost been drowned. "I am Thorhild," she said sullenly. "Why is it you want to murder my people?"

"Look, we've got to get moving," Starkad said. He ignored the girl's question, but he did release her arm. The flesh was already starting to bruise.

"Yes," Mael agreed. He bent over and raised the half-cloak the chieftain had worn. The upper part of it was blood-sprayed, but the wool was dyed nearly black so the stain was not evident. "She can wear this," Mael said. "It's not much, but it's what we've got at hand."

Gingerly the girl wrapped the garment around her. It fell almost to her knees. Obeying Starkad's peremptory gesture, she followed the Dane. Mael brought up the rear of the file until they had again reached the beaten track. There was no sign of the other villagers or of anything at all human in the woods. As they stepped through the runaway privet which must once have been planted as a boundary hedge, Mael cursed. "Forgot to fill the damned water bottles," he explained.

Starkad was using both arms to force the locked growth apart for his companions. He laughed. "Can't keep a thing in your head any more, can you? Don't know what must be wrong with you."

They marched stolidly along the trail, Mael leading again. When he judged they had come farther than any of Thorhild's kinsmen were likely to have fled, the Irishman dropped back as nearly alongside the girl as the track allowed. "We didn't murder your folk," he said earnestly. "Only the one fellow there—and him we had to kill to save you."

The girl looked over at Mael with a blank expression. It slowly grew to distaste. "You ended the gift to Lady Nairthus," she said. "Now they'll all starve."

"Manannan MacLir, girl!" Mael exploded. "Did you *want* to smother in that ditch? You were sure fighting hard enough about it from what I saw." In his anger, Mael brushed against a beech tree. It flung him back onto the trail, cursing and using his palms to dampen the clangor the trunk had raised from his shield boss. Starkad snorted.

Thorhild ignored the Irishman's stumble. Her brow furrowed. "I thought I could give myself. But I didn't want to, not really, when the—time came. But that was me.

"It was—" she paused to count on her fingers—"five years that we sold everything to buy a ship so that Borgar could bring us to this land. We would be rich, he said—Borgar, your man—" she jerked a nervous thumb back at Starkad, afraid to turn her head in the slightest to face him—"killed him. Borgar said a great king of the British had called us over to guard him. He would give us fine land. But the first year and the second there was blight. We harvested little. The third, our harvest was good, but we owed the seed to rich folk in the city. Their interest rate ate the corn as surely as the blight had before. Last year all was well, until the hail came just before the harvest. And if this Spring is so wet that the seed rots in the ground, we all . . ." Thorhild shrugged. "Lady Nairthus was angry with us. And now she'll kill all of them, all my family, my friends."

Again the girl glared straight at Mael. "What business of yours was it?" she demanded. "Why did you want to murder us?"

Mael shook his head and lengthened his stride instead of trying to answer. Behind him Starkad called, "Some day you'll learn, little brother. Stay away from any woman unless you want to screw her. And *especially* don't try to do one a favor."

They ate, completely enveloped by the branches of a weeping peach beside the ruins of a villa. The rain had finally ceased, but the tree's ground-touching tendrils were protection against eyes as well as rain. Within their cover, the earth was bare and fairly dry. The light that seeped through the foliage was pale green, insofar as there was any light at all. "We're going to need more food," said Starkad in Irish, popping the last of a cooked pork sausage into his mouth. Two of their bread loaves had been wetted through the Dane's pack. They had deliquesced into a gluey mass. Besides, the travelers had three mouths to feed now.

Mael shrugged agreement. The girl was watching them, but with no sign that she understood the Celtic tongue. In the same language Mael answered, "We needed directions, anyway. We've come about as far as we can on the little that Arthur mentioned. What I figured we'd do is find a lone hut towards evening—we've passed a few already. That'll be British. They won't dare refuse us whatever we ask—and they'll be enough afraid of the local Saxons, if they're smart at least, that they won't go running off to report us when we've gone. Anyway, we can leave them enough money that they won't take a chance of losing it. They'll know that sure as sin the Saxons'll strip them bare if they learn there's anything to strip."

"And the girl?"

Mael grimaced. "We'll figure out something. Maybe we'll let her go in the morning. She doesn't know what we're about, and she isn't too near her own people now. She'll be no real danger to us." He looked up at Starkad's smile, then added, "I do some stupid things, don't I?"

The Dane's smile broadened. "Oh, well," he said, "we all do."

By late evening the clouds had cleared and Mael could see the single finger of smoke etching the pale mauve sky. They had met several other travelers on the path by then. No one had spoken, letting a glance and a glower suffice to safeguard privacy. One old woman, alone save for the sow she drove in front of her, signed the Hammer at their backs. Starkad had turned and showed his teeth, thrusting the woman on like a blow.

Now the big Dane pointed at the smoke. "It's a ways off the trail," he said, "and there's only one, so it's not a village. Looks to me like what we're after—and none too soon for my feet."

A hundred yards farther on, another track joined the one they were following. Even the long twilight would be fading soon. There was little choice but to take the path to the dwelling. The building lay a quarter mile back from the main trail, surrounded by trees on one side and a small hand-sown garden plot on the other. It was a rude hut, a dome like a huge beehive. There was a cupola on top to shield the smokehole from the rain. The lowest two feet of the walls were of wattle and daub on a frame of bent saplings which provided the roof stringers as well. Down to the wattling, the dome was thatched. The low doorway was covered by a rush mat that leaked light through its interstices. As the travelers approached, the mat was flung open from the inside, silhouetting a bent figure in the opening against the dull glow of the fire inside the hut.

To the rear, Starkad swore under his breath. Metal chimed as the Dane gripped his shield with

a beringed left hand. The stooping figure called to
them in British, "Welcome, travelers. I've waited
for you." The voice was high and feminine, the
words so reminiscent of Veleda's to Mael in the
Laigin that the Irishman froze. But this was an old
voice, a cracked one. As the travelers stepped
closer, the firelight showed them that the woman
in the doorway was as crabbed and sexless as an
ancient fruit tree. Mael's memory stayed with
him, though, bursting out of the scab laid over his
longings by the chill and the days of heels thudding on the ground.

The three of them ducked one at a time into the
hut. Mael went first, darting his head to either side
to be sure there was no one waiting flat against an
inner wall with a bludgeon raised. There was only
the woman. When Mael saw how the shawl of gray
homespun bulked about her body, he realized she
was even smaller than she had first seemed.

The interior of the dwelling was a single room,
dry and warm but thickened by the smoke that
swirled from the draft through the door curtain.
There was little furniture. To the left was a low
bedstead with a rush mattress and a covering of
cowhide. Surprisingly, it seemed clean. Across the
hut from the bed were a half dozen large storage
jars—the pantry, filled with grain and oil and
beer, perhaps. A small ham, whittled far down on
the shank, hung from a stringer above the jars.
There were no chairs, but a three-legged stool
stood near the tripod over the low fire. Suspended
from the tripod was a covered bronze pot of something savory. There were no other furnishings or

decorations in the hut, save the bundles of dried
or drying herbs festooning the whole ceiling.

Starkad grunted as he entered the room. A
bundle of dried parsley brushed his hair when he
straightened up; his hand batted the herbs away
reflexively; then he moved a step out of the way.
"What do you mean, expect us?" he demanded
bluntly. "Are you another of them?"

The woman smiled. It made her more attractive,
though she was still neither young nor a beauty.
Without pretending ignorance she said, "A wise
woman? In a way. I'm not what the folk about here
think I am, Saxon and Briton both . . . but I'm not
the fraud they pretend to think when they talk in
the daylight. 'Old Gwedda, too foolish to find her
nose with both hands. For charity, we give her
some bread and a flitch of bacon now and again.' I
can't keep their lovers true to them, and I won't
make their neighbor's cow go dry . . . but I can do
more to cure them than anyone else in a day's ride,
and I learn things from here and there. I learned
that you—two of you, at least—would be coming,
and that the world had need of your safety."

They were speaking in British. Thorhild looked
from one face to another without comprehension.
The girl was first sullen, then restive as her eyes
took in the variety of gathered herbs and the paraphernalia half hidden at the head of the bed. The
Saxon girl edged toward the door. Starkad's arm
stopped her and walked her quickly back. The
Dane's index finger curled beneath her shift,
plucking one breast out to view. "Not so soon,
little one," he said in German. "The party hasn't
even started yet."

"You must be hungry," said Gwedda in a businesslike tone. "Sit down and we'll eat."

The two men stripped off their wet cloaks and formed them over their shields to dry a little in the warmth. Starkad leaned his axe against the corner of bed and wall, then hung his dagger belt over the upraised haft. Mael took off his body armor. This time the Dane continued to wear his mail shirt without commenting on his reasons.

Gwedda began dishing a stew of game and vegetables out of the hanging pot. She paused suddenly, realizing that she had only three plates.

"The girl and I'll share," said Starkad. His hand guided Thorhild to the bed where he sat down beside her. The three travelers set to work hungrily on the stew, round loaves of barley bread to sop the juices, and a handful of leeks. Gwedda ate also, with good appetite though she kept an eye out for her guests.

"Oh," she said. "Would you like some beer to drink? Or I even have a skin of mead. A Saxon gave it to me for setting his son's leg straight after a tree had broken it."

Mael grimaced. "Mead's too sweet to drink and too thick to piss," he said. "I leave the muck to Germans. Their tongues all froze in the cold so they don't taste it. But I'll take beer, indeed, and thank you for it."

"Never knew an Irishman with any sense about liquor or women," Starkad chortled happily. He reached for the tied-off goatskin Gwedda was handing him. "Come along, girlie, this'll put a little fire back in your guts." Thorhild twitched her head away from the Dane's caressing hand.

Starkad appeared undisturbed by her attitude—
unaware, in fact.

"Do you know whereabouts there's a village of
Saxons under a thegn named Biargram?" Mael
asked Gwedda. The Irishman leaned back against
the wall with a pottery mug of cool ale in his hand.
The room felt safe, cozy in a way that went far
beyond its warmth and dryness. The smoke and
dimness of the fire provided a curtain of sorts,
dulling the images of Starkad and Thorhild across
the room. It even seemed to mute the sound of the
Dane's clumsy endearments.

"The village isn't that near," the old woman was
answering with a frown, "though you can walk the
distance in a day, I think. Now let me see. . . ." She
closed her eyes and continued, "There are three,
no, four forks in the road between here and where
you want to go. You'll have to go around another
village about a mile from here where two brothers
rule together. First . . ."

The room and its sounds faded as Mael listened
to Gwedda's words. The Irishman found a picture
of the intended route forming in his mind. It could
have been just careful description coupled with
images formed from Mael's own years of travel; it
could have been something more. Mael was never
certain. But as the witch spoke, Mael seemed to
walk the trails step by step. He saw the groves and
the pattern of chalk cropping out on a hillside, the
stream near a crossroad and even the fallen tree a
hundred yards downstream from it where men
could cross without wetting their feet.

Starkad lay back on the bed, continuing to swig

the thick mead and trying to force some on Thorhild. The Dane was still drunkenly good-natured.
Underlying his pleasantries, however, was the
assurance that he was a stronger man than any
other he knew, strong enough to take almost anything when he decided he had waited long enough
for it to be offered freely. Thorhild had been edged
against the wall. By turns she had been petulant,
then taut and sullen. None of her moods made any
useful impression on the big Dane, any more than
her clenched hands could keep his fingers from
prodding and fondling her at will.

Starkad leaned toward the girl to nuzzle her
hair. Her singlet had been pawed free of her
bosom. A fold of the Dane's chain mail caught her
right nipple and pinched it. Thorhild shrieked and
leaped away. Starkad shot his arm out to grab her,
but the girl was already stumbling over the pile of
his equipment. Metal crashed as Starkad threw
himself to his feet. Then the girl's small hands
were thrusting the point of his own dagger
straight in the Dane's face.

Combat reflexes had kept Starkad alive a hundred times before, as they did now, but he flung
himself back without thought of the fact that his
right heel was under the bedstead. The dagger
swept harmlessly in front of the fluff of his moustaches. The tendons of the Dane's ankle popped
audibly, even against the din of the girl's screams.

Thorhild turned and ran for the door. Mael was
on his feet now, eyes bright with the disoriented
terror of a man roused to battle from dead sleep.
Starkad was already striding for his prey, but his

right leg folded beneath him. As Thorhild darted into the night, the Dane pitched forward helplessly. His forehead fetched up against the doorpost. The ground-shaking thud that impact made stilled his roar of anger.

Mael tried to force his way past his friend's bulk. First Starkad's prone body blocked him. The Dane rolled to his side. Shaking his head to clear it, Starkad put out a hand to bar the passage deliberately. "No," he said. "Let her go."

"What?"

Starkad's face was streaming blood from the pressure cut in his scalp. He lowered the hand he no longer needed to keep Mael away, trying to smear the runnels of blood from his eyes with the palm. Gwedda was there at once, interposing herself between the men and expertly daubing at the wound with her scarf.

"Let her go," Starkad repeated, "because she earned it." Before Mael could protest, the Dane added, "Look, we were going to let her loose in the morning, anyway, weren't we? We just did it a few hours early, think of it that way. That little hellcat's a real woman after all, by Frigga. I'll be damned if I'll have her carved up for it. After all this is over, I just might come back this way and see if I can't look her up. You know?"

"You damned fool," Mael breathed in wonderment. He shot his half-drawn sword back into its sheath. "And you say you like 'em better filled out than Veleda?"

"Don't stand!" Gwedda ordered sharply as the Dane started to get to his hands and knees.

"I can—" Starkad began, but the old woman cut him off.

"You can ruin your ankle forever, or you can stay off it for a few days now," she snapped. "Here, let me see." The shapeless boot slipped off easily, but Starkad winced at even that slight friction. The ankle was red and angry already, so swollen that the big bones were hidden in puffy flesh. Gwedda probed the injury with her eyes.

"The shield and spear," Mael said slowly. "If we wait to get them for this to heal . . . Veleda said to hurry."

The witch's face paled even in the orange light. "The Veleda? *She* sent you after—"

"Shut up, woman," the Dane snarled, "or I'll shut you up."

Mael blinked in surprise at his friend, but Gwedda understood the reason for the threat. She said, "I can see there might be need for haste. If a —seeker of ability said to hasten, I would take her word for it, Irishman. I would take her word for anything."

"Look, I'll be ready to leave in the morning," Starkad said.

Mael caught the woman's grimace and demanded harshly, "Ready to go without slowing me down? Ready to hike twenty miles, to climb hills and ford streams without falling on your butt and pulling me down, too?" The Dane made a moue of frustration but said nothing. More gently Mael continued, "I know you're tough, old friend. And I know that even hurt you can do things that most people wouldn't be able to do healthy. But there're

212 of our own."

limits. You can't fly without wings, and you can't walk without two ankles to support you. Remember, we aren't here for any reasons of our own."

"Help me to the bed," Starkad said dejectedly. The ankle was sending jagged black pains up his whole side. "We'll see how it looks in the morning."

CHAPTER ELEVEN

It looked bad in the morning, as they all had known it would. There was no need for further argument, though. Starkad was delirious and mumbling demands to a chieftain Mael knew had been dead for twelve years.

The Irishman looked at Gwedda. "Look, take care of him," he said. "I'll be back as soon as I can be. If that's not in a week and Starkad can walk again, tell him to head back to where we came from and take care of Veleda. Until I get back."

The Briton nodded, catching at her lower lip with her teeth. "I've poulticed his forehead," she said. "The cut there won't get infected. But he's very strong. When he slips and turns that strength on himself, he's no less destructive than at other times. But I can lower the fever and the swelling soon, I'm sure."

With food in his pack again and his cloak spread across his back to dry as the sun rose clear, Mael strode along the path. The help Gwedda had given him made his direction as certain as if he had walked that way daily for a year. Mael was perversely sure, however, that the wise woman herself almost never left the narrow bounds of her clearing.

Mael had intended to let Starkad carry the burden of entry into the closed society of a Saxon village. The big Dane had a measure of fame, even though he had never capitalized on it by welding masterless men about him into a pirate band. Starkad could have stalked into the village, roaring that he needed protection during his outlawry and that, from what he'd heard, Biargram was one of the few men big enough for him to swear to. The thegn would have been flattered, the men who had not heard of Starkad might be doubtful but would keep silent because of the Dane's size . . . and those who *had* heard stories about Starkad would keep very silent indeed. Mael, as a hanger-on and a foreign one at that, had hoped to be lost in the impact of his friend's personality. That would have given the two of them time to locate the arms and remove them at leisure.

Without Starkad, the job became much harder. If Mael were accepted at all, it would be with suspicion. The women would shun him, the children spy on his every movement, the men find his alien face annoying and pick fights with the Irishman any time they were drinking. It was quite possible that the villagers would simply set on Mael and kill him out of hand. But Veleda's urgency was still fresh in his mind, and there seemed no way around it. Mael hadn't really expected to come home from this one, anyway.

Well into the afternoon, the Irishman saw the first signs of the village. A hillside, rolling up to the right of the trail, had been cleared and recently plowed. No one was working in it at the moment, but the chink of tools could be heard in the near distance. There was an occasional soughing that was not the wind. Mael shrugged a little to settle his body in his armor. He went on at the same pace as before. As he expected, the village was over the rise.

There were a dozen buildings on either side of a small stream, laid out as haphazardly as if they had dropped from the sky. The settlement as a whole was not palisaded—it was too far back from the War Zone to be threatened by Arthur save in event of a major disaster. Each of the houses, however, had a separate garth surrounded by a fence. The buildings had been dug down a foot or so and the turfs set around the excavations. These formed the foundations for the wall posts. The posts were joined with wattle and daub. The largest of the houses gleamed with plaster over the mud; its walls had been strengthened by cross-timbering. Like the rest, however, it was thatch-roofed and had no chimney. Smoke from the central hearth was expected to find its way out through the triangular openings at the peaks of the sidewalls. In the winter, their own fires were a worse enemy to the Saxons than Arthur more than dreamed of being. Now in the spring, the heat of a score of bodies was enough to warm the houses without flames.

The first challenge to Mael's presence came from a pack of nondescript dogs. They had lain in pairs and triplets, sharing the shade of the houses with the village's chickens and hogs. When the dogs scented Mael, they leaped up and ran toward him yelping and snarling. The Irishman kept his stride steady. His lips were a little tighter. When the rangy, stiff-legged bitch who led the pack came close enough, Mael swung his spear butt up from under her jaw and cut the barking off within her teeth. The rest of the pack gave back, prancing. Mael continued to advance, using his spear butt freely on whichever dog was the nearest or noisiest. He wetted the point only once, on the shaggy brute who slipped up behind him and snapped at his heel. The shock of that death silenced the other dogs for a moment; then they were yapping as enthusiastically as before.

The dogs had been the first to notice the intruder because the Saxons were all at work in the fields. The eyes of the laborers, men and women both, were unable to reach beyond the plowshares or the wavering stone fence at the field edge toward which they dragged their equipment, staggering. The explosion of barking drew their stares to the approaching stranger in armor. Dropping their tools, the Saxons began running down the hillsides toward the village. Only a few small children stayed where they were, freed from their own duties by their elders' rush to arms. The children set down the long switches with which they had been lashing birds away from the seeds. Depending on their mood, they began either to play or to watch the drama below.

Mael was a quarter mile from the village at the time he was noticed. He made no attempt to hurry. The Saxon warriors gathered in front of the nearest house to await him. They were hastily equipped; at every moment another man raced out of a building to stand by his fellows. From the shuttered windows peeped the women. The panic, Mael knew, was not at what he was but for what he might be. He was unexpected, inexplicable: a scout for an enemy, a messenger from King Cerdic —who knew?

By the time Mael reached the band of warriors, it was some sixty strong. Half a dozen at most wore ring mail. Perhaps twice that number had leather jerkins, hardened with scales or at least metal studs. The rest, though the village was clearly much more prosperous than the one in which Thorhild had grown up, wore only boiled leather or no body armor at all. Almost all of the Saxons carried shields, round or kite-shaped and made of wood or oxhide. The fancier ones had iron rims and sometimes designs worked in their faces with metal. None of the shields looked out of the ordinary, the famous object Mael had come to steal.

Nor were the remaining arms exceptional. Most of the warriors carried spears six to eight feet long. A few made do with axes or agricultural implements, hoes or metalshod dibbles intended for planting. The wealthiest Saxons wore double-edged swords the length of a man's arm. More common were heavy fighting knives, scramasaxes, often thrust sheathless under a belt. The knives averaged a foot and a half long, sharpened only on the lightly curved inner edge.

The headgear was generally leather with a mixture of iron and bronze pots; it was here that the leader's equipment was most unlike that of the other Saxons. The apparent chief wore an iron helmet whose face was closed from nose to throat by a veil of fine ring mail. All the metal surfaces were silvered, and the cap itself was parcel gilt as well. Though striking, the helmet was not a modern design and probably had been handed down through several generations.

The thegn was as tall as Mael and broader. His face was unreadable for the veil and the bushy blond brows that twisted above his eyes. The Saxon took a step forward, his spear half poised, and called to the Irishman, "What's your business here?"

Mael halted within a spear length. He kept his own weapon upright. The dogs were backing away. Though Mael was well aware that the wings of the Saxon line were edging forward to encircle him, he ignored them. "I am Mael mac Ronan, of the Cenel Luigdech," he declaimed with deliberate formality. "Exiled from my own people for saving a Saxon trader's life, I have come among his folk to take the service of the thegn I am told is the greatest of them all. I come to join the chieftain Biargram Ironhand."

The intake of breath among the Saxons was swift and general. Many of the warriors signed Thor's Hammer at Mael, twisting their spears sideways in order to hold out their clenched fists palm-upward. One man gasped, "A miracle!"

Even the thegn had started at the Irishman's words. Very carefully he asked, "What do you come here to do?"

Mael was uneasy. The Saxons were not reacting hostilely, but the reason for their religious awe was unclear; therefore, it was potentially dangerous. Had some priest foretold an outland savior appearing to aid Biargram at a crucial moment? If Mael's luck had been that good, then surely the gods were behind him in this mad quest! "I have come to join Biargram Grim's son," Mael repeated.

The Saxon chief clashed his spear against his shield boss in an access of joy. "And so you shall!" he thundered. "I'm Biarki, Biargram's son. My father died three days ago, but you'll join him tonight—in his barrow."

Mael's arm was quick, but a dozen Saxons had already launched themselves onto him. They pinioned and bound the Irishman before he could strike a blow.

"How far is it to this damned barrow?" grunted Mael to Biarki. The young thegn walked beside Mael in the midst of the procession of happy Saxons. They were keeping holiday. Some of the women had even bound flowers into their hair. As for Mael, he too was bound—by a pair of nooses

held by three men each before and behind him.
The cords were long and slack enough for comfort, but if Mael balked or ran, they would choke
him at once. Mael was furious—with himself and
his luck and his captors. He had cursed them all
loudly from the beginning of the march. What
could the Saxons do to him if his insults angered
them, after all? Condemn him to death?

Little the Irishman said, however, could penetrate Biarki's buoyant mood, anyway. "Oh, well,"
the Saxon said, "a couple miles yet. We didn't
want my father staying too close, you know . . .
and not just any place would have done for his
barrow. We needed a cave so that the walls would
be solid and he couldn't . . . well, you know."

"Look," Mael snapped, "if you're going to kill
me, you can at least tell me why. I don't know a
damn thing."

Biarki laughed. "My father was murdered," he
explained, "by magic. He had a spear and a shield,
you see, heirlooms of our house." Mael shot a side
glance at the thegn but made no overt indication
of his particular interest in the weapons—or of his
surprise at Biarki's inappropriate good humor.
"They were the arms made for the hero Achil by
Wieland the Smith. That was long ago, at the Troy
fight. No one ever had arms like those.

"We came here to take service with King
Cerdic," continued Biarki. "He gave us good land
and we were happy. Only, Cerdic has a councillor
named Ceadwalla, a Briton who commands his
housecarls. This Ceadwalla is a very great magician, and after a while he learned about my

father's shield and spear. He came to my father and demanded them—a nasty little man with a birthmark like a spider on his right cheek. If Britons lived like men, they would have thrown Ceadwalla onto the kitchen midden the day he was born."

"Well, why didn't you do it yourself?" Mael asked. "You folk seem quick enough to murder strangers. Or do you do that just to people who come alone and friendly?"

"Ceadwalla was too powerful to kill," Biarki admitted easily. "He never came to us with less than a hundred men, and . . . we knew he was a magician, too, remember. But still my father held him off. Then last year, Biargram's head began to pain him both day and night. He called Ceadwalla to him and gave him the spear but kept the shield. And that was enough for one year, but last week Ceadwalla came back. My father refused him the shield again, and so my father—died."

Mael grimaced in utter bewilderment. The men at the head of the procession were singing a cheerful, bawdy song. Closer by, a group of women were chattering like daws in a cornfield. "If this is how your mourn your chiefs," the Irishman said, "you must dance yourselves to death at a marriage feast."

"Death isn't the worst that can come to a man," Biarki said, his smile wiped away as cleanly as smoke in a windstorm.

They marched along together in silence for a time, as if they were comrades. At that the two men were more similar than different to look at except for their hair color: two big fighting men in armor, young for any profession but the one they followed. "You've started your story," Mael said at last. "Now tell me the rest."

Biarki nodded. "You may as well know," he agreed. His expression became grim. It might better have suited the prisoner being led to death. "We held a wake for my father," he said, "laying his body out on a bier in his house garth. We feasted around him, lighting lamps after sunset. Each one of us told stories about how we'd ambush Ceadwalla and avenge Biargram. And then the moon rose, and so did my father, there in the midst of us."

Biarki swallowed thickly. Nobody looking at him could have doubted his sincerity. The Saxon went on, "He stood and tried to walk, but his legs didn't work and he fell. He was making sounds like a carp sucking air. His eyes had been closed. They opened again but I don't think he could see anything. He lay there on his belly, crawling with one hand and one foot. We all ran. We locked ourselves in our houses and didn't even look out at the garth until the morning. My—father—was still lying there, dead again. He had pulled the trestle out from under one of the tables and eaten most of the food there. He'd shit, too, great sloppy trails of it that stank like a bear's. . . ."

Biarki shuddered in a way that Mael could now appreciate. His own mind glanced back a few days to his horror in the ship, the purple hell-light writhing from Veleda's fingers. Mael trembled also. Magic was for those who understood it. And

surely there were few human beings so evil that
they understood it.

"We would have raised a true barrow," Biarki
said, "but there wasn't time and—maybe it
wouldn't have been strong enough. From the
inside. So . . . there was a cistern not far away,
near where a villa had stood. They'd cut it down
into the rock, the Romans had, and it was fifteen
feet deep. Deep enough. So we took m-my—" and
this time the Saxon could not get out the word "father," so he said, "Ironhand there, with his shield
and his horse and his dog. . . . And we hoped that
he could lie still now that he had his grave goods,
but we covered the cistern over and put guards by
it. And the guards heard Ironhand begin to move
when the moon rose again. They heard him smack
and slurp and eat.

"So we knew we would have to give his soul a
human before his body would lie still. Some said a
slave would do, and some said Thora, because she
had been his woman for a year before he died. And
a few of them said perhaps his son was the gift
Ironhand sought," Biarki added with a fell smile,
"but none of them said so when they thought I
might hear them. When you came, there could be
no doubt but that Wotan had answered our
prayers and sent us the sacrifice he demanded."

Mael laughed. He could accept Biarki's story.
He could accept as well the Saxons' belief that
their god had listened to them and sent an Irish
alien to take the place of one of them—or a valuable slave. It just seemed a pity that the best proof
Mael had yet found for gods taking interest in the

lives of men was about to end with him being
eaten by an animate corpse.

The Saxons' destination was only a few minutes
further. The ruined villa was a jumble of masonry
overgrown with honeysuckle, recently disturbed
by the burial party removing stones to heap over
their chieftain's grave. Already the leaders of the
procession were beginning to scatter the low cairn
to open the cistern again. It lay some fifty feet
from the other ruins, far enough that rain from
the house gutters could be piped into it without
being contaminated by surface runoff from the
latrine and the stables to the rear.

"Just clear enough stone to lift one timber,"
Biarki ordered his men. "That's enough room to
let him down." It was a low tumulus anyway, less
a marker for posterity than an additional burden
in case something from inside began to push up.
The cistern had been a rectangular prism, six feet
by twelve feet, cut into the rock. The original lid
had been replaced for Biarki's purposes by a roof
of logs. They were then covered with stone. The
result was not airtight—the feed pipes would have
allowed a prisoner to breathe, anyway—but it
would be quite impossible to open from the inside
without tools and a platform. The Saxons had left
Mael his body armor, but nothing with an edge or
a point or even a lip that could be used to dig. Mael
greatly doubted that anything useful had been
buried with Biargram, either. Grunting with
effort, three of the Saxons tugged at the end log to
pivot it away from the hole. "Enough?" one of
them asked, wiping sweat from his lips with the
back of his hand. The Saxons—the whole village

was present, nearly two hundred of them—had
grown silent. The six men holding Mael tensed for
the first time.

Biarki strode to the edge of the cistern, motion-
ing the guards to bring Mael along, too. "He'll
fit," Biarki said, measuring the Irishman's chest
against the opening. Then, after obvious hesitation, the thegn knelt to peer into his father's
grave. Mael, shading his eyes, bent down also to
take a first look at the barrow in which he was
expected to die.

The walls were deep and sheer. The bar of sunlight through the opening fell across a low bier on
which nothing lay. Instead there was a man in the
far end of the chamber, slumped over the dim bulk
of a horse. The stench of the pit was sickening, but
it was not the effluvium of decay.

"You said you put his shield in with him?" Mael
remarked, no longer concerned about what his
captors would think of his interest.

Biarki nodded, pointing. The heirloom had presumably been leaned at the head of the bier. Now
it lay half under the legs of the corpse, a circuit
gleaming dimly in the light reflected from the
plastered sides of the cistern. Another object on
the floor among the disordered grave goods
caught Biarki's eye: the head of a large hound,
ripped or cut crudely away from its torso. The
thegn gagged and turned back from the grave.
Mael stared at him in surprise. Swallowing
heavily, the Saxon explained, "Thunderer—his
dog . . . we tied his feet, but he was alive when we
put him in the barrow."

Mael straightened, looking with contempt at

Biarki and the white-faced throng of Saxons waiting beyond. "Oh, you're fine brave men to do that to a dog," he said.

Biarki also stood. "Do you want us to kill you first?" he asked without meeting the Irishman's eyes.

Mael shook his head briefly. His limbs were weak with rage and fear. "No," he said, so that no one would think that he had been unable to speak. Then he added, half in bravado, "You think you're going to lay a ghost this way. But keep your doors barred, Saxons—because I won't stay down there forever, and I don't think I'll forget you while there's a one of you alive." He glared like a demon at the men holding him. "Now, slack your goddamn ropes so that I can get down in there with your bogie."

One of the guards suddenly began to vomit on the ground. The others backed away, not actually releasing the ropes until Mael had lowered himself to full arms' length into the cistern. He clung to the stone lip for a moment. Just as the Irishman let go, a boot heel clunked down where his fingers had been. The rope ends writhed down into the pit beside him. Only seconds later, the men above had levered the heavy timber back into place. Mael was in darkness allayed only by chinks of light which dimmed as stones were piled back atop. The thud of rock against rock continued for what seemed an impossible length of time. When it ceased, the blackness within the tomb was unrelieved.

Mael sat on the edge of the bier and considered

his situation. It was unpleasant and very probably hopeless, but it did not appear to be immediately desperate. The air stank, as was to be expected in an enclosed room fouled with liquescent feces. There was enough ventilation through the old pipes to keep it life-sustaining and, fortunately, his sense of smell was swiftly numbed. Mael had no way of getting himself out, though. By leaping from the top of the bier he could probably touch the roof, but that would not allow him to dislodge the tons of wood and stone above him. If he was to be released, it must be from outside—Starkad, searching for him in a week or a month, or perhaps Veleda, somehow learning of his plight and somehow aiding him. . . .

The thought of Veleda's witchcraft turned Mael's thoughts where he had not wanted them to go, to Ceadwalla's curse and the body with which the Irishman shared the grave. Sighing, Mael got up and shuffled carefully to the rear of the chamber in order to examine his companion.

Biargram Ironhand was as still and cold as any man dead three days could be. The Saxon had been a big man and seemed even bigger in the dark with only touch to guide Mael's judgment. Biarki's description of the corpse's rise had been so circumstantial, his terror so genuine, that Mael had not really doubted the account. Now, confronted with the flesh, the Irishman found death's reality more convincing than words ever could be. Muttering to himself, Mael felt over the grave goods to see if there was anything among them that could be useful to him.

As he had expected from the first, there were no tools or weapons. There was, however, food and a sealed cask of wine or beer. A few mouthfuls torn from a joint of boiled pork satisfied Mael's hunger. The meat was only a texture since his taste buds had been stunned by the fetor of the room, but it was no less nourishing for that. At first Mael could not decide how to open the cask without a point or blade. Finally he smashed in the top with a chunk of stone that had fallen down when the grave was reopened. The ale within was cool and sharp and satisfying.

After that, Mael waited. He had been a prisoner before, but never so thoroughly one or in such solitary fashion. There was probably no human being within a mile of him. For a while, Mael tried to concentrate on Veleda. No message of comfort or succor came to him, and besides, Kesair's thick black hair seemed to wave in front of his vision of the witch. At least, Mael told himself, he could ignore the false fear of Ironhand. It was certainly after sundown, and Biargram was no less a corpse now than he had been when the grave was opened.

Except that Biarki had been talking about moonrise, not sunset, hadn't he?

And then boots scraped in the corner by the dead man.

Had it not been repeated, the sound could have been Mael's fancy. It was followed by a thick, slobbering noise like that of a beast trying to drink with its nostrils under water. Then Biargram managed to tear the gobbet of horse meat loose with his teeth. The chunk was too big for a human throat, so more than a minute of wheezing and grunting followed before a smacking gurgle ended the process. Mael, who had remained as motionless as a fawn who scents the hunter, heard Ironhand pause and the leather of his harness creak as he turned from the horse. The dead Saxon stood up.

It was neither an easy process nor a swift one. Ironhand's fingers scrabbled on the wall for purchase. Mael could hear the nervous patter of bits of plaster falling away under the dead man's grip. From what Biarki had said, Mael had assumed the corpse was at least too discoordinated to move except by crawling. Now, one heavy step at a time, the thing was walking toward Mael. Very quietly, the Irishman eased himself to the far end of the bier. He could hear the breath whistling in and out of Biargram's mouth. Air did not seem to be sucked deeper into the dead man's lungs, however.

The low platform on which the body had been laid was over two feet wide. Mael had risen quietly on one side of it. Ironhand moved past on the other, a step, another step—he was parallel to Mael—*thick fingers brushed the Irishman's cheek*.

Mael screamed and flung himself back against the wall. The dead man lunged at him, tripped over the bier, and crashed headlong. Mael ran to his right, toward the end in which Biargram had lain. Mael's first stride set his foot on the slimy dog's head and he, too, skidded to the floor. His hands touched the shield which he had come to take. The dead Saxon was trying to regain his foot-

ing and was doing so more easily than he had
stood the first time. A detached part of Mael's
brain searched for a correlation. He remembered
that the moon was waxing toward full. If the moon
ruled this creature, than he would not reach full
strength for another day yet.

But that calculation was almost unconscious.
Mael, gripping the shield by the rim, was swinging
it edgewise like a great axe blade toward the
wheezing sound that marked the monster's face.
The impact felt like hitting a statue. The creature
toppled, but his flesh did not give the way a man's
should have, spattering fluids away from the
blow. Even as the corpse fell, his hands closed on
the shield. Mael pulled back to save his sole
weapon. There was no comparison between his
strength and that of Biargram. It was like tugging
at a full-grown oak tree, hoping to uproot it. Mael
cursed and backed away. The corpse came after
him, dropping the shield with a clang.

Those were the first moments. The creature's
coordination seemed to improve slightly as the
hours drew on, but still he stumbled like a two-
year-old. A two-year-old with the strength of
Starkad's axe. In one of their circlings, Ironhand
snatched at Mael's arm and touched the ale cask
instead. In an onset of rage or perhaps emotion-
less destructiveness, the creature smashed the
sturdy container to splinters. He brought the cask
down again and again on the stone bier, spraying
ale and ruptured oak across the tomb. Then Ironhand began searching again for Mael. The tenor of
his shallow, wheezing breaths never changed.

The monster, however slow and clumsy, was indefatigable. He could not see in the dark any better than Mael could, nor did he seem to hear Mael's breathing over the constant rasp of his own. His very motions appeared as mindless as those of a worm crawling back and forth across the bottom of a jewel box. But if the worm is ceaseless, it will cover every inch of the box a thousand times—and Ironhand was ceaseless.

The deep-dug cistern had felt cool when Mael first dropped into it. Now his exertions had heated the chamber into a steamy oven. The Irishman sucked in painful gulps of air through his open mouth. The ale was gone. Even if Mael had somehow saved it, there would have been no time to slurp a drink.

Mael was beginning to stagger as badly as the thing pursuing him. Once he horribly miscalculated in the narrow darkness and ran squarely into the creature's chest. As the Irishman ducked away, Biargram's hand flailed across his cheekbone and seized his right ear. Mael screamed and tore free. The pain was terrible, a dull ache like a hammer blow overlaid with piercing agony, but pain was a proof of life, and the pain would have stopped very suddenly had Mael hesitated in pulling away.

The Irishman's life depended on the bier. It was just wide enough that the monster could not reach across it to the far wall without overbalancing— yet. Had the corpse's motor control been a little better, had Biargram been able to step up onto the two-foot platform, he would have caught Mael at once. Instead, Biargram had to drive his prey into the arms of fatigue.

In all likelihood, another night would give Iron-hand that needed agility, even if Mael survived this night.

At the end, Mael was so exhausted that he would have been blind with tears and sweat even had there been light in the tomb. He tripped and fell across the shield, then skidded to the floor again as he tried to rise. Mael lay there sobbing hopelessly for twenty long seconds before he realized he was no longer being pursued. The Irishman could hear the slow scratching of the corpse's fingers on the stone floor, but the breathing sounds had stopped. After a moment, the scratching ceased also.

The moon had set. Mael was to have peace until it rose again.

Mael stood with the metal shield of Achilles in his hands. Using his toes as antennae, he edged his way toward where the last sounds of the corpse had come. Biargram was there. Prodding from Mael's hobnails brought neither motion nor resilience. Mael had thought initially that the corpse was stiffened by rigor mortis; now he realized that the condition was more nearly akin to petrification. He brought the heavy shield edge down three times on the Saxon's skull, arm's-length cuts that would have sawn through a tree trunk.

Biargram was as unmarked after the third blow as before the first. Each hair was in place, and the teeth were still bared in a snarl.

Crying again, Mael dropped the useless shield and threw himself into the corner away from the dead horse. He was utterly wrecked by fatigue, physically and mentally. It was in abdication of his responsibilities, even for his own life, that he slept.

But there was nothing he could have done that would have been of more use that day, or of less.

CHAPTER TWELVE

Mael awakened to a sound. He lashed out with feet and hands in blind panic. He knew in instant terror that he had slept for hours, believed that the clinking against rock was the monster, moon-risen again and reaching for him. The sound came again. It was from above, from outside the tomb. Someone was clearing the stones away.

Mael almost shouted. Instinct strangled the cry in his throat. It might be Starkad, might be Veleda or Gwedda, and any of them would continue with or without Mael's encouragement. Equally, it might be the Saxons returning for reasons of their own. If they thought Mael were dead, they might be relaxed enough to allow him to leap from the bier to the cistern's lip and squirm out. They might cut him apart on the surface, no doubt they *would* do so—but they would not return him alive to Ironhand's grave.

One of the logs stirred and fell aback. The hands above that tried to remove it had proven too few for the job. A voice, harsh though muffled by the timbers, snarled in British, "Quickly, you idiots. We have less than an hour before moonrise, but I swear I'll send you into that pit whether you've got it open before then or not!"

The timbers shifted again, creaking as crowbars were levered under one in the middle. The log was prised upward. Light gleamed briefly through the crack before the same contemptuous voice ordered, "Close the lantern! Or do you want all the Saxons down on us to see what we're doing at their chieftain's barrow?" Metal clicked as the slide of a dark lantern shut again. Grunts and low-voiced curses were the only sounds for some minutes as the men above struggled to manhandle away the roof log.

As Mael listened silently to the grave robbers, his mind turned over the cramped layout of the tomb. There was no perfect hiding place, so he took the best he was offered. As swiftly as he could move without kicking any of the scattered grave goods, Mael stepped to the part-eaten carcass of the horse. He pressed himself against the wall in the angle it formed with the body. It was not truly concealing, but it blurred his outline. Mael did not think the Britons would look farther than Biargram's sprawled corpse at the other end of the chamber, anyway.

The log heaved up into the night, dropping a rain of rock fragments to the floor and bier as it swung away. Mael resisted the instinct to crouch lower. Movement would certainly have betrayed him.

The lantern, a candle in a baffled canister with a
shutter, thrust down into the opening and fanned light across the chamber. The illumination
seemed much brighter to Mael's shrouded eyes
than it really was. The quick sweep did not reveal
him to the one directing the light. Rather, the
lantern focused on the upturned shield, steadied,
and winked out. There was muttered conversation
above. Ropes slapped wood. A figure, swaying
against the vaguely starlit opening, began to
descend in a sling.

When the Briton had been lowered shoulder-
deep in the pit, he slid the lantern open again. The
light flashed over the roof timbers. The command-
ing voice snarled through the opening, "Keep the
bloody light down or keep it out!"

"Then keep this bloody rope still!" the man in
the sling cried back. He trained his light on Biargram's glaring visage as if it fascinated him—or as
if he expected it to move. The hot metal of the
lantern stank in a different way from the fetid air
of the tomb.

The sling dropped by jerks as the men above
handed the rope down. When it touched the
surface of the bier the man stepped off it, then
down to the floor. The Briton's back was to Mael,
his body silhouetted by the circumscribed candle-
light. The man bent to pick up the shield. It was
heavier than he suspected. He grunted in surprise
and his thumb slipped off the slide of the lantern.

Mael swung to his feet at the moment of darkness. Like a dancer to his partner, he stepped to
the grave robber just as the other began to stand

up. The dim light through the roof was enough for
Mael's eyes after their deprivation. He struck with
the strength of frustration built up during his long
pursuit by the monster.

The Briton's neck broke under the double-
handed blow. The shield and the lantern clashed
together against the stone. "Conbran!" someone
demanded from the surface. "What's wrong?"

Mael tugged the shield out from under
Conbran's body. Both the Irishman's hands were
numb from the impact. "Just dropped the damn
thing," he said hoarsely. He leaped to the top of
the bier, holding the shield to mask his face
against watchers above. "Pull me up," he ordered.

The rope swung upward more swiftly than it
had lowered. The shield rim scraped against the
logs. Hands reached to take it from Mael, but the
shield was his only chance of survival and his
fingers were locked on it. The sling drew Mael
waist-high to the lip of the cistern and he stepped
up to the ground. There were a dozen men around
him, all armed, and a babble of muted questions.
Suddenly one man cursed and threw back the
velvet curtain shrouding a lighted oil lamp. The
light flared across Mael's face.

"Lord Christ!" a Briton shouted. "It's not Conbran! The Saxon—"

The lamp fell to shatter on the rocky soil. Yellow
light bloomed from the spreading oil like a
beacon. The grave robbers were screaming,
running, all but their harsh-voiced leader whose
cheek crawled with a birthmark like a spider.
Ceadwalla shouted another vain command, then

turned to Mael. He carried a silver-chased spear which he raised to thrust.

Mael caught him across the bridge of the nose with the rim of the metal shield. The bones shattered like porcelain under a sledgehammer.

Ceadwalla's spear had a tubular socket and a blade as long as a man's forearm. The metal was iron or steel, but deeply incised and filled with silver. Mael hefted the weapon, then set it beside him as he fumbled with the dead Briton's sword belt.

There was a sound in the darkness, someone approaching. Mael tried to stare beyond the wavering circle which the oil flame illuminated. The belt buckle came loose. Mael rolled Ceadwalla's body aside. He tossed the ends of the freed belt around his own waist and snugged them before he rose. The shield was in his left hand and he balanced the spear on his right. The person coming toward him could be seen now. It was a man by his size, a big man porting an axe high so that its edge was a yellow crescent in the flames.

"Aye, come and be killed!" Mael shouted. He raised the long spear to hurl.

"Mael!" roared the figure. "It is you, you damn fool!" Starkad lowered his axe and bounded fully into the circle of light. He was not favoring his right leg. His arms opened to clasp his friend.

"Idiot!" Mael gasped as they pounded each others' backs. "You could see it was me, couldn't you? God knows I was so close to the fire that my bloody eyebrows were singeing."

Starkad took a step back, still clasping the Irishman's shoulders. "Oh, I could see you, all right," he agreed, "but—well, your mother wouldn't recognize you now at a glance."

Mael frowned. There was a dagger on the belt he had appropriated. The hilt was delicately jeweled and chased in gold. He was not surprised to find the blade had been silvered as well. It made a fair mirror, enough to test Starkad's statement. Mael's right cheek had been plowed with triple furrows. The blood that sheeted from those surface wounds had been runneled in turn by sweat. Far more blood had poured from the veins feeding the torn-off earlobe and the tuft of scalp that had been plucked out at the same time. That gore had splashed on Mael's shoulder and down the side of his armor.

"Oh, yes. . . ." the Irishman said. He touched the throbbing remnants of his ear, grimaced, and re-sheathed the dagger. "There're two things I still regret about this business," he stated deliberately, "and the first is that I killed this offal, this Cead-walla—" he toed the dead Briton contemptuously —"instead of stunning him. I'd like very much to be able to drop him down into that barrow alive."

"Sure," Starkad agreed, "but with all the com-motion we've set off up here, don't you think it's time we moved on?"

"Right, before moonrise for sure," Mael said. He picked up the weapons he had dropped. Pursued by memories, he led the way north down a track through the pine woods which had once been a metaled road serving the villa. "The other thing I regret is that we've got to get this gear back," the Irishman continued, shaking the spear and shield to identify them. "If we didn't have to do that, I think I'd take a chance and give those Saxon swine a better reason to remember me than some silly threat I shouted as they dropped me into their hole."

"Umm, you don't need to worry about that," the Dane said.

"Sure," Mael agreed, "I know. There's no worse waste of time and effort than worrying about revenge. And hell, they didn't do anything that my own people might not have done. If they'd run into the same sort of—problem, that is."

Starkad began to laugh quietly. Mael glanced back at him, but there was not enough light to catch the Dane's expression. "You're sounding like a woman," Starkad said through his chuckles. "I'm ashamed of you, Irishman."

"Well, what the hell do you want me to say, learned one?" Mael blazed back.

"I just meant I burned the village last night," Starkad said. "They were all drunk and sleeping. I found the place late and lay around outside till near dawn when somebody came out to piss. He told me what they'd been celebrating, and I . . . well, I got a little pissed myself. If I'd been smarter, I'd have kept one of them as a guide and saved myself a day of stumbling around these hills till I saw the lights up here. But I just wedged the doors of all the houses shut and set torches in their thatch."

"My god," Mael murmured. He had spoken truthfully about how like his own people those of

Biarki's village were. Now it was his own family which his mind saw screaming in the flames, children in the arms of women with their hair afire—

But what would he have done himself to folk who had sacrificed Starkad, though they were his own kin?

"Hey," he said at last, punching the Dane's armored chest, "you shouldn't take chances like that, you hear me?"

Starkad guffawed. "Oh, well," he said, "maybe some day you'll do something for me, do you think?"

They walked on, chuckling without speaking further. When they crossed a north-leading trail, they followed it abreast with linked arms until, deciding they had come far enough from the tomb site for reasonable safety, they bedded down in a beech copse.

There was leisure in the morning to sort matters out before moving on again. Mael's pack, along with his own shield and weapons, lay somewhere in the ash of Biarki's village. Fortunately, Gwedda had restocked the Dane's store before sending him off.

"How in the Dagda's name did you get here?" Mael asked between mouthfuls of cheese. "You were supposed to be off your foot for a week, and here you are."

"The evening after you left," Starkad explained, "Gwedda dropped the bowl of soup she was handing me. Her face went white as the grime would let it, and she said that I had to get to you as soon as I could. Seems she'd gotten a message. She also got some help—somehow—that let her fix my ankle when she couldn't have done it herself. She put her fingers on the swollen part and didn't say anything, and she wasn't looking at anything either, not that I could see. And the pain left right away, and the swelling started to go down." The Dane frowned in apology for his weakness. "It wasn't that it hurt, you know," he said. "It was just that I couldn't walk without falling on my ass again."

Mael was still thinking about an earlier comment. "Help," he repeated.

"Yeah. I didn't ask who, but I wouldn't be surprised if she had white hair and was waiting for you when we get back to the barracks," Starkad said.

The trophies they had come for, the shield and spear of Biargram, presented a problem when the friends examined them by daylight. The intaglios of the spear head appeared to be of silver, but they showed no tendency to tarnish. The symbols etched and filled there were surely meaningful, but they were part of no script with which Mael was familiar.

But whatever the characters meant, they were certain to arouse attention as the two men trekked back to the British lines. Starkad suddenly guffawed, thrusting the spear head down into a puddle and smearing the mud carefully over the metal. The result looked slovenly, but it would be ignored by everyone they passed.

The shield was more difficult to deal with. It

was about the size of the one Mael normally
carried, a four-foot circle. At some sixty pounds,
the trophy was much heavier than most shields.
The man for whom it had been made must have
been impressive if he could carry it through the
course of a long battle. The man who had forged it
had been impressive, too—if a man *had* forged the
shield. Biarki's claim for Wieland seemed less
foolish now that Mael had seen the object. The
facing was without doubt the most exceptional
work of art the Irishman had ever laid eyes on. It
was of metal, laid out in concentric circles, each
with its individual subject chased in reliefs of the
utmost delicacy. Where humans were carved, they
were so real that they seemed to speak and sing.
Mael stared at the center where the boss was
formed by the Earth encircled by the sun and
planets. He had an eerie feeling that were his eyes
good enough, he could even have seen men moving
on the surface of the tiny world.

"Tyr's *arm*," Starkad muttered. "That damned
thing'll shine a mile away. Mud'll just flake off a
big surface like that when it dries, too." Without
real hope, the Dane splashed muck across the
shield anyway—and the two men watched in surprise as the dirt streamed away instantly, as if it
were being hosed off under pressure. Not a fleck
remained on the glistening metal.

"What would you say this was made of?" Mael
asked suddenly, tapping the shield.

"The backing's hide, looks like oxhide," Starkad
said. "The rest, well, from the weight it's got to be
metal all through. Iron, I'd guess, for the core. And

the facing's silver, gold, looks like copper and tin
and—and Surtr knows what all else.''

"Not much doubt about the gold, is there?"
Mael agreed. "Nice soft gold." He touched one of
the golden figures with his dagger point, then
forced his full strength against it. The steel
skidded away. The gold remained unmarked.
Starkad shrugged.

"I'll sling it on my back and wear my cloak over
it," the Irishman decided. "Makes me look like a
fool, binding my shield up where I can't get to it if
there's trouble. But hell, I feel like a fool a lot of
the time, anyway. Let's get moving."

To avoid trouble, Mael and Starkad went thirty
miles due north before heading west, instead of
going back directly the way they had come. There
was no telling what they had stirred up behind
them. Although the return was no less dangerous
than going among the Saxons had been to begin
with, they both felt lighthearted. The sun was
bright, and they had already been successful.
Intellectually they knew that neither fact im-
proved their chances of a safe return, but sub-
consciously there was an attitude of arrogant triumph that carried the friends well through one
Saxon patrol.

They met Cerdic's men around a bend ob-
structed by hedgerows. There was no chance to
hide. Mael simply snarled to the leader of the
Saxons that they were a Dane and an Irishman
landed at Portsmouth and headed north to join
Aelle. Behind him Starkad thumbed his axe edge
and muttered audibly that he'd as soon play hack-

skull with mop-brained Saxons as he would with
the British. There were a dozen of the Saxons,
housecarls of Cerdic, but they looked uneasily
from one to another and back at the grim men they
had stopped. Mael had washed off the blood and
filth of the tomb. His cheek was still freshly
scabbed, and pus oozed from the swollen remainder of his right ear. Starkad had never
needed injuries to look like a troll.

After some hand-muffled communication
among themselves, the patrol let Mael and Starkad continue. It was the only significant encounter the friends had until they came upon a
group of Companion cavalry near Cirencester,
commanded by the same officer who had seen
them off a week and a half before. By that chance,
entry into Arthur's Britain was a matter of hand-
slapping congratulation instead of arrest for
investigation. The ride back to Moridunum was
brutal, but it was toward what was for the
moment home to Mael and the Dane.

For most of the ride, Mael and Starkad straggled
behind the courier whom they accompanied from
Gloucester. Then Mael heeled his horse into a trot
when he saw the guard post, the westernmost of
the scattered structures of the villa. Starkad followed with less enthusiasm.

The pickets, bored with inaction, rose and began
to peer toward the approaching riders. Then
another figure stood beside the Companions,
shorter than they by far. Her hair was a white fire
in the breeze. Mael whooped and kicked his tired

beast into a full gallop. Instead of reining up, he leaped from the saddle and plunged into the group of guardsmen. It was a technique which the Ard Ri's men were trained to use against hostile infantry when their horses could not be trusted to charge home. Surprised, the Companions did not react quickly enough to cut the newcomer apart. Mael came to a halt with his right leg braced against the wall of the guard post, Veleda in his arms, and a huge smile on his face. Witch and warrior kissed, oblivious to the half-drawn weapons of the startled men around them.

Veleda nuzzled the Irishman's ear, but instead of love the words she was whispering were, "Don't let anyone see what you brought back. You wouldn't be allowed to keep it."

Mael released her with a comfortable grin. The shield was still under his cloak, the spear head harmlessly mudstained. Mael had been a mercenary too long to flaunt extreme valuables. Circumstances change quickly. A wanderer with a golden sword hilt—or a silver shield—might find his skill of less interest to a lord than the goods he carried. With one hand, Mael unpinned his cloak and loosed the buckle of the shield strap beneath it. He offered both to Veleda as a package and its wrapping, saying, "You tie this to the saddle and mount my horse. I'll walk alongside."

"To the Leader," directed the captain of the guard. "Nobody comes in from the East without being taken to the Leader."

Escorted by two Companions who were by no means a guard of honor, Veleda, Mael, and the

Dane went the half mile to the villa instead of forking off toward the barracks. Starkad, too, had dismounted, saying that he was not going to be on horseback if anybody had that choice. The transfer of the shield had gone unremarked. The camouflaged spear nodded innocently in the lance socket where it had ridden since Mael was issued a horse at Cirencester.

Arthur and Lancelot, Merlin, and several officers whom Mael knew only by appearance were drinking in the shade of the west portico of the building. Three tables had been set up in a squared-off U around which the captains reclined Roman-fashion. A score of servants and guards stood or squatted nearby. Mael unbelted his sword and handed it without comment to the guard who blocked his approach. Starkad scowled but followed suit with his axe. The discussion around the tables paused as the two men stepped into the hollow of the U, facing Arthur who lay alone at the center table.

The king set his cup down. He wiped his mouth and moustache with the back of his hand. "You returned, did you, Irishman?" he said in a voice half playful, half not. "That's a little surprising, isn't it?"

"That's bloody impossible if they'd tried to do what they said," snarled Lancelot from his position at the head of the right-hand table. "You're being played for a fool." The Gaul slurped down the rest of the drink in his cup and signaled peremptorily to a cupbearer for a refill.

"We were too late," Mael explained, speaking to

Arthur and not his Master of Soldiers. Lancelot
was wearing only an embroidered tunic and was
unarmed, as were the other men at the table.
There were, however, enough armed guards at
hand to dice Starkad and Mael if the order were
given. "Biargram had already died, so we just
came back."

"Every word a lie," said Lancelot. The squat
Briton beside him laid a restraining hand on the
Gaul's ankle, but Lancelot kicked it away. "They
went to carry word to Cerdic so he can plan to hit
you—now. They came back because their oh-so-
British traitor sent them to spy some more."

Arthur laughed. "Shall I have them both killed,
then?" he asked.

Starkad growled. Mael clamped him by the
elbow, taut as a lutestring himself. He was looking
for the weapon handiest to seize if Arthur carried
through with his whimsy. Merlin grinned, the only
man relaxed in the sudden tension.

"Show him the spear, Mael," Veleda called.
"The one you stole from Ironhand's barrow!"

Mael turned. Lancelot was rising. Veleda stood
beyond the pillars at the edge of the throng of
guards. She was holding the spear toward the
Irishman, butt-forward.

"No!" a Companion snarled, snatching the
weapon away. Mael had made no attempt to take
it.

Arthur gestured. The guard, his eyes flashing
sidelong toward Mael and Starkad, scuttled
around the table and handed the spear to his
Leader.

Arthur took it without speaking. He frowned at

the mud-smeared head, then dipped a napkin in his cup and used it to rub the metal.

"We broke open the grave to make sure he was dead," Mael lied. "That's proof we were doing what we said—and didn't have time for anything more."

Merlin's face had lost its look of repose as he saw the spear being carried forward. He stood, leaning over Arthur's shoulder to get a closer look at the inlays as they were cleared. "Leader," the wizard breathed, reaching out with his index finger to trace the markings, "I must have this. . . ."

Arthur twitched the metal away in irritation. "Don't be silly," he said. "There's nothing here for you." Mael, ready to protest if the spear were given to Merlin, eased. "It's a royal weapon," the king continued. "I'll keep it." Arthur looked up at Mael and Starkad, holding the spear by the balance. "You two can go back to your barracks now," the king said. "Be ready to march in the morning. We're going to teach my Saxon brother Aelle the lesson that Lindum is to remain a British city."

Mael licked his lips but did not try to claim the spear. He had seen the glitter in the king's eyes. Lancelot either missed that warning or was too drunk to care. The Gaul stood up, his anger so sharp that blood was spotting his face where tension had popped open the old scabs. He cried, "They're making a fool of you, I say, and everybody else knows it! You *must* nail them up, the both of them, or—"

"Must, Roman?" Arthur whispered, and there

was suddenly no other sound in all the crowd. The king hurled the spear expertly, the motion smooth and backed by an arm as strong as that of any of his men. Lancelot moved at the same instant, tilting the heavy table up as he ducked his body into its shadow. The silvered spear head smashed its full length through the parquetry, slamming the table back down onto all four legs. The shaft stood quivering, an exclamation point between the king and his slowly straightening Master of Soldiers. No one else moved.

Arthur giggled. Turning to Mael and Starkad, he said, "I told you to leave, didn't I? We march in the morning." Then he looked back at Lancelot. "I think you'd better leave, too, Lancelot, and I'm for bed as well. We have a hard fight coming, and right now I seem to be too drunk to throw a spear straight."

Mael tugged circumspectly at the Dane's elbow. The two of them retrieved their weapons and stepped away with the quickly dispersing band of courtiers. Mael caught a final glimpse of Lancelot's face as the Gaul, too, strode toward his quarters. Lancelot's expression was as dead as a bowl of rendered fat.

CHAPTER THIRTEEN

"If we aren't going to do anything but stand here," Starkad complained, "I'm going to get some sleep." He threw his pack down for a pillow on a likely patch of turf and stretched out.

Before dawn the recruits had been roused and marched to a store shed. There they waited behind four troops of Companions also being issued rations for the campaign. After that they were marched back to the corral for horses. Now they waited again on one of the drill fields, trying to quiet their unfamiliar mounts. In the near distance were the lights and murmuring of one of the line troops, also awaiting the order to march. Down the road from the headquarters building clattered a messenger, one of the staff officers who had dined with Arthur the day before. Maglos, the aging Briton in charge of the recruit troop, waved the courier over with a torch.

"We're ready to mount," Maglos said.

"No, you're not," replied the courier without dismounting. He was the squat man who had tried to restrain Lancelot. "You've been moved back from third to ninth start, after Theudevald's troop over there. Run your men through another kit inspection and make sure none of them are trying to carry their gold around in their blanket roll."

"Second to the end?" Maglos shrieked. "Christ's bleeding *wounds*, you know how most of these sows ride! If you start me ninth, it'll be the bloody watch after midnight before I make camp!"

"Well, better you and not everybody behind you as well," the staff captain said unsympathetically. "Check 'em out good. If any of these oafs panics because the Saxons are in the baggage and they're afraid they'll lose their loot—well, it'd be better for them if they'd banked it here with the camp prefect, and it'd be better for you if you'd never been born."

Nodding, the courier rode off toward Theudevald's troop across the field. Maglos cursed and turned back to his own unit. The three other Companions of the cadre were murmuring among themselves. "Everybody on your goddamned feet for kit inspection," Maglos roared. Mael, already standing, pulled Veleda a little closer. His eyes were on the captain. Starkad, of course, ignored the shouting.

"Christ, what sorry whoresons," Maglos said. His frustration was real as he looked down the line of parti-equipped men, many of whom were not able to ride or speak a common language. "I'm going to tell you people something, and I don't want anybody to think it's a joke," the Briton continued. "You aren't being marched to Lindum to fight. You're going because there won't be enough trained men back here to control you if somebody gets some smart-ass ideas about desertion or looting. You're a burden on the war, and we don't need any more burdens. So if any one of you—or all of you together—steps out of line for one instant, you're dead. You're nailed up to a tree in less time than it takes to shit. Do as you're told, do *just* as you're told, and maybe some of you can live long enough to be worth keeping."

Maglos and his men began working down the line of recruits one by one. His voice blurred by his cloak, Starkad said, "Why put so much of his army back here where it's five days' march to any place the Saxons are going to be? And five more damned days on horseback for me."

"A safe place to train recruits," Mael guessed idly, his attention still on Maglos.

"No," said Veleda unexpectedly. "One troop would be enough for a cadre and a guard, love. Arthur doesn't keep ten back here for training or for the Saxons. They're to keep the landowners in support."

"Huh?" Mael said. "They do support him. They always have."

"Together they *have* to support him," the woman agreed, "or the only question is whether the Saxons or your Irish kin will pick their bones first. But one by one, it's different. They're self-willed men, these magnates. They're powerful,

each in his own right. Who's to say that one's grain
levy wasn't excessive, or the weight of bronze for
armor wasn't more than another's smelters pro-
duced?"

"So if there's any trouble, Arthur sends in the
troops and burns their roofs over their heads,"
Starkad chuckled, his eyes still closed. "Then the
rest of them ante up."

"He doesn't have to burn anything," Veleda protested. "If a delivery's late or the weight is short,
Gawain or one of the other captains takes a troop
or two to the landowner's villa. He just stays for a
while. After feeding a hundred men and horses for
a month, the landowner makes his next tax payment on time even if his children may have to go
hungry. Arthur's taught him that they most certainly *will* go hungry if he scrimps the levy again.
And there's no fighting or need for it. No one
magnate is so foolish as to think he can drive off a
troop of Companions, and no group of magnates is
so foolish as to think they'd live for long if they did
all rise and defeat Arthur."

Maglos had reached them. Mael, knowing that
Biargram's shield, the only thing of note he had,
was hidden back in the barracks, was relaxed.
Pointing at Veleda, the Briton snapped, "What's
she doing here?"

"Waiting for the fools in charge of this botch to
get moving," Starkad rumbled before Mael could
get control of his tongue. "Then she'll tell us good-
bye. And until you *do* get moving, just leave us
alone. Neither I nor my friend ever left a fight for
fear of losing our bedrolls."

The captain froze. He might in his frustration have carried the matter on, had not one of his cadre tugged at his arm. "Theudevald's troop's moving out," he reported, pointing.

Maglos sighed. "Prepare to mount and form column of fours," he ordered. "We won't get the word for another half hour—but it'll take that long for some of you hogs to get straight."

When the horn finally blew, Mael leaned over his saddle and kissed Veleda again. The Greek in the rank behind cursed as his horse balked to avoid the Irishman's. Starkad turned and stared back. The curses stopped as the Greek's throat froze.

"I'll think of you," Veleda said. "Of you both." Then she was gone and Mael and Starkad were headed into the first of five days of brutal route marching.

The ten troops of the Western Squadron were being sent off at half-hour intervals, interspersed with lightly escorted strings of remounts. There was no baggage train. Without fanfare, wagon loads of supplies had been sent forward weeks earlier to supplement the sparse forage available at the edge of the War Zone. The rations of biscuit, cheese, and dried meat which each man carried were for use after the battle, when the pace of flight or pursuit might not allow normal measures.

The squadron followed Roman roads for the most part. Cracked by subsidence, rutted by centuries of wheels gouging their surface, the roads were still straight and broad and as useful to

Arthur's army as they had been to Hadrian's. The troops crowded civilians to the side and off onto muddy shoulders to curse at the miles-long road-block. Where the civilians were driving animals to market, the cursing became mutual. The column, regular enough at the start, began to bunch and straggle. One of the horses in Mael's troop found itself in the midst of a flock of sheep. It suddenly went into a whinnying funk. When the horse bucked him off, the rider broke his neck by land-ing on a milepost instead of the mud.

"First blood to Aelle," Starkad laughed. But the next time his own mount shied, the Dane sawed his reins as if he meant to pull the horse up on its hind legs.

Near noon the forlorn hope reached the pre-arranged bivouac site at Pen-y-Gar. In theory the rear guard should have joined them in three hours or so. Actually it was long after sundown that the hard-faced Companions chivvied in the last of the recruits. Streams to ford had caused confusion and delay. Hamlets along the route were built out onto the ancient roadway, narrowing it to the width of one horse and leaving the flagstones slimy with offal. All the recruits were fighting men, but a good number were not riders. Even the ones who were used to horses were unready for a regimen of fifty miles a day. Saddles became weapons which pounded and chafed. Toward the end, two of the recruits had to be tied to their pommels. When the cords were cut, the men fell as if heart-stabbed.

That first night the recruits were too late for a

hot meal and too tired to care. If they had been
less exhausted, they would have mutinied. As it
was, even the failure to place guards as ordered
was the response of inability rather than disaffec-
tion.

The next three days repeated the first. Mael had
less trouble than most of the other recruits. He
had ridden since childhood and was in as good
condition as any man in the army. Starkad rode by
dogged stubborness. Others were able to make the
journey; therefore he would. The Dane spoke very
little after the first hours, dismounting mechani-
cally at Mael's direction and swallowing food as if
oblivious to its taste or texture. Starkad was not a
natural horseman, but his strength and sense of
balance were enough to keep him mounted. Grace-
less, hulking, and silent, the Dane looked like a
bear on horseback. Even in their most savage ill-
tempers, none of the other men mocked the spec-
tacle he made, however.

At twilight of the fourth day, the squadron
entered the walled city of Leicester. The population was already swollen to triple its usual size
by refugees, the troops of the Southern Squadron
who had been pulled north for this thrust like
those of the West, and the jackals who always
batten or soldiers nearing combat. There were
whores and their pimps, gamblers, ale merchants
and silk sellers. Men need release as death ap-
proaches. Each has his own way of seeking that
release, and the cost no longer matters.

There were no Saxons save prisoners within

fifty miles of Leicester. That did not keep the farm families from pouring in to the protection of the walls. The civilians knew only generalities: Aelle was moving north—or was it west? Arthur was gathering his whole force to block the Saxons. To the households on lonely farms, there was little to choose between the two sides on the march. Either might loot and rape, would perhaps kill and burn. . . . Better to hide in a city where only one side was to be met, where the officer's eyes were sharper. At any rate, there were more potential victims and the resulting better chance of being overlooked. Leicester stank of excrement and animals sickened by hard driving and lack of fodder. The streets were choked with people, moving and eating and trying to sleep. The householders kept their doors locked and prayed for deliverance.

Like the stench, rumor was everywhere. The recruit troop dismounted in what had been the market square, now converted to their bivouac—the Southern Squadron had usurped all the permanent quarters available. Mael heard one well-dressed townsman saying to another, "Yes, they massacred every man of the Northern Squadron. Only half a dozen managed to get out with their skins. Geraint himself was captured. It won't take Aelle a day to storm Lindum, now—and how long do you think we can last in Ratae with Lindum gone?"

The speakers passed on, ignoring the hundreds of armed men around them. Mael grimaced and said to Starkad, "Just tents for us. Anything I can get you?"

"A drink and a cunt," the Dane replied with un-expected animation. The city—always a place of excitement to a countryman like Starkad—seemed to have revived his spirits. The Dane nodded at the warren of streets leading off the square. "Bet we can find both of them out there pretty quick."

Mael frowned. "How about the horses?" he asked.

"I can't drink 'em," Starkad grinned, "and I'm damned well not going to try to fuck 'em either if there's better stuff around. If somebody wants to steal mine, he's welcome to it."

Mael looked around the milling throng. Nearby was a Lombard recruit he knew slightly. "Vaces," the Irishman said, putting his hand on the Lom-bard's shoulder, "get my horse and my friend's here fed and stabled, will you? I'll make it worth your time."

"Hey, why me?" the other man yelped, but Mael could already see Starkad disappearing into an alley. The Irishman followed him with only a hand waved back at Vaces.

Leicester had inns, but they were stuffed with officers. There would always be entrepreneurs ready to care for the lower ranks, though. One of those benefactors had set up in what had been a fuller's shop before the influx of soldiers. The owner and his family now kept to their living quarters upstairs—the trap door in the ceiling was bolted. The ground floor was rented to a Moroccan at an exorbitant rate. The Moroccan, of course, was getting his profit quickly from watered beer and a percentage of the dice game in the corner, despite the expense of the three bouncers who kept a semblance of order.

Noise bloomed even out into the street, and within the big room it was at first hard to think. There was no furniture except the rough-sawn bar. Behind that barrier, the Moroccan and a vacant-faced girl dipped beer from open tuns. The bare walls echoed the din of a score of languages. Virtually all of the customers were armed; it was not a dive in which a civilian could have survived, had one been foolish enough to enter. "I'll get it," Starkad rumbled to Mael as he eyed the press around the bar.

A blond veteran with bandages on his left foot stood near them. When his ear caught Starkad's accent, he brightened and said, "Hey! Danish?"

"Yeah, a long time ago," Starkad agreed, watching the Companion sharply.

"Hel take it, we're next to brothers here in this snakepit," the blond man said. He thumbed coins out of his purse. "I'm Tostig Radbard's son, got a squad in the Northern Squadron. Geraint sent me back here when I got gimped up at Lindum." Tostig gestured at his injured foot. "Thing is, I can't even fight my way up to the bar with this. I'll buy if you'll bring me one back. No, two—stuff's so pissing thin it's not worth it to drink one at a time."

Starkad clapped the other Dane on the back. "Sure, I'll bring you beer and you don't need to worry about paying," the big man said, his momentary suspicion forgotten. He began to bull his way to the bar, ignoring the curses of the men he thrust aside.

"What *did* happen at Lindum?" Mael asked Tostig. The Irishman and the Dane were about of a size. The blond man had obviously seen his share of service.

"Same thing always happens when the Saxons come play with us," Tostig chuckled. "We killed 'em by the shit-load and sent the rest off screaming for their mommies." The Companion was speaking loudly, but Mael had to strain to hear in the surrounding racket. "Two weeks ago, Aelle marched north with his whole levy. Must'a been ten thousand of 'em. We're based at Lindum, right? But we pulled back to Margidunum and the fort there. There's only five hundred of us and that makes the odds a little long, even for Geraint.

"So the Saxons throw up earthworks to blockade Lindum. And the people in Lindum don't do anything, and we don't do anything—and the Saxons get pretty damned hungry. There wasn't a goddamn thing to eat bigger than a field mouse left outside the city. You know the Saxons; they couldn't organize a supply train from the rear any better than they could've flown to Mikligard. So after a week, Aelle went back home with all but a couple thousand farmers. Them he left at Lindum to keep the place bottled up. He'd be ready to move the main body as soon as something happened on our side."

Tostig chuckled again. "Only what happened is, we caught the blockading force at dawn with their pants down. They hadn't even set up outposts, much less built a proper stockade against whoever might come up from the rear. We slaughtered

Saxons from Lindum to the River Dubglas. I don't
know half a dozen besides myself of our boys who
aren't ready to ride again today. And I could if I
had to."

Starkad, three mugs of beer in each hand,
pushed his way back in time to catch the last of
what Tostig was saying. "If you hadn't been in
such a hurry to do it yourselves," he remarked as
he handed the drinks around, "the bloody Saxons
wouldn't have had time to get their shit straight
again, like I hear they have now. The army together could've cleared Lindum and then gone
through Aelle's whole kingdom before he got his
breeches laced."

Starkad's tone was friendly, but the criticism
made the Companion bridle. "Bloody general,
have we here? Knows more'n Geraint or the
Leader himself. Well, let me tell you what it's like,
buddy. We can beat a Saxon army any goddamn
time we like—you'll see that in a day or two or I'm
no fucking squad leader. But there's a *lot* of them.
Not just the soldiers, but back home. And we've
got three squadrons, maybe fifteen hundred men
counting every bugger and ass-wipe.

"We can beat 'em—" Tostig paused to slurp a
long draft from one mug. The vessels were terra
cotta, unglazed and already dark with the brew
oozing through the porous material—"because
we're mounted, we're armed, and we're *trained*.
And all the training in the world doesn't matter a
fuck if you're trotting down a lane and some hick
behind a hedgerow puts a pike through your back.
Or you're riding some bitch in a stable and her

husband cobs you with a wooden hay fork. *That's* why the Leader knows what he's doing."

Mael waited for Starkad's reaction. To his relief, the big Dane only laughed and downed his own beer. "Well, you've had your fun already," Starkad said to Tostig. "You ought to be willing for the rest of us to have some, too."

Relaxed, the three men finished the round. Starkad fetched another. As they drank he asked Tostig, "You want to come with us and find a whore?"

The Companion shook his head. "Hard enough to get a drink," he explained. "Damn if I'm going to try to get into a knock-shop. Not with a bum foot and a thousand extra troopers in town."

Bawling happy good-bye's, Starkad led Mael out into the street again. The night air was cool and the relative silence itself palpable. "You know, I'd just about settle for a bed to sleep in," the Irishman suggested.

"Balls," said his friend. "Now, if you were a whore, where would you be?"

They followed several narrow streets blindly, meeting other soldiers as drunken and confused as they were. All the doors were barred, the windows uncompromisingly shuttered. "Look," Mael protested, "this is a pretty good district and we sure as hell aren't supposed to be in it. If we run into the Watch—"

"Then we'll ask *them* where to find cunt," finished Starkad good-humoredly. "Anyway—"

There was a scream from the house beside them, a two-story structure of brick and tile. The front door flew open and a woman darted two paces into the street. The man chasing her seized her hair in his left hand and tugged her to a stop. He raised his bloodstained sword. Mael recognized his face in the moonlight; it was the Herulian recruit he had watched Lancelot pulp a few weeks before. Without thinking, Mael grabbed the raised sword arm and yanked the Herulian back into a knee in the kidneys. The weapon clanked to the cobblestones. Mael heard a grunt behind him. He turned. A second Herulian, this one wearing the medallion of a trained Companion, had started out of the house to his friend's assistance. Starkad hit him in the pit of the stomach with his axe helve. The struggle was over seconds from its start.

Starkad was holding the sobbing girl with his left hand. She was British, perhaps sixteen years old now that Mael had a chance to look at her closely. "Now, let's see," the Dane murmured, pushing past the Herulian he had disabled. An oil lamp was alight within. It shone on a room that seemed to have been painted scarlet. A middle-aged woman and a boy of about eight lay on the floor. They had been hacked at repeatedly. One of the child's hands had been flung separately onto the cold hearth. A balding, corpulent man in a night shift had fallen on the stairs and skidded face-downward almost to the bottom. Blood was oozing onto his body from above, down the treads from the upper floor.

Mael had followed Starkad through the doorway. There was a loud clatter and shouting behind them. Six Companions with drawn swords and the white armbands of the Watch burst in. The British girl looked up wildly. "Not these!" she cried, throwing her hands over the Dane who still supported her. "The others!"

"Check the upstairs," the squad leader snapped to one of his men. "And what *were* you doing here, buddy?" he asked Starkad.

Mael spoke before his friend could. "Got lost looking for the bivouac," he said. "We heard screams, and when those two—" the Herulians' hands were being bound expertly in front of them —"chased the girl out, we grabbed them."

The Watch leader grunted. "At least you didn't do all this," he agreed. "Not without getting more blood on you than you seem to have."

From above, his subordinate called in British, "Two more kids up here, sarge. The shutters're open on one of the back windows. Dunno if those fucking Germans were just drunk or if they planned to get in a little early looting."

"Christ," said the noncom. "You two," he added to Mael and Starkad, "get the fuck back to where you belong. We'll get these slime off to where *they* belong."

The Watch filed out. Each of the prisoners was walking, secured by a baton thrust between his back and elbows and held on either end by a guard. Starkad followed them out and closed the door softly behind him. When he saw that the Watch had forgotten about him and Mael, he opened the latch again silently and tugged the

Irishman inside with him. The bodies lay as they
had. The girl, bent over a table weeping, looked
up.

"What in hell are you doing?" Mael whispered
hoarsely.

"Comforting the bereft," Starkad whispered
back. Rising, the girl threw herself into the Dane's
arms. She was sobbing uncontrollably.

Mael knuckled his lips in disbelief. Finally he
started up the stairs, walking very carefully. "At
least there'll be a softer bed here than back in the
square," he muttered to himself.

The war horns aroused Mael and Starkad as
surely as they did the troops billeted under canvas
in the market. The two friends stumbled back to
their unit, earning a black look but no comment
from Maglos. Starkad had filched a skin of
Spanish wine from the house in which they had
slept. It was enough to square Vaces. "Her kin, her
mother's folk'll be appointed guardians," the Dane
said. "They'll strip the place. I figured we had as
much need for the booze as they did. And she
didn't mind. Her name was Luad."

The two Herulians had been crucified to either
side of the North Gate, through which the
combined squadrons rode on the final stage of
their advance.

The way to Lincoln was deserted, stripped of all
peaceful traffic by the threat of war. The Companions rode easily, four abreast. Even the lowering clouds were a boon for fending off the hammer

of the sun. One brief shower set the cursing regulars to checking the fastenings of their bow cases, but few of the recruits were archers. Though their troop was near the end of the column as usual, the recruits reached Lincoln well before sundown. Geraint's force was in its normal barracks within the city, but they had palisaded a camp outside the walls for the two reinforcing squadrons.

Maglos and the rest of the captains attended a staff meeting at dusk. When the Briton returned, he summoned his motley troop together. The recruits stood around a cresset flaring in front of the four tents allotted to them. "Listen good," Maglos said in British. "You that can't understand, wait till I'm done and ask somebody who could." Realizing that what he had said made no sense, the captain scowled at himself and added, "Well, you know what I mean.

"Tomorrow's the real thing. Geraint left scouts across the Dubglas, that's the river just east. They rode back yesterday. Aelle's there and he's got a *lot* of men, maybe ten thousand. That's all of his own crew and anybody else who wanted to get in on the loot they're planning on. He's camped just across the river. We're going to meet him there in the morning."

The veteran Companion rubbed the knuckles of his hands together. "You guys aren't trained. You can't ride and you can't shoot, most of you. That doesn't mean you can't fight. It better not mean you can't fight. We'll be right in the center of the whole fucking line. The Leader'll be with us, *us*, and it'll be our job to protect him against any Saxons who get through. They'll be keying on him, don't kid yourself."

"If we're so goddamn worthless," demanded one of the Franks, "then why put us in the center?"

Maglos nodded as if unaware of the hostility of the question. "Everybody else'll have to ride or shoot," he said. "All you have to do is wait for the Saxons to run up to you. Then you spear them. Nobody who can't do that ought to'a come looking for a berth with the Leader."

The grizzled Briton looked around the faces of his troop. "One more thing," he said. "You'll stand where you're put and wait. If anybody runs away, they'll be hunted down after the battle by whoever wins. You saw those two bastards at the gate this morning. That's not half what the Saxons like to do to Companions *they* capture. You're fighting men, that shouldn't be any problem.

"But none of you is going to leave your position and charge early, either. There's no glory in getting an arrow in your back, and that's just what you'll have before you've taken three steps. You don't know, you *can't* know what the Leader's going to do. But he's got to know exactly what every man in his army does. That's how we've beat the Saxons before; that's how we'll beat 'em tomorrow. Anybody who doesn't think they can live with that had best consider falling on his sword. It's apt to be quicker than disobeying orders."

Maglos was breathing heavily with emotion. His eyes caught Starkad's. The Dane was as calm as a

269 The Dragon Lord

block of granite, impassive and untouched by anything that had been said. "Believe me or don't!" Maglos snarled. "But you'll learn tomorrow! Now get to bed!"

"When we get into line," Mael said very softly to Starkad as they trudged to their tent, "let's just wait for the Saxons to come to us."

"Because that loudmouthed Briton tells us to?" the Dane snorted.

"Umm," Mael temporized, "because Arthur plans his battles so he can win them. And I've got a taste for wanting to be on the winning side. More loot."

"You kill everybody on the other side, then you win," Starkad muttered, but Mael was no longer afraid of his friend deciding to break ranks. When the Dane went berserk he was beyond reason or argument, but Starkad could control the onset of the rage—and Mael was now sure he would do so.

CHAPTER FOURTEEN

The Northern Squadron marched out of Lincoln in the middle of the night. Mael heard the gates squeal, then the soft thudding of hooves. Geraint's men knew the terrain well enough to be able to take up their positions in the dark. They were reinforcing the troop left as pickets at the Dubglas ford when the rest of the squadron pulled back to await Arthur.

The two remaining squadrons rode at dawn. For the first time, Arthur's men left the network of wide, stone-dressed Roman thoroughfares. Their captains led them along narrow tracks in single file through woods and between tall hedges. The forks would have been bewildering had not Geraint left guides at each doubtful turn to direct the unfamiliar troops. When the rear guard came by, the guides would join it.

Near Lincoln, the dead Saxons had all been dragged into mass graves by conscripted civilians, but from a mile beyond the walls there were constant reminders of the rout. The bodies were bloated and so blackened by decay that their skins were indistinguishable from their leather garments. Perhaps the cows and the flies who lay across the corpses like sheets had risen when the first horsemen approached. By the time Mael and Starkad passed near the end of the column, they could ride within a foot of a cadaver rolled barely to the margin of the lane. The carrion eaters would still ignore them. The horses' hooves stirred up the scent of death along with the dust.

"None of them fought," Starkad noted idly as he and Mael rode side by side on a stretch wide enough to do so. "All the wounds are from behind."

"They were afraid," Mael said, realizing that the Dane's comment was accurate. Sometimes the stub of an arrow shaft protruded, broken when the archer tried to retrieve it; sometimes a diamond-shaped wound gaped between the shoulder blades where a lance had driven in with the stunning impact of a horse and armored man behind it. Less frequently, the victims had died when swords bit through skulls or collarbones in a huge, black fan of blood.

Starkad snorted in disgust. "You can't run away from a horseman," he said. "If you stand, you can maybe take a few of them with you to Hel."

The words were not braggadocio, Mael thought to himself. The big Dane really could not imagine panic, fear so great that a man would rather die than face it . . . though the fear itself was generally of death. Mael could not be like Starkad, but the Irishman knew from a hundred bloody fights that there was no fear so great that he could not function despite it. And invariably in the past, his opponents had proven to have had the greater reason for fear.

Forest opened onto plowed land, a narrow canal of sunlit ground between wooded dikes. In the cleared area, men and beasts were milling in disorder. Unarmed handlers from the support sections were leading clumps of riderless horses out of the way of the troops debouching from the woods to the west. Beyond the handlers, dismounted Companions were filing into the eastern woods, carrying all their equipment including the spears they seemed to be bearing instead of lances this day. The men in sight all appeared to be from British tribes, armed with long self bows instead of the more handy composite bows Arthur imported for the mercenaries of other nationalities. The western Britons had grown up with their highly effective weapon. Though the shorter bow of horn and sinew bonded to wood was more useful for a horseman, Arthur had not attempted to retrain his own countrymen.

Maglos rested his hands on his double pommels, counting his men as they appeared. "All right," he shouted. "Recruit Troop, dismount! Give your horses to the handlers, four to a man. Then follow me. And bring all your goddamned gear, especially your water skins, or by god you'll parch like raisins before this day is out."

Stumbling, his legs not working quite like legs after long days of gripping a horse, Mael followed Maglos up a recent slash in second-growth forest. Just behind him strode Starkad, bubblingly happy to be afoot again. The Dane's axe arced out in fun and nipped a two-inch branch from a pine tree. One of the cadre yelped a startled protest as the blade looped back at him. The Dane laughed and wiped sap from the steel.

A Companion stood at the head of the trail where the slope flattened and occasional glints of armor and sunlight could be seen through the trees. "Which unit?" the guide snapped at Maglos, then noticed the varied gear of the men beyond. "Oh, Christ, the recruits," the Companion muttered. "Straight on ahead and spread to the right, three feet between men. And keep 'em the fuck back from the edge of the trees. Every three feet, forming on the command staff."

Ten yards further were knots of men and horses —Arthur and a cornicine, Lancelot, and a blocky man holding the red dragon standard. A fifth man walked from behind a tree at the sound of the recruits trampling through the brush. Mael recognized Cei in a helmet whose long iron nose-strap seemed to split his face. The four subordinates were on foot, though their horses stood drop-reined just behind them. The king himself was still mounted.

Mael took his position to Cei's immediate right where Maglos motioned him. He met the seneschal's eyes, then turned and knelt by a tree. Pre-

tending the command group was not present, the
Irishman slid forward to where he could look out
over the east slope of the hill. Maglos was spreading the rest of the troop along the crest, man by
man.

The valley below had the cross section of a
shallow U, half a mile from ridge to ridge. The
floor was broad and flat, marked with the darker
green of reeds where the Dubglas meandered
down the middle. The slopes were gentle but
noticeable, grassy except for an occasional out-
cropping of limestone. At the base of the hill were
a pair of incongruous pennons set on staves some
two hundred yards apart. They were apparently
centered on the command staff. Mael's eyes
narrowed as he saw the flags. To either side the
Dubglas glittered in a narrow band, but in front of
Mael the water purled and whitened over
shallows. Twenty of Geraint's horsemen, the only
Companions in plain view, patrolled slowly up and
down the meadow to the west of the ford.

Across the stream were the Saxons. The rumor
that they were ten thousand strong might have
been an underestimate. They were in such disorder that it was hard to say. The far side of the
valley was covered with a litter of tents, cook
fires, and wagons. Men sat or sprawled among
draft animals and the sheep and swine driven
along with the levy for food. The Saxons had built
no palisade. The only guards apparent were the
parties of housecarls formed in front of the largest
tents around the war standards.

The Saxons were disorganized, but their
numbers were stunning.

Many of the Saxons were awake and straggling down toward the stream in small groups, some to draw water but many to shout insults at the mounted vedettes on the other side. The Dubglas was no more than a hundred feet wide at the ford, though the current there was swift enough over the slick stones to make crossing an awkward business. Standing at the edge of the water, a few Saxon archers shot at the Companions. Their shafts wobbled harmlessly short. Arthur's men appeared to be paying no attention.

There was a bit of discussion among the vedettes. One of the horsemen, a Hun with a naked torso and hair streaming down his back like a horse's tail, uncased his bow and nocked an arrow. Lancelot caught the motion out of the corner of his eye. The Gaul broke off his conversation with the king. The Saxon archers began stumbling back away from the stream in sudden panic. The mud clutched at their feet. Several dropped their weapons to scrabble on all fours.

The Hun ignored them, arching his back and his bow together. He drew and loosed the arrow in a single motion. The nearby Saxons froze, but the arrow curved high beyond them. It plunged down into the group of armored housecarls in front of the largest tent, three hundred yards away. The high-pitched hiss of the dropping shaft was enough warning that the Saxons looked up from their banter in the instant before the arrow struck. Then the guards exploded apart. They left one of their number screaming on the ground with the arrow through the flesh of his right leg. The standard he had held, a boar's skull on a ten-foot

pole, wobbled and dipped to the earth before any
of the other housecarls could catch it. The Hun's
laughter pealed into the sudden silence of the
Saxon camp.

Lancelot was swearing in Celtic, his knuckles
white on the hilt of his sword. "They were told not
to shoot without orders, not to do *anything*
without orders!" he snarled. "I'll have him flayed
alive when he—"

"Be silent," said Arthur, without particular
emphasis. The king was squinting for a better look
at the archer. There was a slight smile on his face.
"That was Edzil, was it not?" he asked, as much of
Lancelot as of anyone. "One makes allowances for
Huns, you know, Roman."

The tall Master of Soldiers said nothing, though
his face grew pale. After a moment, Lancelot released his sword so that it could slip the six
inches back to home in its scabbard.

Starkad nudged Mael and gestured to the left.
An armored horseman from the flank was picking
his way along the tree line toward Arthur's position. The rider was alone, but the gilt and silver of
his arms suggested his rank. Lancelot noticed him,
too, and said, "Here's Geraint. He'd better have
everything in order or . . ."

Geraint nudged his horse into the command
group. "Or what, Lancelot?" he asked. He was
older than most of the Companions and rode with
the stiffness of a man laced together with scar
tissue. "Everything's fine. We set them between
the two lances, from there up the slope to maybe
forty yards from here. All of them you sent for-

ward. They're waiting for the Saxons to come."

"Well, that's what they're doing now," said Cei
expressionlessly. Every eye in Arthur's force
riveted itself on the ford and the Saxons beginning
to splash across it.

Not all of Aelle's army was advancing, nor were
those who were crossing the Dubglas in as good an
order as even the footing would allow. Bands of
men, two or three or up to a score, plunged into
the water, wearing long swords and full armor.
The froth rose to their knees. They shouted, keeping their heavy shields raised to cover their faces
and torsos against the expected sleet of arrows.

None of the patrolling Companions fired. Their
officer gave a quick command. The squad rode
north along the stream, then turned sharply away
from the water and up the hill. The Saxon rabble
on the other bank shrieked triumphantly and sent
a useless volley of missiles after Arthur's men.
Most of the arrows did not even reach the west
side of the Dubglas. The last of the riders to dis-
appear into the woods cloaking the British left
flank was the Hun, Edzil. He turned toward the
Saxons. They cried out in fear, but instead of
firing again the Hun laughed and pumped his
finger at the footmen unmistakably.

Cei and Lancelot had mounted their horses.
Mael, who had been lying on his belly, rose and
ran his left arm through the loops of his target.
"Give me a minute, will you?" Geraint requested
without concern. The squadron commander rode
back toward his position at a canter.

The leading Saxons were berserkers and cham-

pions from among the housecarls, and thegns with
a reputation for valor or the desire to gain one.
When those leaders had waded ashore on the west
bank, the mass of the army began to follow them
across the ford in a brown wave. The Saxons
slipped, spilling themselves and their neighbors in
tangles of limbs and equipment. "Now!" Starkad
shouted. The Dane had risen to his feet and slung
his shield around to his back where it gave no protection but would not interfere with his axe.

Arthur gave his cornicine an order. Mael could
not hear it in the din from the Saxons and the
excited exclamations of the recruits nearby. The
horn sounded a five-note series. Maglos and his
cadre ran behind the untrained men shouting, "No
farther than the standards!" as the whole British
army shuddered forward into the sunlight.

The king was splendid at its head and center. He
wore full mail, including chaps which covered his
legs without preventing his inner thighs from gripping his horse firmly. All Arthur's armor had been
silvered. The bronze wings flaring to either side of
the helmet had been picked out in gold as well.
The midmorning brightness made the king a lightning bolt rather than a man. The dragon standard
borne at his side filled with the first breeze and
unfurled its scarlet terror. The scales of bronze
and gold worked into the standard's fabric hissed
as though the serpent were a living creature. The
Saxons fell silent, save for a few shouts of bravado
which rang more fearful than frightening.

Arthur drew up just clear of the trees. His
armored squadrons, tightening ranks which the

forest had disarrayed, halted to either flank. And the Saxon swarm which had stopped in fear, divided by the river at the king's appearance, raised a great shout and rushed to reunite on the west bank.

Whimpering with frustration but not quite mad enough to charge alone, Starkad turned from the enemy and hugged Mael to his breast. "What's he waiting for?" the Dane demanded in a voice that half the army could hear. "We could—while the river cut them—"

"Don't worry," Mael murmured, patting his friend's iron back like someone consoling a child on the death of a pet, "it'll be all right for us, yes. . . ." Mael's eye caught the glitter of the king's helm. He looked up at the monarch. Arthur, cold and remote as a statue from Karnak, was staring at the two of them. Mael stared back, repeating, "It'll be all right."

Starkad shuddered, regained control of himself. He gave the Irishman a final squeeze before loosing him.

Arthur's force, now that Mael could see it whole for the first time, was drawn up as a line of infantry between two solid masses of ranked horsemen. The center was made up of the native Britons and the recruits, dismounted to either side of the king. The Britons were setting their spears butt-first in the soil and propping their shields against them. That accomplished, the Companions strung their longbows and waited for orders.

The cavalry on the flanks was more restive.

Mael noted that the mounted Companions, too, were handling their bows. Their lances pointed vertically upward—ready, but waiting.

Like a crystal with a core of glittering steel, the Saxon host grew by accretion. Men still wandered down the hillside to the ford, yawning and shifting their equipment into more comfortable postures. When they reached the river they paused, then splashed through it to find places among the thousands of warriors already knotted on the other side. In the center of the Saxon line, the nobles and their paid men were ranked ten deep around the standards. Those placed in the forefront were there of their own will. Already they stamped and clashed blades against their shield bosses. From the second rank rose Aelle's own standard, the Battle Swine, raised from the dirt to lower over the array.

The men on the fringes of the formation, two-thirds or more of the Saxon force, were of another sort. These were the peasants who owed their thegns produce at harvest time and their bodies in war. It was men like these—freeborn and free-holders, but living at a subsistence level—whom Aelle had left as a tripwire at Lincoln. They had no mail coats nor even the long tunics of iron-studded leather which some of the housecarls wore. In linen and wool and occasionally a steer-hide jerkin, the peasants eyed the archers waiting on the hill before them. They shuddered, then edged a little closer inward toward their armored betters. The peasants' weapons were generally spears, leavened with a few axes and billhooks—tools on any day of the year save days of battle. There were a few men carrying bows. Since the bowmen generally lacked even the flimsy bucklers carried by most of the carls, they were especially determined to worm their way in from the exposed fringes where they might have been of some use.

In a clear, carrying voice, Arthur cried, "Now to grind the vermin away! Loose the horse!"

The cornicine lilted out a call that horns on both wings echoed instantly. The twenty troops of horsemen under Gawain and Geraint scissored down from the flanks at a fast walk rather than a gallop. The Companions began shooting at two hundred yards. Their targets, the mass of Saxon peasantry, crumpled like grass in a hailstorm. Each horseman carried two dozen arrows in his quiver. The front rank of nomad mercenaries, Huns and easterners to whom horses and horn-bows were a way of life, spent their loads in less than a minute. The remaining Companions were mostly Germans of one nation or another who had been as innocent of archery as the Saxons until Arthur trained them. They were slower to fire, but there were eight hundred of them.

The Saxon wings disintegrated under the weight of fire. The carls had no protection but shields of wicker and unstrapped wood—and the bodies of the men dying in front of them. Arthur's men were using broadheads that slashed wounds as wide as paired thumbs. In the soft targets the arrows still penetrated completely and pinned men to their dying neighbors.

Without any defense or means to retaliate,

without any stiffening from the chieftains who
were concentrated in the center of the array, the
surviving peasants broke and ran. The Dubglas,
more an incident than an impediment when the
Saxons advanced across it unopposed, became a
bloody deathtrap. Men who slipped were trampled
into the rocks. Disabling wounds left others to die,
trying to scream in the frothing water that
smothered them. The ford was only a hundred
yards wide. It packed the thousands of fugitives
into a still denser killing zone for the arrows that
ripped among them. Fallen bodies dammed the
water into a bloody pond. The surface foamed
repeatedly as it broke through the obstruction,
then stilled again when fresh corpses took the
place of those washed downstream. Mael turned
to speak to Starkad as the last rank of Companions
wheeled their horses. Only then did the Irishman
realize that he could not shout over the cries from
the river a quarter mile away.

The cavalrymen were reforming and again fill-
ing their quivers from stores borne from Lincoln
by mule train. A few horses had stumbled. Their
riders had either remounted their own animals or
swung up on the pillions of neighboring riders.
Arthur's fighting strength was undiminished.

But so, despite the carnage, was that of the
Saxons.

Aelle's thegns and housecarls had not been
touched by the arrows. Their shields were broad
and thick, wrapped and studded with iron. Raising
them, chanting a war hymn, the Saxons began to
plod forward toward the thin British line. Aelle's

men still outnumbered their opponents two or three to one. Rightly, they feared neither lances nor the arrows with which the squadrons were being feverishly replenished. The Saxon formation was a wedge of interlocked shields, the inexorable swine-array whose invention had been Wotan's greatest gift to men of valor.

"Look there," Starkad said and pointed. Half a dozen horsemen still loitered near the Saxons. As the wedge began to advance, these Companions cantered even closer. Extra quivers were slung across the withers of their mounts and their bows seemed extensions of their arms. They were Huns.

Saxons in the center of the array raised their shields overhead; those on the left flank facing the horsemen crouched down so that their heads and torsos were covered by their shields. Completely protected, the Saxons waited for the arrows to come.

Come they did, stabbing into the bare calves and ankles of the outermost men of the swine-array. The screams and clash of falling armor masked the machine-like snap of bowstrings and the laughter of the Huns. Every time a Saxon fell or dropped his shield to clutch at his bleeding leg, a second arrow took him in the chest or belly.

"They aren't using broadheads any more," Mael muttered. "Those must be bodkin points to do that, I don't care how strong their bows are." At fifty yards the Hunnish arrows were driving through even good ring mail.

As if the sudden clutter of bodies were an anchor dragging it back, the whole formation faltered. Then, from the front where the boar's skull threatened, Aelle's deep voice boomed, "Wotan loves brave men! Forward!"

The bellow and the clashing of armor in answer to Aelle's shout startled even the seasoned war-horses of the Huns. The Saxon ranks closed; the swine-array resumed its advance upon eight thousand feet.

Hooting and yipping more to themselves than to frighten, the Huns guided their mounts with their knees to within ten yards of the Saxons. There the little men of the steppes opened fire again. They were so close that their shafts pierced even the sturdy shields raised against them, pinning the wood to the arms that held it or gouging deeper into faces. Starkad's knuckles went white against the unyielding helve of his axe. The Dane was not an archer, and he could identify all too easily with the Saxons below.

One huge Saxon broke ranks and charged the tormentor whose arrow had lodged in his left eye-socket. The German was deaf to the shouts of those trying to bring him back. Iron medals cast in the shape of Roman horsetrappings glittered against his chest. The Hun who had pricked him wheeled his horse and retreated a dozen paces. The archers to either side waited until the foot-man had drawn abreast of them. They shot to-gether. The goose-quill fletching of their arrows bloomed against the Saxon's rib cage without the hindrance of the heavy shield to penetrate. Dead on his feet, the warrior staggered on.

Shouting in high-pitched voices, the pair of

Huns slapped six arrows apiece through the Saxon's cuirass. Each clump of feathers was so tight that a man's palm could cover the entry holes. The victim's arms slowly straightened so that his spear and shield were hanging as dead weights instead of weapons. Still the Saxon kept advancing.

When the dying warrior was within a yard of the Hun who was his quarry, that horseman shot once more. This time the shaft entered the right eye and clanked against the helmet at the base of the skull. The Saxon stiffened and fell backward like a tree sawn through at the roots. The Hun who had killed him bent without dismounting. He swung up again with the iron medallions in his hand.

Starkad cursed on the hill from which he watched the lethal toying. Beside him, Mael slapped his fist again and again upon his pelvis. The Irishman could see this game was almost over. It would be the Saxons' turn to strike next. Arthur's line overlapped the wedge to either side, but the Saxons were ten ranks deep and faced only a single row of longbowmen and recruits. Horns cried fierce, brassy commands from Arthur's wing squadrons. That was too late, Mael thought—the Saxons had reached the edge of the hill, only two hundred yards from the British. Aelle shouted and his men broke into a bellowing charge. Arrows could perhaps needle the margins of the swine-array, but missiles alone could never break it.

Then Mael gasped as the wedge disintegrated of its own accord at almost the instant the rush began. The whole Saxon front rank began to scream and stumble like their comrades who had been leg-pierced by the Hunnish arrows. The weight of the ranks behind the leaders pressed the charge onward. Men hopped and fell, shrieking as they stood one-legged and pulled black metal from the bare soles of their raised feet.

"Crows' feet!" Mael shouted, recognizing from the result what was breaking the Saxon line. The Irish used the devices, too, when time and location permitted. Crows' feet, caltrops, tetrahedrons—they were simply four iron nails welded with their heads together so that a spike was upward no matter how the object fell. Strewn in high grass, they were almost invisible. Their spikes ripped buskins or bare feet like so many two-inch spear blades.

The crows' feet were disabling but they could not kill. The arrows that now darted from three sides of the broken array accomplished the killing. Longbows from the hilltop thrummed as Saxons dropped their shields to pluck iron from their feet. From either flank rode three hundred archers, firing from refilled quivers. The Companions' fingers were bloody from earlier shooting and many riders were unable to draw their shafts to full nock. The body armor of the thegns was often able to turn a missile anyway, even when it missed the shields. Still, many arrows found targets and Saxons gurgled and fell.

Mael part drew and resheathed his sword a dozen times in nervous exultation. "If they run!" he was shouting. "If they run—"

Warriors in the rear of the array broke. That

was their death, for the last two ranks of Arthur's horsemen whooped and charged with their lances couched. The wave of steel lance heads bit into the backs and necks of the running Saxons like saw-teeth in soft pine. The victims flew forward. Their arms windmilled; sometimes a bright froth of pulmonary blood sprayed from their nostrils. The killers rode over the fallen Saxons, pivoting their wrists at the balance of the lance shafts and dragging the points free. Then the Companions could strike again, either with butt spikes or the already bloodied heads.

As a week before at Lincoln, as other armies for a thousand years, the Saxons proved that to run from a lance was to die. The darting steel left them food for the battlefield crows, whether they were thegn or carl, naked or mailed.

Some of the Saxon peasants who had survived to recross the stream lay on the far bank watching. They were shivering spectators for whom the price of admission had been the death of the men to every side of them. Now, as their screaming superiors rushed toward the water to die, the carls turned again. They began to straggle off toward their homes as swiftly as exhaustion allowed their legs to move. War was coming too close again, and the peasants had had their bellies full of it for this day.

Not all the Saxons ran. The men in the front ranks thrust forward and up the hill because it never occurred to them to go in any other direction. Some wore wooden-soled sandals which turned the points of the crows' feet. Some were simply lucky, skipping across ground which, though thickly sown, was not interlocked with spikes. A few showed enough intelligence to shuffle forward instead of striding, scuffing the devices harmlessly out of their way. Most of the Saxon champions, however, twisted the bloody iron from their feet and walked on, treating the wound as one more incident of war like a beesting or sunburn. Men who could not do that fled and died fleeing, but among warriors whose honor and livelihood was physical valor, it would have been surprising had there not been many who ignored injuries in order to close with the enemy.

The longbowmen, their quivers emptied, were snatching shields and spears. "All right, you bastards!" Maglos roared to his recruits. "Time to earn your pay!"

Mael shrugged once more to settle his armor comfortably. With a shout that tried to equal all the battle noise around him, Starkad bounded toward the nearest of the oncoming Saxons. Mael ran at the Dane's left and a step behind him. The Saxon, a great walleyed ruffian in chain mail, thrust his target forward to block Starkad's axe. The axe blade sheared the iron-bound linden wood from one rim to the other, gouging so deeply that it opened the Saxon's forearm as well. The Saxon screamed, spinning off balance from the torque of the blow he had received. Mael's sword tip laid the falling man's throat open, drowning his cries in a spray of blood.

Still bellowing his berserk challenge, Starkad met a clot of a dozen Saxons. They split apart at

his fury. Some of them were engaged by the other
recruits and Britons following the Dane to battle.
Starkad's axe was making broad figure-eight
passes in the air before him. One housecarl
counted on the pattern he imagined in the Dane's
offense. Starkad, reversing the direction of the axe
in mid-sweep, dashed the Saxon's brains out with
the peen. A thegn to Starkad's left saw the Dane's
back open, forgot Mael, and raised his spear. Mael
thrust and the thegn took the Irishman's sword
through the rib cage. The Saxon fell, his bones
gripping the blade. Mael tried to tug his weapon
clear as two of the dead man's housecarls pressed
him. The blade bent as it came out, cocking up in
the middle at a thirty-degree angle.

Cursing and suddenly in fear of death, the Irishman jumped back to avoid the spear which licked
at his face. Mael's missing earlobe burned as if
afire. The sword he carried was the one he had
taken from Ceadwalla's body, a well-polished
blade and solid to look on. But the metal was soft,
and now it would be his death for not testing it
earlier. . . . The Saxons struck together, both holding their spears overhand at the balance. Mael
backed again, letting the points notch his shield
facing. He set his blade under his right sandal and
tried to straighten the weapon.

The leftward Saxon howled and thrust with
both hands, driving his spear six inches deep in
Mael's shield. The Irishman slashed from a
crouch. The stroke severed the Saxon's wrists before he could step away from it. The dying man
threw his spurting stumps in the air and turned,

fouling his companion's blow so that the spear
only ripped Mael's side instead of splitting his
breastbone as intended. The Irishman's mail shirt
was as good as could be forged, but its links
parted before the spear head.

Mael countered with a backhanded slash at the
remaining Saxon. Ceadwalla's blade had twisted
axially under the stress of lopping through the
previous opponent's wrists. The edge did not bite,
but the effect on the Saxon was that of being
slapped across the head with a long iron club. The
man went down. Mael finished him with his shield
edge. He dropped his useless sword so that he
could use both hands to slam the iron rim down on
the Saxon's neck.

Ignoring the swords sheathed at the dead men's
belts, Mael worked the spear out of his shield to
rearm himself. The weapon had a long, double-
edged blade, and its shaft for several feet back was
wrapped with iron wire. To free the spear, Mael
pumped the shaft up and down. His eyes darted
about the immediate battlefield to be sure that
none of the men brawling nearby was about to
stab him.

Lancelot's fine armor had drawn more than its
share of attackers. The Gaul was handling them in
easy—almost leisurely—fashion, striking with
both the head and the butt spike of his lance. As
Mael watched, Lancelot cleared a Saxon from his
left side with a jolt from his buckler.

Arthur's own style was as lethal, though more
frantic than that of his Master of Soldiers. The
king was wheeling his horse in a tight caracole

that intimidated footmen while he slashed at them to either side with his sword. Arthur's silvered armor danced as he moved. A blow of some sort had severed one wing from his helmet and scarred the plating beneath it. The war-horse foamed as it trampled over the bodies of two slain Saxons. Nearby lay the British standard bearer, his teeth locked in the throat of the berserker who had killed him. The red dragon lapped over both men like a shroud. Cei was nowhere to be seen, but his horse trotted riderless at the edge of the woods.

Below, the melee begun when Starkad had struck the foremost Saxons had expanded into a full battle. Men had flowed together from both sides. Now the lines were beginning to disintegrate again from attrition. Aelle, the Saxon king, traded spear thrusts with two Companions. Twenty feet away, Starkad and a Gothic swordsman fought a trio of Saxons. As Mael wrenched his own weapon free, Starkad finished one opponent by chopping through his left thigh. At almost the same moment, the Gothic Companion doubled over with a surprised expression and both hands spread to catch the intestines spilling out of his torn jerkin. Starkad turned to block the bloody sword which had killed the Goth, leaving his right side and the Saxon there unattended.

Mael took a step forward with his spear cocked in his right hand. He loosed. The Irishman's legs were rubbery from exertion and the heat, but they held him. The shaft flew straight. The Saxon's upraised sword glanced off Starkad's shoulder, but dead fingers had released it even as the blow had started. The impact of Mael's spear punching into his chest drove the Saxon a step backward. He fell there, hemorrhaging bright streams from mouth and nose.

Mael knelt, panting hugely against the weight and constriction of his armor. His eye settled on the Saxon king. Aelle was not a young man; his beard was a grizzled red like the fur of an old fox. But the Saxon was as cunning as a fox as well, survivor of more battles than most men could dream of fighting. Mael saw him thrust one Briton through the thigh and drag him like a harpooned fish into the path of the second. When that Companion stumbled, Aelle's shield boss laid him out as surely as a club to the head could have. Pulling his spear point free, the Saxon king stepped over the litter of bodies and hurled his spear at Arthur.

Arthur had just dispatched the last of his attackers. He was shouting with triumph when the Saxon spear took his horse in the right ham. The beast gave a whinny that was almost a scream. It reared. Arthur, terrified of being afoot, screamed himself. He dropped his sword and clutched his saddle with both hands.

Lancelot's eyes were as cold as the iron frame of his helmet. He spurred his horse from a walk to a gallop. His lance was couched under his arm, the point aimed at the center of Aelle's breastbone where the impact would knock the Saxon down even if he managed to interpose his shield to the blow. Aelle had drawn a hand axe from his belt. With a feral grin and the timing of a man who had

seen thirty years of battle, Aelle brought his axe
around in an overhand arc. It intersected the lance
an inch behind the head. The wood sheared and
the point flew away, its sharpened edges glistening like the facets of a gemstone. The shaft, swung
downward by the blow, drove into the ground and
lifted Lancelot by directing his own momentum
onto the sudden fulcrum. With hideous perfection, Aelle made disaster certain by sweeping his
target around. Its boss took the horse on the left
eye as the beast drove past him. The horse shied.
Its feet skidded out from under it, narrowly missing Aelle as the hindquarters slewed around. The
beast's weight pinned the struggling Lancelot's
right leg against the turf beneath it. The animal's
rib cage thudded like a drum. Man and horse cried
out together.

Aelle, midway between Arthur and Mael, regained his balance. He cried, "You at least will get
your death this day, Unfoot!" As if in response, the
legs of Arthur's wounded mount collapsed. The
king slid to the ground despite his screams and his
grasping at the mane and saddle. Brandishing his
shield and hand axe, Aelle ran toward his fallen
opponent thirty feet away.

To either flank, lancers were riding uphill to
help finish the Saxons, but there was no Briton as
close to the two kings as Mael was. The Irishman
grunted and took a step toward Aelle. The Saxon
was moving away from Mael, and besides, Mael
had no weapon left but his target. He slipped his
left arm out of the loops and gripped the rim with
both hands. The shield was five layers of birch ply-

wood, faced with leather and locked together by
an edge band of iron. Slightly convex at the face, it
weighed almost forty pounds. With all his remaining strength, Mael brought the shield up from his
left side and released it. The target spun like a
huge discus, curving uphill toward the point at
which Aelle and Arthur were about to meet.

Aelle was raising his axe high overhead and
shouting down at Arthur when the shield caught
him in the back of the neck. It killed him instantly.
The Saxon's cries snapped off as his spine parted.
His head scissored back and met his shoulder
blades while the target spun off to the side. Aelle's
axe flew high over Arthur to stick in the ground
near the fallen standard. Aelle's flaccid body
slammed face-first at the feet of the British king.

Arthur stood up very slowly, bracing himself
with a hand on the ground. His eyes were on Aelle,
ignoring Mael and the riders spurring toward
their Leader from both flanks. The Pendragon's
face was white except for his moustache and the
blood trailing from his bitten lip. With his twisted
foot, Arthur kicked at Aelle's head. It lolled on the
broken neck. The helmet rolled off and the sun
gleamed on the Saxon's bare pate. Arthur kicked
him again and spat. "Swine!" he shouted. "You
Saxon swine will *all* kiss my feet or burn, *burn!*"

Arthur suddenly straightened and glared at the
men around him. The Companions had paused
when their Leader rose. Now the naked fury of the
king's stare drove at them like a gust of chill wind.
"Lancelot! Where are you, Lancelot?" the king
shouted.

Mael turned. Lancelot's horse had scrambled to its feet. The Master of Soldiers raised himself to his left knee. Blood was dripping from the top of his other boot. Though Lancelot's leg had not been broken, its flesh, pinioned against the bone by the horse's half ton of weight, had been torn as if by an axe. When the Gaul tried to stand, his face went sallow and his right leg buckled under him.

"God damn you, Roman!" Arthur shouted. "You always fail when I need you!" Mael's own expression blanked. The Irishman had a momentary urge to put a sword through Lancelot's heart as a mercy, despite his hatred for the tall captain.

The king's eyes flicked aside. They focused for the first time on Mael. "You, Irishman, you'll not fail me. I need you to ride to Merlin. Tell him to loose the dragon now." Arthur's face was growing red. He paused, then the words began to spatter out again. "Tell him it must kill and burn and waste the whole land from here to the seacoast. Tell him to sear the Saxons until they either wade into the sea or beg me, *beg* me, for mercy! And that mercy I may grant or not grant!"

Mael licked at the sweat rimming his upper lip. "I—I'll need equipment—"

"Yes, yes," Arthur snapped, "anything, horses . . . Lancelot, write him out a warrant to take whatever he needs along the way. Hurry!"

Two men were helping Lancelot sit up. He had taken off his helmet and was sucking wine greedily from a skin bottle. He winced. "In my saddlebags," the Gaul muttered. "There's parchment there and an ink stick."

One of the pair holding the Master of Soldiers leaped up and caught the nearby horse before Arthur could flare again in rage. The Companion rummaged in the bag for the materials, then brought them back quickly. Lancelot spat on the ink and began to scratch words on the scroll with a reed pen.

Arthur had unlaced his helmet. He mopped his face with a towel soaked in water. There was a long welt on the left side where the cheek piece of his helmet had been driven into the skin. Otherwise, the king had his normal color back. "There'll be Saxons scattered from here to Glevum," he said to Mael.

The Irishman was examining the sword he had just taken from Aelle's body. It was a long horseman's blade of Roman pattern and Spanish manufacture, old and well cared for and deadly.

"Plenty of British cutthroats, too," Arthur was saying. "Battle draws them." He looked back down the slope. Some Saxons were still writhing amidst the crows' feet, trying to crawl away from the squads of Companions who carefully picked their way in to finish the wounded. Nearer the river, there was a denser carpet of men with arrows and sometimes broken lance heads protruding from their vitals. The Dubglas still choked on bodies. Its current had not yet washed all the blood away from them.

With unexpected insight, Arthur added, "Maybe that's the only kind of men that battle does draw. But I'll send Gawain with you. I want the message to get through."

Mael looked up. "Leader," he said, "send Star-kad along instead of Gawain."

The king glared at the Dane who was now shambling up the hill to his friend's side. Starkad's smile was contented. He had lost his steel cap somewhere, and blood, slung from his axe head after his first stroke, speckled him all over. He himself appeared to be uninjured. "The Dane?" Arthur said. "He rides a horse like a sack of grain."

"He fights like any three of your Companions," Mael said, with no attempt to keep the edge out of his voice. "Send him with me or send someone else in my place."

The good humor of victory held. Arthur shrugged and called, "Lancelot, add the Dane to the warrant."

The Gaul's face was impassive as he scratched a flourish on the parchment. He handed the docu-ment and pen to his Leader. Arthur signed his name laboriously, chewing at the corner of his lip as he formed each letter. He gave the result to Mael. "Don't fail me, Irishman," the king said. "Don't even think of failing me."

CHAPTER FIFTEEN

Mael led a pair of remounts while Starkad rode alongside him unencumbered. The two of them were on the best horses available after the battle, steeds which had carried longbowmen to the site and had seen no further use that day. It was late afternoon. Even with hard riding, it would be a full day before Mael and Starkad could reach Moridunum.

The pace that Mael set was jolting and would wreck the horses in thirty miles. That was expected, and the mounts were replaceable. Starkad was riding as clumsily as Arthur had suggested he would, clinging to the saddle as if it were a spar and he a shipwrecked sailor. Each step hammered the Dane's spine and the insides of his thighs. He treated the punishment as he had that which he had received in the battle: something to be ignored or, if it could not be ignored, endured. At some point, even Starkad's strength would fail him and he would roll out of the saddle like a bundle of scrap iron. Until then he would ride.

As when they hiked toward Winchester, the two men kept general silence. Hoofbeats sounded on the metaled highway and their harness creaked around them. At a patrol station west of Lincoln, they left the horses they had been riding. There were no mounts there to exchange for them because the stables had been stripped for the field army. Trusting that stations farther west would have a better selection remaining, they pushed on astride the remounts the Irishman had been leading.

Night fell. At the post at which Mael and Starkad next stopped, the keeper's wife—her husband had been carried along with the army as a horse holder—demanded to know how the battle went. "Dead Saxons," Mael said, thrusting his head in a horse trough to clear away some of the grogginess. "All shapes and sizes, all dead. I doubt a thousand of them got away." The woman was chortling with joy as they remounted and rode away. Mael thought of the thousands of piled bodies, men he had never known and whose families would never know them again.

There were three more watch stations in the War Zone. Mael and Starkad changed horses at each of them. In the more settled country to the west, there were no longer military posts and stables to supply remounts, but the farms were more spacious. Privately owned horses were avail-

able. At a villa near Mancetter, they traded their
blown army steeds for a pair of gangling bays,
draft animals but the best that circumstances
offered. They rode them twenty miles until they
met a landowner rich enough to be accompanied
on the rounds of his estate by a mounted bodyguard.

"Hold up," Mael called to the pair. He rode
alongside the civilians and fumbled in his scrip for
Arthur's warrant. Rubbing his eyes with his free
hand, he held out the paper to the landowner.

While the bodyguard, a lanky man whose tunic
half hid a mail corselet, lowered at his side, the
magnate read the warrant. "We need your
horses," Mael said. "Arthur will make it right in a
few days."

"We'll exchange horses on Arthur's say-so?" the
landowner asked, his eyebrows rising with his
voice. He had a cultured Latin accent. "And what
has that barbarian ever done for me?"

Behind Mael, Starkad grated out his first words
in ten hours: "He left your head on your shoulders, scum. I won't, if I hear your voice again."
Mael glanced back at his friend. The Dane was
hunched forward in his saddle. The morning sun
was low enough to throw his hulking shadow
across both the Britons. Because Starkad had not
taken time to clean it, the axe in his hand was
crusted with dried blood.

The bodyguard was already swinging out of his
saddle by the time his blanching master ordered
him to dismount.

Starkad did not speak again until mid-afternoon

of the day after the battle. They had exchanged horses for the tenth or twelfth time—Mael had lost count—and were on the last stage of their ride. Sounding surprisingly hoarse, the Dane croaked, "Brother, what do we do after we get where we're going?"

Mael opened his mouth. Though he tried to speak, his tongue did not want to bend. He spat toward the roadside and made another attempt. "We'll give Merlin the message. Bathe. Sleep. Drink. Drink first, yeah. Maybe Veleda will be waiting for me. . . ."

"Then let's stop here for a few hours."

"What?" Mael turned to stare at his friend. Starkad gripped both front pommels of his saddle. His legs hung straight down, toes pointing to the ground. The Dane's face and beard were white with dust except where tears had broken paths from the corner of each eye. "Are you all right?" Mael asked. He reined up sharply and reached out a hand to steady Starkad.

"I said these dwarf-begotten horses would have to kill me before I fell off," the Dane said very softly, "and neither thing has happened yet. But if we ride straight in there now, my friend, you won't have a man behind you. Only meat, raw and tender. And they'll see me like this, those women and the burned-out men we left behind. And I'll be no better than they, Mael, no better at all, and I don't . . . want that.

"Please."

"Manannan, you didn't have to ask," Mael lied in embarrassment. "I was going to suggest we lay up here myself. I figure there's a good chance they aren't going to believe us right off—Merlin or the rest of the crew, either. If I stumble all over my tongue and can't remember what day it is, which is the kind of shape I'm in right now, we'll be thrown in the hole as deserters until the rest of the army gets back.''

The friends dismounted in a willow coppice near a stream which they muddied in washing themselves. Mael kept his back turned so as not to see the agony on the Dane's face as he forced his legs to move again. Mael's own thighs could not have been more painful had the femurs been broken. He could imagine how the less experienced Starkad felt. Stretched on the ground in front of their tethered horses, the men slept for five hours to the rim of twilight. Then Mael lifted his head from his pillowing saddle. Starkad, aroused by the creak of the leather, crawled to his feet as well.

''Feel okay?'' the Irishman asked.

''Weak as a baby,'' grumbled Starkad. He grasped a two-inch willow beside him and tried to break it off with one hand. The supple trunk bent but would not part. Suddenly the root end flew up, spattering mud over both men. Mael cursed. ''Maybe not quite as weak as a baby,'' said Starkad with a grin.

They rigged the horses and rode on at the same savage pace as before. The exercise loosened Mael's sleep-tightened muscles as lard loosens before a fire. The touch of the saddle was fire indeed to his bruised thighs.

With the sun low and in their faces, the riders approached the villa. The women in the enlisted lines, high-built behind the main building, caught the glint and jingle of harness first. The watchers began to drift toward the flagged entranceway. The women had been sitting in little groups in the cool of the evening, talking and mending garments. A few of them ran inside, shouting on rising inflections to their friends within. Those, wives and mothers and daughters, tumbled downstairs and out of doors, stumbling in haste and pinning on their cloaks as they ran. The gentle motion became a rush akin to panic. A hundred yards from the doorway of the villa, the crowd struck Mael and Starkad like hens around a farm wife at feeding time. "Is my man—" "Tell me about—" A hundred variations on the theme sounded in as many languages.

Over the babel, using his spear shaft as a lever to thrust away the hands groping for his reins, Mael cried out, "We won! We won! But let us through, women. . . ." Then, "We don't know the names of anybody, *anybody*, and we've brought a message for Merlin."

The Irishman had to shout the same thing repeatedly since only the nearest of the crowd could hear in the clamor. As some melted back like ice in a torrent, other women as quickly took their places. Starkad was unexpectedly gentle himself. He said over and over, "Unless your man was a Saxon, he'll be back in a few days. It was no more trouble than a pig killing, it was."

The two spearmen at the door of the villa were a

twenty-year-old with blond hair and one leg and an older veteran still weak with the dysentery that had kept him back from the campaign. The youth held out a flaring torch toward Mael to see him more clearly than the waning sun allowed. "Merlin," the Irishman demanded. "Where is he? We've got a message for him from the Leader."

The guards glanced quickly and oddly at one another.

"With the monster he raised," said Veleda from behind Mael. "With his dragon. Welcome back, my love."

Mael turned. Veleda was on horseback, as beautiful and free as the wash of her hair. The Irishman nudged his horse toward her. The press of clamoring women still separated them. Mael leaned sideways and Veleda caught his hands, bridging above the crowd for a moment. Starkad watched with an indecipherable expression.

Mael released Veleda. "Arthur sent us to tell Merlin to loose his beast," he said.

Veleda's laugh was real but harsh. "No," she said, "god sent you to destroy that dragon before it destroys the world and more. There is no limit to the number of universes, and there will be no limit to the size of the beast with all infinity to draw on . . . unless it can be killed while it is still able to die. *If* it is still able to die." Veleda stretched out her hands to touch Mael's, but she leaned away as he tried to gather her into his arms again. "Not now," she said. "It—it's at best very close to being too late. Did you bring the lance?"

Mael straightened and cursed sickly. "I could

have," he said, remembering Arthur's dying horse and the spear still in its saddle scabbard. "I don't think."

Veleda smiled unexpectedly and kissed the Irishman's fingertips. "The time's here, and we're here, the three of us—and I brought the shield." She rang her knuckles on the cloaked circlet lashed again to her saddle. "Everything is the way god willed it to be. Let's see if he wills us to kill a dragon." Veleda clucked to her horse. It wheeled, picking its way through the clots of women still nearby. At the fringe of the crowd she turned north toward the cave.

Mael spurred after her. Starkad followed them with a wry grin and a curse as his mount jolted his bruises anew. "Well," Mael called to the witch-woman, "I'll learn never to take you for granted."

Veleda looked back at him. Her face was dim in the faded sunset. "I wouldn't ask you to do this if it weren't necessary," she said quietly. "If there were anyone else but you, you two . . . but there isn't, and things are as they are. If you're killed—and you may well be killed—I won't long survive you. And if you fail, the world itself won't long survive."

"Be the first wyvern we chopped, won't it, brother?" Starkad noted placidly. The Dane was polishing his axehead on his thigh as he rode. "Don't worry about us, Lady. This sort of thing may be all we're good for—this and women. But we're very good at this."

"And you'll not do anything stupid if something goes wrong," Mael added in real irritation. "I've enough on my conscience without adding your blood to it." After a moment, he frowned and added, "I thought that sound I was hearing was thunder. It isn't."

"No, that's the wyvern," Veleda agreed. "It roars as though the sound alone could bring down the walls that hold it. But the sound won't have to."

Blue-white fire stabbed suddenly from ahead of them. The hillside framing the jet was a dark blot against a sky which the thin moon lighted. The bellowing that followed the flame reminded Mael of the squeals of the tiny creature which he had slapped across the cave so recently—reminded him as the sun reminds a man of the stars its glare extinguishes. The vivid fire silhouetted the crabbed figure of Merlin near the clump of poplars. He was bent over a brazier like the one on which he had raised the creature. The jet of fire had come from the throat of the cave. The iron gate-posts still stood but they were red-hot. Only scraps remained of the panels themselves. Previous gouts of fire had burned away the oaken leaves entirely and had left only the hinges and reinforcing straps.

"The spell keeps it from crossing the doorway," Veleda explained. "It doesn't stop the flames, though. And it's only the cave mouth which the spell can block. No one, not even I, has the power to bind the whole hillside. Perhaps if I'd realized sooner what was happening . . . but. . . ."

As Veleda's voice trailed off, flame exploded suddenly from the rock far above the doorway.

That azure flare limned a narrow opening. It
widened perceptibly as the limestone burned
away. Mael frowned, trying to superimpose his
memory of the cavern's interior against what he
now saw of the cliff face. The stone at the top front
of the cave must have been very thin, separating
the hollow from the outside air by only a few
inches. It was through that weakness that the fire
had burst.

Briefly silent, the three newcomers dismounted
beside Merlin. They lashed their horses to the
poplars. Wheezing and the sound of crumbling
stone were loud within the cave. Even through his
thick sandals, Mael could feel the ground shaking.

"What in god's name have you done?" Veleda
whispered to the wizard.

Merlin's face was as pale as the waning moon. "I
don't know," he said simply. He still carried a
willow wand, but his fingers had shredded it into
little more than a belt of fabric. When Mael had
last seen Merlin, the wizard had been as awesome
to look upon as a Roman aqueduct: ancient and
mighty and seemingly beyond human change. All
that strength had wasted out of the man in a
matter of weeks, leaving something pitiable in its
disintegration. "Did Arthur learn?" the magician
asked. "Did he send you to kill me?"

"What?" Mael said in surprise. "Kill you? He
sent us to tell you to let the dragon loose against
the Saxons."

Merlin burst into cackling laughter. "Let it
loose? It's about to let itself loose, don't you see?"

Another jet of flame slashed through the

hillside. A slab of rock collapsed with a roar which merged with that of the imprisoned beast. For an instant, the wyvern's head thrust through the opening high in the cliff. The shape of the head was the same as it had been when Mael first saw it. In size, however, it was now almost a yard from crest to muzzle. When the creature slipped back, its scales rasped more stone down into the cave with it. "It's grown large enough to tear its own exit," Veleda observed. "This one, this *magician*, depended on the rock to hold it forever if he couldn't control it himself. And it's grown too large already for anyone to control it through spells. Just as you told the fool it would."

Merlin shriveled away from the witch's scorn. He made no attempt to deny the statement.

Starkad shrugged. "We'll control it," he said. He loosed the strap of his buckler and gripped its double central handles with his left hand.

Veleda handed Mael the ancient target from Biargram's tomb. The Irishman took it by the rim. Its weight was a subconscious surprise. "Starkad—" he began uncertainly.

"Don't try to give *me* that thing," the Dane said. "You want to load yourself down like a mule, that's your business. This—" he gestured with his own buckler. It was also round, but it was less than a foot and a half in diameter—"is as much as I'm going to lug, dragon or no."

"Yeah, well...," Mael said. He turned away from Starkad as he slipped his arm through the loops of the target. He did not see Veleda's hand touch the Dane's and squeeze it briefly.

Veleda thrust a stick of brushwood into the brazier. After a moment, the end smouldered. It flared as she whipped it over her head. Answering flame cut deeper into the stone of the cliff thirty feet above the ground. The roar of the wyvern echoed again across the otherwise-silent countryside.

Raising the torch so that it would not blaze in the eyes of the men following her, Veleda began to walk toward the bluff. Starkad and Mael were side by side. The Dane carried his axe at high port across his shield face. The Irishman rested his lance on his right shoulder. None of the three bothered to look back at the huddled wizard.

Veleda skirted the original doorway at a safe distance. Though the wyvern was now concentrating on the vent in the roof of its cavern, it would have incinerated anyone passing the doorway within reach of its flame.

Mael used the butt of his lance to brace him as he began to climb the bluff which had been lifted out of the surrounding soil a million years before. Beside him, he heard Starkad twice slip clangingly onto his shield. The hole which the dragon had ripped stared darkly at the men as they approached it. It was an irregular oval, big enough now to drive an ox through. Its edges were thin where ground water had hollowed out the limestone to within inches of the outer surface of the hill. Mael edged forward the last sword's-length on his belly. The inner face of the cave showed deep gouges from the monster's claws. Rock near the opening had been burned to quick-

lime by the flame. The white caustic crumbled as
Mael's shield brushed it.

Within the cave, the waiting dragon cocked an
eye which reflected enough moonlight to glitter
Veleda cried a warning, but Mael was already
twisting his head back. A gout of fire leaped thirty
feet and tore the rock like a saw. A spatter of the
flame heated Mael's whole shield by touching the
rim.

The dragon's wings boomed as they flapped in
the confined space. The beast heaved itself up on
its left leg. Its right foot, triple claws extended,
scrabbled a purchase on the lip of the opening. Its
snout was braced against the upper edge of the
hole. The dragon strained. The rock began to crack
away. Mael had risen to his knees. The shifting
surface flung him prone again. The wyvern flapped its wings and lunged upward, getting its
head and neck completely through the opening.
The tips of its left claws and the thunderous
clapping of its vans held the monster poised there
although even its right leg must have been above
the cave floor.

Starkad rose on the high side of the hill and
chopped at the wyvern's neck. His axe glanced
away from the dense, black scales in a shower of
sparks. Mael shouted. The creature twisted more
quickly than Starkad could recover. The jaws
slammed. The Dane thrust out his shield more by
reflex than by plan. It wedged at the hinge of the
monster's jaw. The sturdy buckler was gripped
top and bottom by the dragon's teeth, but it pre-
vented them from closing on the man. Mael raised

is lance as a furious snap of the beast's neck
flung Starkad high in the air. When the Dane
loosed the handles, he cartwheeled against the
night sky. The buckler disintegrated in blue-white
flame. The linden was blasted like thistle-down in
the jet from the monster's throat while the iron
boss scattered in a shower of burning gobbets.

Mael stabbed at the back of the wyvern's skull.
His lance refused to bite. Sweat was washing the
Irishman's body. His target glowed like the crown
sheet of a boiler from its brush with the dragon's
flame. The thicknesses of ox-hide backing the
metal were barely enough insulation to permit
him to carry the shield.

The wyvern strained upward again. The whole
weakened cliff-face began to crumble down into
the cavity. The ground dropped out from under
Mael. He tried to stay upright, but the stone beneath him twisted and threw him on his back.
Rocks as large as the Irishman's torso fell with
him. Only his armor kept them from pounding him
to death. Dust rose in a gray pall. It hid the walls
of the trench which had been formed when the
front of the cave collapsed. The dust hid also the
jumble of rock that blurred and buried Merlin's
blocking spell. The symbols were useless anyway,
now that the cave gaped fully open to the sky.

Above everything, the dragon raised its mighty
head and bellowed its victory to the moon.

The beast slammed the air with gem-scaled
pinions which roiled the dust into ghost shapes.
Falling limestone had briefly bound the wyvern's
left foot. The wingbeats now tore the claws free.

Mael, stunned by the fall, lay on the rubble which
covered what had been the cave entrance. Momentarily, the creature roaring above him was only a
nightmare. Then the Irishman was alert once
more, realizing that the dragon was growing as he
watched it. In his mind echoed Veleda's voice saying, "There is no limit. . . ."

Mael fought upright, coughing from the dust.
Splinters had cut his cheek and right thigh. His
torn ear was draining down the side of his jaw
again. The Irishman had not let go of his lance,
and his shield was strapped firmly to his left arm.
He gauged the wyvern's distance. With all his
strength, and with both hands guiding the shaft,
Mael drove the lance up against the creature's out-
thrust keel bone.

Sparks danced like fairy lights as the flint-hard
scales shaved curls from the steel. The beast bent
toward Mael and opened its jaws. Fire spurted.
The air itself grunted as it flash-heated, making
the powdered stone *whuff* away from the arm-
thick jet of flame. The fire struck the center of the
ancient shield, the silver-gleaming boss that was
the world in every detail. The impact of the flame
was like that of a battering ram. The metal glowed
white and the hide backing stank like a slaughter-
house as it charred. The facing did not melt.
Though the iron core of the shield soaked up much
of the blast, Mael burned as though he had
strapped a lighted stove onto his arm.

Screaming with pain, the Irishman hurled his
lance at the wyvern's sparkling eye. The weapon's
point glanced off a bony scute and flickered into

the night. Perhaps the silvered blade of Achil
would have bitten, have penetrated, but honest
steel was useless. The beast roared and rocked forward, reaching out with its right leg. The three
toes were folded under for walking. As the foot
glided toward Mael through the dust, its claws
flared out like black horn scythes. Their thrust
drove Mael backward. He fell into the crevice between two slabs of rock. The claws curled over the
rim of his shield. Their needle points pricked the
Irishman through his mail. The wyvern rolled its
weight forward, crushing the unyielding circuit of
the shield down on Mael and the tumbled stone
beneath him. The metal sizzled where it touched
the bare flesh of his thighs and the base of his
throat. Mael could not fill his lungs to scream.
Rocks were being driven through his back.

The wyvern cocked one eye down at the Irishman like a grackle studying a worm. The beast
leaned forward, bending from the hip joint, and its
jaws began to gape. One of its eyeteeth had
cracked jaggedly; the other was a gleaming spear-
head touched by the moon's cool light. Mael's
right arm was caught under his shield. He had
half-drawn the Spanish sword when the beast's
weight crushed him against the rocks. Now he
dragged the weapon an inch further from its
sheath, feeling his skin tear and slip in his blood.
The dragon's mouth stank like a furnace stoked
with old bones. Mael whined curses into it. The
blast of fire from the jaws would leave his helmet
a pool of incandescent slag amid the ash of his
head and shoulders.

Starkad leaped down from the hillside onto the dragon's withers. His beard and hair were tangled like a gorgon's locks. The shock of the Dane's mass was staggering, even to a monster fifteen yards long. The wyvern took three steps forward, all the weight of its first stride bearing on Mael's shield. The beast passed over the Irishman like the shadow of death. It was trying to twist its serpentine neck to the left to tear at the man on its back. Starkad had locked his heels around the wyvern's throat, just ahead of the wings. The vans crashed against the Dane, hiding him momentarily. When they lowered, Mael saw his friend still astride the monster.

Mael rolled to all fours. "I'm coming!" he wheezed. His flesh had swollen cuttingly to the straps of the target. The circuit of burning metal tried to anchor him to the rubble, but he lurched upward and the shield came with him. Before him, earth spewed high as the wyvern pivoted. It was trying to turn more sharply than its bones allowed.

Starkad lifted his axe high over his head, peen forward. For a moment he was a bellowing statue against the night sky. Mael, staggering forward with his spatha out, raised his own banshee war cry, but the darkness drowned in the dragon's roars.

There was no sound and no movement. Starkad poised and Mael hung in the midst of his own attack. The Irishman could see Veleda in the corner of his eye. Her arms were outstretched and her lips pursed in the middle of a chant. The

woman's slim body was glowing violet. The cliff
face brightened with the reflection.

Mael was cold. The ghastly color enveloped him
and became a force created deep within his being.
It was an amalgam of motion and fury and soul,
all focused on Starkad's axe. Mael knew for an
instant that there was something more dehuman-
izing than merely being the object of inhuman
forces. Motionless himself, the Irishman strained
toward the motionless tableau of dragon and axe-
man. The great axe began to shimmer violet.

The Dane brought his weapon down in an arc so
perfect that it seemed the dragon was raising its
skull to meet the blow. The stroke was swift
enough that a line of steel hung in the air. Iron
struck bone and rang and rebounded as it had
when the axe head smashed the stone in Lancelot's
hands. The dragon missed a half step, shaking its
head. The eerie light had vanished. Starkad raised
his humming weapon again, but the first blow had
numbed his whole side. The creature's wings
batted the Dane. His feet were no longer locked
beneath its throat. Mael saw Starkad flung away,
losing even his grip on his axe. Man and weapon
struck the ground twenty feet apart.

The Irishman's legs drove him forward. The wyvern pivoted. Its head was twisting toward Starkad. The jaws were open. Mael howled and cut
with his spatha at the beast's tail, the only portion
of the dragon he could reach. The blade clanged
and skittered away harmlessly. Mael raised his
sword again, gripping the hilt with both hands.
Through the rising arc of the blade, he saw the

wyvern's head. The axe blow had caved it in. As the creature swung, its brains dripped from the open wound.

The beast turned further. Its jaws slammed shut and tore a huge gobbet out of its own left flank. The dragon screamed. It threw its head back, then forward and down with a gout of fire. The soil blew apart as moisture exploded into steam. Then the monster found its own right foot with the flame and sent itself sprawling like a broken-backed snake.

Starkad was crawling. Mael shouted to him. The Dane was not attempting to escape but rather to reach his axe. Beside Mael the wyvern began hammering the ground with its head and tail. The rocky soil shook in syncopated thunder. The dragon licked its side with another tongue of flame. One wing fell away. Scales, thrown high by the gases of their own destruction, spun back to the ground like dead leaves.

Mael shambled toward the Dane, letting his sword fall on the ground unnoticed. The shield was a fiery deformity which warped his body with its weight. He was past noticing even that. When it suddenly slipped off, the Irishman's back still bent to its imaginary burden.

Starkad looked up. With an effort that made his jaw sag open, the Dane rose to his feet. Some time during the night the left side of his beard had been scorched away. Blisters pocked his skin. He embraced Mael, each man cursing and praying in his own language.

Veleda stood beside them. Together, the knotted

killers' arms reached out and drew her close. The blonde woman's touch was cool and clean in a way that nothing they could remember had ever been.

Mael croaked, "You said you couldn't kill it."

"Alone, I couldn't have," Veleda replied. She nuzzled the bloody armor on the Irishman's chest. "I wasn't alone."

Starkad looked past her to the dragon. It was no longer thrashing. Scales were already sloughing away from the huge body. "What's happening to it?" the big man asked.

Veleda followed his eyes. "It grew on this earth a thousand times faster than was natural," she said. "Now that its reality is death, it decays the same way it grew. There won't be anything left by morning—except perhaps as much dust as a large salamander's skull would leave."

"We'd better get away now," Mael said. "Before Arthur learns what happened to his pet. Do you think you can ride as far as the nearest fishing village, friend?"

"Oh, I can do anything," Starkad grumbled. "Haven't I proved that already? But I don't see what you're worried about. We had to kill the thing, even Arthur's tame wizard—" the axe gestured toward where Merlin had been standing, but there was no one there now—"could tell hi— Oh. Yeah. Could tell him. But sure as Hel won't, not and admit how bad he'd fouled up. Hel and Loki, another damned ride."

"Well, maybe we can find a wagon at one of those farms," Mael said as they stumbled toward their mounts. "I've still got that warrant to commandeer anything in the kingdom. We can get a boat and sail for Ireland—"

"Spain, I remember the women."

"Well, wherever. . . ."

"Wherever god wills," said Veleda. She threw her arms about the waists of both men and began to laugh.

EPILOGUE

The war standard snapped in the breeze.

The walls of Arthur's tent had been rolled up, leaving its roof as an awning against the bright sunlight. Even after a week, smoke from the Saxon village tinged the air, though by now it was more an odor than a haze. Merlin lay in the dust between Gawain and the seated king. The lithe Companion toed the wizard, saying, "I brought this one back, but the others were gone. If there was ever a dragon, I couldn't find a sign of it. I'd have chased after the Irishman, but I figured the boat he and his friends stole would carry him farther than I wanted to go."

"So," Arthur said quietly. He stroked the arms of his high-backed throne. "Where is the dragon, wizard?"

Merlin raised his haggard face. "Gone. Dead. Finished."

"So," Arthur repeated.

He stood up, his scabbard knocking against the oak of the chair. The surrounding guards and courtiers stiffened. "But *I* haven't failed," the king said. His eyes were on nothing but the eastern horizon. "The Saxons, the world. They'll know me, *know me!*"

Men looked at their hands or at the ground or even, in horrified fascination, at their Leader. Only Merlin seemed oblivious to the king. The wizard was scratching at the dust with a fragment of willow twig.

"Do you hear me?" Arthur shouted to the world. *"I will not die!"*

Beneath the king, Merlin gestured and an image shimmered between his fingers. It was a silver chalice, jeweled about the rim. For a moment the sunlight haloed it.

Then the grail tumbled and fell back into the dust from which it had sprung.